Miss Ava's Scandalous Secret

Merry Spinsters, Charming Rogues Book 2

Sofi Laporte

http://www.sofilaporte.com

sofi@sofilaporte.com

c/o Block Services
Stuttgarter Str. 106
70736 Fellbach, Germany

Editor: Donna Hillyer
Proofreaders: Jessica Ryn, Stacey Ulferts
Cover Art: Victoria Cooper

ISBN: 978-3-9505190-8-2

 Created with Vellum

Chapter One

TRISTAN EDWARD SYDNEY, EARL OF RAVENSCROFT, had to marry.

He had until his thirty-third birthday to find a bride. Midnight. Sharp.

"And if I don't?" Tristan gripped the brandy glass so hard it nearly pulverised.

"If you don't, I'll cut off your purse strings and donate everything to charity," his father roared, the spittle spraying all over the table. Alastair Sydney, Marquess of Livingstone, had never been known to be soft-spoken, but his anger raised his tone a few notches and would have terrified even the most hardened of men.

Tristan flicked away the moisture on his cheek. "You won't," he said with a sang-froid he didn't feel.

Livingstone jabbed a finger at him. "Watch me. You'll inherit the title and the land, but none of my fortune. Not a shilling. Not a penny! Not a-a—"

"Farthing. I am beginning to apprehend the gist of the matter, sir." Tristan set down the empty brandy glass on the table. He started to feel that his waistcoat was cut a tad too tight and wished he could loosen his cravat.

"To be enforced immediately, a minute after midnight. Without my blunt, you'll have to see for yourself how to pay your gaming debts, your tailor, boots, and cravats and all this other nonsense on which you fribble my money away." Fires of wrath sparked out of the older man's eyes. "With the lifestyle you lead, you'll end up in debtors' prison, and I won't move a finger to get you out."

Tristan swallowed. He'd heard they used thumbscrews and skullcaps on the poor inmates in Marshalsea prison. He rubbed his thumb involuntarily.

It was all fudge and nonsense, of course. His father's bluster was intended to browbeat him into submissiveness. He was an earl, and earls were untouchable. Everyone knew that the nobility could live off their debt for years on end and that they couldn't be thrown into prison like that.

He remembered the fate of poor Brummel, who'd had to flee to France to escape his creditors. Well, the poor sod hadn't been an earl, so there.

But there was Lord Hyatt, who'd lost everything including his mind, and he'd eventually ended up in Bedlam. Which might be a tad worse than Marshalsea.

Tristan studied his fingernails. "What prompted this unanticipated resolve, may I ask?"

Livingstone slammed a sheet of paper onto the tabletop with such force that the Ming vase wobbled. Tristan's hand shot out to steady it.

"This. This scandal sheet. This leaflet of shame. This picture of ignominy!"

Tristan looked at the sheet and repressed a groan. It was a Cruikshank caricature depicting himself draped over a park bench, dishevelled and evidently drunk, surrounded by a group of demi-mondes who were cheerfully pulling on his clothes in an attempt to undress him.

He rubbed his neck, which had started to feel uncommonly warm. "It was just a prank," he muttered. "Where is your sense of humour?"

"My sense of humour ends when you impugn our family honour." Livingstone's voice shook with quiet rage. "That includes mine, yours, and your sister's. Have you even considered what example you're setting for her? You have disgraced yourself and our family name in the most shameful manner possible."

It was a prank that had gone badly awry. All because of his friend Miles, blast the man. Granted, he only had himself to blame, for Miles might not have resorted to such extreme measures of retaliation if Tristan hadn't provoked him in the first place.

Tristan had set up Miles, who had an affinity for royalty, to meet Princess Alexandrine of Prussia, who was currently visiting England. He'd been tickled to see his gullible friend fawn over the beautiful princess, as he'd set them up for a tête-à-tête picnic in the moonshine. The princess, however, turned out to be a Drury Lane doxy in the grey morning hours. Tristan had hired a pretty actress and paid her well to play the part of the princess. The girl had told him afterwards, when she'd collected her money, that the look on Miles' face had been priceless.

It'd been a silly prank. Nothing more. They'd done this to each other since they were at Eton, cementing their friendship through mutual teasing and playing ridiculous jokes on each other.

The problem was Miles' revenge, which did not wait long.

Miles had invited him to one of his orgies and, as it inevitably happened, he'd been foxed. So foxed that Miles had been able to cart him to Hyde Park, deposit him on a bench, and perch a pair of donkey's ears on his head with a wooden board around his neck: "Who will marry me?" When Tristan had awoken with a splitting headache, his body stiff from having laid on the hard bench the entire night, he'd found himself surrounded by a large group of giggling women of all kinds. Fisher maids, milkmaids, flower girls, seamstresses, and prostitutes.

He'd stared blankly into the wrinkled face of an old woman, who'd revealed a set of black teeth as she'd grinned. "I'll marry ye." She'd cackled a laugh.

The story was splashed all over the papers. The *ton* was riveted. In this battle of pranks, Miles Davenport had won. Wagers were placed: would Ravenscroft retaliate with yet another, bigger prank?

Only the real Princess of Prussia was not amused. In a miff, she'd cut her visit short and returned to Prussia. In a letter to the Queen, she'd complained about degenerate English noblemen and their craven lust for amusement at the expense of innocent others.

The Queen, much affronted, had summoned Livingstone, suggesting that he had better gain control over his son as she handed him a copy of the caricature.

Livingstone had squirmed. His son had brought

disgrace upon his family name. He'd clearly failed in raising a dutiful son. On return to his residence in Grosvenor square, he'd summoned Tristan.

"You are causing a diplomatic scandal!" he roared. "Men your age have died on the Continent, fighting in one of the worst wars ever. For England. For King and Fatherland. And what do you do? You fritter away your time and fortune—*my* fortune—and undermine our alliance with the Prussians by insulting the princess." He poked a finger at him. "In the end, it will be your fault if we lose all our allies."

Tristan felt inclined to remind his father that the war was long over, Napoleon was tamed and packed away on a forsaken island, and peace had been reigning ever since.

"It's not that bad," he protested instead.

"You have no idea how bad things are. Thanks to you, the title Ravenscroft and our family name Sydney have become synonymous with philandering, gambling, and drinking."

Tristan rubbed his neck. He had acquired the reputation of a philanderer, that much was true. And yes, he drank now and then, but so did everyone else. His biggest fault, it seemed, was that he spent too much time in the company of Miles, who kept dragging him from one prank into another.

"It is time to mend your ways. You will marry."

"Marry!" Tristan stared at him aghast. He knew he needed not fear debtor's prison, but what Livingstone was suggesting was worse, for marriage was a kind of prison, except this one carried a life-long sentence.

"Why do you think marriage would change anything

about my situation," he dared to ask, "if I am such a hopeless character?"

Lord Livingstone shot barbs out of his eyes. "One word: stability."

"Stability." Tristan pondered on the word. "As in, security. Constancy."

"You do know your vocabulary, I see." Livingstone's voice dripped with sarcasm. "I mean stability as in steadfastness, soundness and maturity." His father leaned forward, and Tristan did not care much for the gleam in his iron eyes. "Find a good woman and start up a nursery. All the Sydney men have married good, virtuous women. Not only that, but the Sydney brides have also been great beauties, all of them. No exception. Our women are our jewels, our pride. There is no greater honour than to go through life with a beautiful, virtuous woman on one's arm. You must find such a jewel and carry on the line. It's time for you to grow up, my boy."

"That's all very well and good," argued Tristan, who was a strapping man of thirty-three and very much attached to his bachelorhood, "but why do I have to mend my ways through marriage? We all know that, in this day and age, marriage doesn't necessarily mean faithfulness." He couldn't think of a single couple where the man didn't have a bit of muslin by the side.

Livingstone gave him a cold stare. "Your mother would've been disappointed in you. She'd clearly intended for you to be a better man than that."

That sat. A clear hit below the belt.

Ice-cold rage took hold of Tristan. *And whose fault is*

it my mother died? he wanted to shout. Yet he did not utter the words that burned in his throat.

Instead, his father continued, "These are the conditions I'll set: your bride must be of good, respectable, solid stock. Her breeding must be impeccable. She will be a beauty, a jewel, like the rest of the Sydney brides. No opera singers, ballet dancers, or widows who are after your fortune. Any breath of scandal and you are cut off. Am I making myself understood?"

"Yes, sir." Tristan gnashed his teeth. Then he pulled himself up. "However, I, too, have conditions. I'll choose a bride. However, on the day of my engagement, I need a certain amount of money to be made available to me without any strings attached."

Livingstone glowered at him under his bushy white eyebrows. "How much?"

Tristan gave him the sum.

"For what do you need it?"

"No doubt to pay back my debts at my tailor and the shoemaker," Tristan answered sarcastically.

"I shall give you half of what you ask."

"The entire sum, not a farthing less. Or I'll be determined to, as you say, trod down the path toward degeneration, destruction, and doom." He clenched the edge of the table for support.

"You bargain like a fishmonger." Livingstone tapped a finger on the tabletop. "Very well. No doubt your debts are considerable. I shall cover the amount you ask for. But a month after your engagement, at the most, you will find yourself in church. On that day you will receive the funds."

Tristan nodded curtly.

"Things are very simple, my boy. You are a Sydney. I expect you to fall in line with the rest of the Sydney men and choose a virtuous woman. If you want my blunt, you will notify me of the happy event by the eve of your thirty-third birthday. Midnight. Sharp. This gives you a good month to look for someone suitable. I'll approve of the bride personally. And that is final."

Tristan felt the iron shackles click shut about his throat.

He was doomed.

TRISTAN DROVE HOME IN A TOWERING RAGE.

He threw his hat and gloves on the floor, took two steps at a time up the staircase, tore the door open to his study and poured himself a glass of brandy out of his decanter. The longer he pondered on his father, the longer he became convinced that the old man was a tyrant, whose sole purpose in life was to torture him. His entire ancestral line was colluding with the old man. All the cursed Sydneys with their fine aristocratic noses, blue eyes, title, birthright, and wholesome wives. May they populate Hades with their infernal beauty and virtuosity.

Livingstone wanted him to be married?

His wife should be wholesome, respectable, and beautiful?

She would be a jewel, the pride of his home?

Pah.

Well, he would marry.

He would marry the plainest, dowdiest woman in the

ton. But she would be so very respectable, Livingstone would find it impossible to object. Oh, how the *ton* would laugh! Yes, they would ridicule him. But the final joke would be on starchy, proud Lord Livingstone and his accursed pride in his beautiful lineage, whose good-for-nothing son, alas, married the ugliest hag of all England. For the reality was that he did not care a whit about how his wife looked; whether beautiful or plain, what did it matter? He would deposit her in Ravenscroft Hall and forget all about her. He would never have to see her. He would have fulfilled his marital duty. He could then return to his former life, surround himself with true beauties and pretend nothing had ever happened.

To blazes with his grand family line.

Tristan toasted himself on his brilliant plan.

Chapter Two

Just at the precise moment that the earl was penning his list, Mlle Violetta Winter hurled a precious Ming vase against the mantle of the fireplace.

It crashed, and the vase splintered into a thousand fragments.

"I won't sing for the Prince Regent!"

"If you could but take a moment to reconsider—"

"Preposterous notion!"

"Please!" The Hon Phileas Whistlefritz cringed behind the great fauteuil, wringing his hands.

"How could you, Phileas?! You knew perfectly that I came here incognito and that it is most important for me to remain so!"

Phileas wisely refrained from telling her that all of London knew already she was in town, that everyone had known she was coming long before she'd even set foot on British soil, and that the Prince Regent himself had insisted on her singing for him personally. He'd been keen on it ever since he'd heard she'd sung for Napoleon and broken a dozen champagne glasses with her coloratura soprano voice. It had made her a legend. Prinny, not wanting to languish in the former French emperor's shadow even in this regard, especially since he was defeated, had declared that his biggest desire was to have Mlle Violetta Winter sing for him and smash a full two dozen glasses with the sheer force of her voice. The gentlemen in their clubs were already placing bets, and the betting books were full.

"But it's nothing grand! Just a tiny, wee opera..." Phileas rubbed his hands.

"Which one?"

"*Don Giovanni.*" Phileas ducked quickly.

But Violetta had clung to the porcelain rider, exhausted. "When?"

"Tomorrow."

Silence.

After a while, he raised his head cautiously.

Violetta had slid down on the floor next to him, hugging the porcelain rider to her chest.

"It will ruin me," she whispered.

"Nonsense." Phileas, seeing that the imminent danger was over, scrambled up and pulled his cravat straight.

"You know exactly what a public performance in London is going to do to me."

"Spread your fame in England even more. The director happens to agree with me. Your coffers will agree with me also."

"It will ruin me."

"Fid-a-diddle dee, the reputation of Violetta Winter

12

cannot be ruined. If at all, it will carry you to even greater heights of fame than before." He flicked flecks of dust from his breeches.

"You don't know them. The British aristocrats." She spat out the word.

"Er, I don't?" asked Phileas, youngest son of the Viscount of Bleckham.

"How vicious they can be. Sticklers of propriety." Violetta paced up and down the room, clinging to the porcelain figure.

"Hm. True. Yet in the end, it is Violetta Winter who they will idolise. Even greater than in Paris! In Vienna! Milan! They will lie at your feet, worshipping. Like we all do."

Violetta stopped pacing and narrowed her eyes at him. "How many operas did you book me for?"

Phileas mumbled something.

"Speak up."

"I said, nine." Phileas moved behind the sofa as a precautionary measure.

But she remained on the floor and rubbed her eyebrow wearily. "Tell me. Why do I put up with you, Phileas?"

"Because I am the best manager you ever had? Because... I am your friend?"

Violetta sighed. She set down the porcelain rider and wrung her hands dramatically. "Try to understand, Phileas: our reputation is at stake. No one knows that the Sackville family is linked to Violetta Winter. It is crucial for Kit that it remains that way. It is crucial for me. Kit, with his new position and title, needs all the help he can get to settle down here. It doesn't help if word goes round that his twin sister is an opera singer."

Phileas scratched his neck. "I see your point. I swear upon my honour that no one will discover your identity. After all, not even Aunt Wilhelmina, whose house you are renting, knows this. She thinks you're the eccentric spinster Miss Ava Sackville who has arrived with her brother Christopher." He plucked a speck of lint from his sleeve and continued. "If you absolutely insist, we can cancel the soiree with the Prince Regent. He will be furious. But you can't cancel the opera."

Violetta groaned.

"No need to despair! I know just what you can do. There is a solution to every problem." He took a turn about the drawing room, his hand on his chin. Violetta sat wearily down in an armchair and watched him. "The trick is to keep on doing what you have been doing and keep the two identities separate. No one need to know that Miss Ava Sackville is in reality Violetta Winter. If you continue to disguise yourself properly, no one will ever know. During the day, when you're with your family you will be Miss Ava Sackville." He waved a white, effeminate hand. "On stage, you are Violetta Winter. You will have the best personal guards. I'll personally see to it."

She rubbed her forehead.

"The alternative, of course, is that you do not seize this once-in-a-life-God-given-opportunity-with-all-the-abundance-that-comes-with-it and pack up immediately and return to the Continent before anyone ever has an inkling of your existence here." Phileas crossed his fingers behind his back. "You would have to leave your brother to his own fate. He is a grown man. He should be able to cope alone." He held his breath. The mantle clock ticked. Outside a carriage clattered by.

Violetta sighed. "I don't have a choice, do I?" she asked bitterly.

Phileas nearly dropped to his knees to thank the gods. For the seats were sold, the bills printed. They were overbooked. There was really no way out. But Phileas wisely refrained from telling her this.

"Well, then, Violetta-Ava—deuce take it, what do people call you these days?"

"Might as well call me Ava and get used to it."

"Right. Well, then, Vio—I mean, Ava—deuced unoriginal name! Never mind about all that broken porcelain. What can one expect from a diva?" He pushed some porcelain shards away with the tip of his polished Hessian boots.

Violetta looked at the broken vase with a slight pang of guilt. "I shall, of course, replace the broken vase."

"I am sure my aunt Wilhelmina will be prodigiously relieved you got rid of some of her horrid pieces. This Sevres plate was most dreadful to behold, anyway. Say, shall I see you at the soiree of Lady Westington on Wednesday night?"

"While I would rather stay home and pack for our trip to Sackville Hall in Berkshire the day after, I believe it would be good for Kit to be seen in society."

Phileas chuckled. "The persona of Ava Sackville is just perfect. You have always been an excellent actress. You will fool the entire *ton*." Phileas popped his beaver hat on his head and grabbed his walking stick, an entirely unnecessary appendage, except it was so fashionable these days to have one, and Phileas was the crème de la crème of fashion. He made a gallant bow and turned to go. At the door, he peeked around impishly, and asked, "Are you sure you cannot make yourself sing one duet with the Prince Regent, after all, a tiny wee one—" he retreated hastily, just in time for a piece of porcelain to crash against the door.

Violetta had finally hurled Aunt Wilhelmina's precious porcelain rider.

Chapter Three

When his butler announced Miles, Viscount Davenport, Tristan scowled. After all, it was thanks to him he found himself in this predicament.

"Is this a bad time?" Miles asked as he strolled into the room. "You appear to be somewhat blue-devilled."

"Not at all, Miles, not at all. I am merely considering all the different ways in which to kill you, which I find to be a creative and invigorating mental exercise." Tristan bared his teeth.

"Oho! Duels at dawn? I'm all for it. But before we shoot bullets into each other, tell me what has triggered your murderous frame of mind." Miles poured himself a drink and sat down, unfazed, crossing his legs.

"My father is less than pleased with the consequences of your last joke and insists I get married, or else threatens to cut my allowance."

Miles winced. "My condolences, dear chap. That is terrible news, indeed. The old blighter never did have a sense of humour."

"Not when it comes to our illustrious family name, he doesn't." Tristan pulled a hand through his thick, dark hair. "This joke went too far and now I'm in the suds. He's serious, Miles. I'm going to be shackled by the eve of my birthday."

"If it's any consolation to you, it's bound to happen to all of us sooner or later. My mother has been dropping broad hints in this regard as well. Drawing up lists of damsels and the like." Miles gulped. "I tend to make myself rare whenever she starts harping on that line. I fear the day will come when I, too, won't be able to escape the inevitable." He stared morosely into his glass. Then he threw Tristan a sly look. "How's Isolde, by the by?"

Tristan shrugged. "As usual. Difficult and demanding."

"And quite a beauty, too," Miles mused as he drew a finger round and round the rim of his glass. "A diamond of the first water."

Tristan shot out of his seat and clutched him by the throat. "Breathe another word about her, and it will have been your last."

Miles lifted both hands to appease him. "Peace. Forget I ever said anything. It was merely a little flirt, no harm done."

"Well, if I catch you flirting again, I won't answer for the consequences."

"You really are in a foul mood tonight."

"It would help if you were to stop pestering me and helped me instead." Tristan released him.

"Very well, Tris." Miles crossed his legs. "What do you want me to do?"

"Can you think of any respectable families with daughters of marriageable age?" Tristan reached for his glass. "She would have to be plain. The plainer, the better."

Miles lifted an eyebrow, a keen look of interest in his green eyes. "So, this is whence the wind blows?"

Tristan lifted one shoulder. "As you have so acutely observed, all the Sydney brides have been so dashedly beautiful, someone ought to break with the family tradition."

Miles whistled noiselessly. "Are you certain? You'll be tied to a plain woman for life, and all to play a short-lived, childish prank on your father? Appears to me you're needlessly punishing yourself. Is it worth it?"

Tristan pulled his lips to a sneer. "To make a laughingstock out of my father, even if but for a second? Let me think." He lifted a finger. "Yes!"

Miles shook his head in amazement.

"You see, I care not about our family name, about maintaining a lineage, a beautiful bride, what not. Marriage is meaningless, a signature on paper, so what does it matter to whom I am married? Anyone will do. Let her be as ugly as Medusa; I care not. We need not see each other, deal with each other, cross each other's paths. She leads her life, I lead mine." He shrugged. "I fulfil my duty, the old man gets what he wants, except it'll be the wrong end of the bargain. Instead of a jewel, he'll get a hag as a daughter-in-law and no grand-children, for that will be the end of our illustrious line."

19

Miles's mouth had dropped open during Tristan's rant. He snapped it shut. "Here I always thought, between the two of us, that I was the ultimate prankster, but you have a calculated cold-bloodedness underlying your devilry that I find most admirable."

"Back to my original question: I need a respectable and plain woman. Give me some names." Tristan tapped his finger on the table.

Miles wrinkled his forehead. "In the marriageable age? That's a challenge. There are ugly women aplenty, mind you. The ballrooms are littered with them. But of marriageable age *and* respectable?" He weighed his head back and forth. "The problem is that the respectable ones of good families are already married. And most of the ugly ones are too old for marriage. Wait, there is one family that comes to mind. The Witheringtons are both a respectable and a hideously ugly family."

"The Witheringtons? Do they have daughters?"

Miles scratched his head. "Come to think of it, they don't. But they have a parrot, as I recall."

"Be serious, Miles. I can't marry a parrot."

"That is an unfortunate conundrum. Might be preferable over marrying a hag."

"What about the Sackvilles? They are said to be awfully respectable."

"Sackville!" Miles' body convulsed. "You're right. The name is as old and respectable as a bag of dry bones. The old baron bit the dust and there's a new baron, apparently, who's recently returned from the Continent. Of the dandy set. Heard he brought a sister with him. But, Tristan, the Sackville name is synonymous with ape

20

leader, for the females in that family are spinsters. If you go for a Sackville, you've fallen low."

"That sounds just the person I am looking for."

"No, Tris. I'm all for revenging yourself on a tyrannous old man, but not like this. The Sackville hag's as old as your grandmother. Heard the baron's sister's not much better. Has an odd name, too. Mava, Java or Ava. You'd better pass. Have a look at Mrs Townsend instead. She's plain enough, but with an agreeable personality."

Tristan shook his head. "She must be respectable. Mrs Townsend's a widow with a dubious background. My father will never sanction it."

"Then there's only the ancient spinsters left. What a terrible fate to choose for oneself." Miles shuddered.

"Isn't there a respectable spinster that is not ancient?" Leaning back in his chair, Tristan locked his hands behind his head.

"Then she would be married," Miles said with infallible logic. "Or worse: a debutante. You know, those half-infants at fifteen, sixteen, who are still in their salad days."

"A schoolroom miss." It was Tristan's turn to shudder.

Miles clapped a hand on his shoulder. "Cheer up, my friend. If you can't stomach a schoolroom miss, then you might as well choose an old spinster. But not tonight. Tonight, my friend, you will set aside all depressing thoughts of matrimony, and you will go with me to the opera as we allow ourselves to be enthralled by the one and only Mlle Violetta Winter. If your free days are counted, you might as well use them well."

"Violetta Winter?" Tristan looked at him with interest. "The new opera diva? I heard she's good."

"Good? She is spectacular. She is a goddess, Tris, a goddess! You are to be pitied that you have never heard her sing. The most beautiful, ethereal creature my eyes have ever beheld. The entire house went crazy for her. And her voice. Her voice! When she opens this glorious mouth of hers and sings, what can one say but—Violetta Winter..." He kissed the tips of his fingers.

Tristan threw him an amused look. "I must see this Incomparable who has the power to bring you to the knees," he mocked. "But not tonight. Tonight, I have to make a list of marriageable damsels—or rather, spinsters."

"Godspeed, my friend. That is an occupation I'd rather not share with you. I'll seek a more joyful pursuit and am off to the opera."

Miles left with a whistle on his lips to seek a gambling hell.

Tristan was glad to see the back of him.

He would make a list of all eligible, plain ladies. He pulled out a piece of paper and a quill.

To work.

Chapter Four

"Stop the carriage, Kit," Miss Ava Sackville told her twin brother, who'd recently come into the magnanimous name of Christopher Edward Richard Sackville, twelfth Baron Sackville. She gripped her brother's arm as their coach rumbled through a forest and out into a clearing. Nervousness and excitement churned in her stomach.

Kit rapped on the roof, and the carriage came to a halt.

They were on the way to Sackville Hall in Berkshire to visit their only remaining family, Cousin Millicent. They knew nothing about her other than that she was their deceased Uncle Richard's only child. She'd written them the letter in which she had notified them of Uncle Richard's passing. Since his brother, their father, had already died, the title had gone to the only remaining male offspring. Which was Kit.

He hadn't been ecstatic. Kit and Ava had been living

a comfortable life in Vienna and had had no intention of returning to England, ever.

"You are Baron Sackville now, Christopher," Millicent had written. "It would be lovely to make your acquaintance."

"She is right," Ava had told Kit as she folded the letter. "We ought to at least visit her. After all, you've inherited her home."

They'd arrived in England several weeks later and had only recently begun to socialise. Thanks to Phileas, Ava's evenings were full of rehearsals and performances. After a week or two of singing, she was glad to leave London, if only for a few days.

Kit rapped on the roof and the carriage came to a halt.

"Would you look at this." His sister stared out of the window at the sprawling estate that unfolded in front of them. A gigantic mansion of sandstone with a Neoclassical façade, Corinthian columns and a central dome greeted them. A sweeping driveway led around a picturesque lake fringed by trees. One could not tell where the park ended, and the forest began.

"There it is, Ava," her brother said softly. "Father's little cottage." He chuckled.

"This is the cottage Father always talked about so fondly. It's somewhat bigger than I imagined." Ava pulled at her earlobe. "In fact, considerably bigger. I always imagined a dainty little house with a red gabled roof. I don't know why, but the roof ought to be red."

"With a cat and a dog," Kit agreed. "Instead, it looks

like there might be an entire stable full of horses. Father evidently forgot to tell us about this little detail."

Brother and sister stared at the estate, put out at the immense wealth that spread out in front of them.

Kit stared broodingly at the house. "Father was infuriatingly vague about many things, wasn't he? While he glorified England on one hand, he downplayed everything pertaining to our family. The size of the mansion, for example. Look at this estate. Good heavens. He only ever mentioned a house with a garden. Is this what he considers a garden? It's a park bigger than anything I have ever seen. What else was he more than vague about? I have a premonition he may have been less than honest about Sackville being an insignificant title as well. It is a shame we can't stay here longer than two days because of your opera performances in London." Kit turned to his sister and stared. "What on earth are you doing, now?"

Ava turned around. His dapper sister with copper red curls had transformed herself into an entirely different person as he talked. No, not through magical transformation, although Kit had to concede, at times, that his sister's ability to disguise herself bordered on magic. She'd merely put on a wig, and with a few strong strokes of face paint from a chest which she always carried with her, she'd drawn heavy eyebrows. This, together with spectacles and a shawl that even their grandmother would've refused to wear, she'd transformed herself into a proper old maid.

"Really, Ava? You will disguise yourself even now when we meet Cousin Millicent?"

"Lord Shackville," she lisped and grinned, baring a gap in her front teeth. "It ish shutch an honour."

Kit warded her off with his hands, horrified. "O thou vile one! A gross hag... worthy to be hang'd."

"Shame on you for mishquoting Shakeshpeare."

"I may have mixed up *Cymbeline* with *A Winter's Tale*—" Kit crossed his arms and leaned back, grinning "—but what is this? Artificial teeth?"

Ava took out the set of teeth and showed it to him. "They are dentures. Waterloo teeth." She grimaced. "Let us not think about where they came from. They are rather uncomfortable to wear, and they make talking difficult, but they make the best kind of buck teeth. No one will recognise me."

"How can you bear to put something like this into your mouth? You look hideous. Absolutely hideous."

"That is my intent."

"I really don't think it is necessary to go through all these extremes, sister. No one knows you here."

"And I intend for it to remain that way. One can never be too careful."

Kit shook his head. "Even with Millicent? Why not just be yourself?"

"Oh Kit, don't be so naive. You know what will happen if they discover my identity. Even if it is Millicent."

"Ah yes. The ever-scandalous, multi-talented, much sought-after Violetta Winter, star of the stage in Milano, Paris, and Vienna. How terrible to discover she dwells among our midst, living a perfectly respectable life."

"They will shun you. English society is so much

worse than in Milano or Vienna. They are unforgiving. Doors will be shut, and you will not be able to be a true heir to all this. All because a woman who sings on stage is considered scandalous." She stared out of the window broodingly. "She sings, ergo she must be a fallen creature. Look at what happened to Mama and Papa."

Their mother had been an opera singer as well, and she had had the audacity to marry their father, Edward Sackville. Both had become social outcasts, and they had left England, never to return.

Kit looked grim. "One would hope that things have changed in the meantime."

"I would not count on it, Kit."

"And I hear your schedule this season is as full as ever. Your manager tells me he booked you for nine operas and a personal performance for the Prince of Wales himself?"

Ava's fingers clawed into the satin covering of her seat. "Phileas agreed to it before asking my permission. It will never happen."

Kit made a soundless whistle. "You will give the Prince a basket. Do you think that is wise?"

"They will recognise me. It will ruin not only me, but you, the entire family. I can't let this happen." Her finger-nails bit into the flesh of her hands. "I will disappear before it comes to this. I won't repeat Mama's fate."

"Yet your reputation has never bothered you before. Remind me again why that would matter?"

Her eyes bore into his. "A home, Kit. The chance for a true home. Where else but here, in England, where our ancestors are buried? Where our father grew up? Where our inheritance—your inheritance—is."

"A home," he whispered as his eyes flew to the magnificent mansion that glinted orange in the setting sun. There was a yearning in his eyes, some wistfulness, but also a glint of scepticism. "You think this is it? You think we have finally arrived? You truly think we have finally come home?"

She grasped his hand and clutched it tight. "Oh, how I hope that all our wanderings have finally come to an end. We've never belonged anywhere. You know that this is what we have wanted—what I have wanted—beyond anything."

"Your hands are icy." He patted her hands. "Let us go, then." He rapped at the roof and the carriage set in motion.

Ava popped in her dentures and huddled deeper into her shawls.

The carriage drove along an alley of massive chestnut trees into a sweeping driveway, and then halted. As Kit helped Ava down, the imposing front door opened.

Silence reigned for a moment.

A lady of indeterminable age with an eagle nose dressed in funereal black stepped forward. "Lord Sackville. Welcome home."

"Cousin Millicent. We finally meet." Kit grabbed her by the shoulders and planted a kiss on each cheek.

The woman recoiled. "Pray unhand me, my lord," she gasped. "I am not your cousin."

Kit blinked. "You are not?"

"Certainly not." There were two specks of red on her cheeks.

"I am Millicent," a gentle voice whispered. A tall, slender woman in a simple brown gown stepped forward, clutching a cat in her arms. "And this is our housekeeper, Mrs Blake."

Kit had the grace to blush.

Cousin Millicent was in her fifties and looked like the typical spinster with her hair drawn back into a severe bun. She greeted them with a barely audible voice. She was clearly shy; however, when she talked to her cats, a smile stole onto her face, and she seemed to forget her shyness.

She seemed to be a kind and gentle soul with a big heart for animals. Ava liked her immediately.

Millicent showed them the house and the estate, leaving the siblings clearly overwhelmed. "All this is yours now," Millicent said as she clasped her hands in front of her. "Now that Sackville Hall has a new owner, I shall, of course, leave."

"But where would you be living, Cousin?" Ava asked.

"You can, of course, remain here for as long as you want," Kit assured her. "The place is big enough for us all."

"I have lived here with Father my entire life. And yet...it has been a rather lonesome life. I was delighted when I learned I had family still, two cousins who were living abroad. I would very much enjoy spending more time with you." Millicent hesitated before continuing. "I have seen very little of the world, you know. I hardly even know London." She twisted her fingers about her shawl.

"I-I would not mind living in London. I understand you lead a busy life in London. I could rent my own place somewhere nearby. ..." her voice petered off.

Ava and Kit's eyes met. "Nonsense, Millicent, of course you can stay with us," Kit said impulsively.

After a moment's hesitation, Ava nodded.

Millicent lifted her anxious eyes. "You wouldn't see this as an imposition? I wouldn't be a burden. I don't socialise, and I am quite happy to stay at home with my cats. That is...if you don't mind me bringing my cats as well?"

"How many are there?" Ava asked.

"Seven," Millicent whispered.

"Goodnesh!" Ava exclaimed while Kit burst into laughter.

"They are my children, and I could not bear to be parted from them." Millicent kissed the head of the ginger-coloured cat she carried in her arms.

Kit laughed harder.

Ava looked at him helplessly. It would be a challenge to maintain her charade if her cousin resided with them in the same house. But denying Millicent's request to live with them in London seemed callous. She was the only family they had left.

Ava touched Millicent's arm. "Of course, you can live with us in London, and by all means, bring your cats!"

Thus, it came that the Sackvilles returned to London in grand style with their cousin Millicent, their carriage packed full of trunks and boxes, as well as baskets filled with seven cats.

Chapter Five

THE OPERA HOUSE WAS BURSTING AT ITS SEAMS. THE pit overflowed with people who sat on top of each other on the benches, with some attempting to sit on the stage. It was hot, the air stale with the rancid smell of sweat, oranges, cheap perfume, and decaying flowers. Chandeliers swung from gilt sconces attached to the white and scarlet boxes, illuminating the massive domed ceiling from which Apollo in his chariot, flanked by half-naked muses, smirked at the folly of the audience beneath. Above the general din of people conversing and laughing, the orchestra frantically attempted to play the tunes of a country dance performed by a set of dancers on stage, which no one watched. Gentlemen in breeches and buckled shoes squeezed into the corridors, where the crush was the greatest, to visit the ladies in the boxes, who simpered and flirted with their fans.

There was a rustle on the left as the Prince of Wales stepped into his box. Golden buttons nearly popped off his dark-blue waistcoat that stretched tightly across his paunch. On his raised hand he led a voluptuous, dark-haired beauty dressed in a white round gown trimmed with flounces of satin.

"The Marchioness of Conyngham," a lady with a massive ostrich feather on her head whispered to her male companion in a neighbouring box. "They say she is his latest paramour."

"'Pon rep, Prinny has become squelch-gutted," a dandy next to her lifted his lorgnette to study the prince. "One can watch him grow fatter by the minute."

"Not only that, but he's also drunk. Again."

The entire opera house watched as the Prince stumbled over a chair. He would have crashed to the ground, dragging the Marchioness with him, had two footmen not rushed forward to support him. They led him to his chair, where he collapsed, panting.

"Five quid Mlle Winter will let him wait an hour," the dandy told his friend, a thin man in a burgundy coat, who leaned against the side of the box.

He studied his manicured fingernails and drawled in a bored voice, "Ten that she won't. She wouldn't dare."

"Deal." The men shook hands.

The Prince shifted in his seat and drummed his fingers against the scarlet velvet dressing of the balustrade.

The people in the audience murmured to each other. Would she, really? Would she let him wait?

She would.

Mlle Violetta Winter would let anyone wait.

Even the Prince Regent.

"You must do something!" the conductor whispered to Ayrton, the theatre manager, in the orchestra pit beneath. "We've already waited two hours. We will have a revolt if she doesn't appear soon. The Prince is already displeased." He clutched his sheets in terror. The manager wiped his forehead. One could not let princes wait, and he would so very much like to keep his job. He stumbled on the stage and bowed in the direction of the Prince Regent, who scowled down at him.

"Silence. Please." Ayrton looked at the people in the pit in desperation. Didn't they understand? She would not sing unless there was absolute silence. Divas were like that. Fickle, unpredictable, moody.

A temporary lull. Someone threw an orange peel at him. It smashed against his coat. A trickle of laughter.

Then the muttering resumed.

"Silence, I say!" a powerful voice roared from the royal box.

The Prince had spoken.

The muttering subsided.

Not a hush was heard.

She stood in the side wing, grasping the heavy brocade curtain with one slim hand, the other pressed to her heaving chest.

The few minutes before a performance were the worst. The roiling in her stomach, the jittering of her hands. The desire to run, far, far away, from it all.

The adulation. The fame. The glory.

The pressure of having to fulfil expectations.

33

Of having to be a goddess.

She would never get used to it. Yet she knew the fame, the adulation, was not for her. It was for the goddess, the diva. It was for the creature she became when she stepped on stage.

They called her a nightingale, a shooting star, an angel's voice.

No one, they said, could sing with that timbre: high, clean, clear, and sweet, enchanting, seductive, bewitching, and wild.

How they adored her.

It was time.

She closed her eyes.

I am the music.

I am the voice.

She took a big breath. One. Two. Three.

She stepped on stage.

The masses of people in front of her blurred, and the jittering in her stomach subsided.

There was silence.

The first strains of the violins started.

It swept her away, the music, as it always did.

All she had to do was throw back her head—and sing.

Chapter Six

Miss Ava Sackville sang.

It sounded as lyrical as a frog croaking amongst the rushes, and some would consider that din to be preferable to the performance the venerable spinster displayed that evening.

Her fingers crashed down on the piano in an off-beat chord that missed the keys, and her pitch was so crooked that the Tower of Pisa appeared straight in comparison. Everyone winced in unison.

The damsel sang on in blissful ignorance. She had her head thrown back, revealing a white throat; her spectacles had shifted on her nose and slid down to its tip, which was graced by an enormous wart.

When she finished with a shrill flourish that made a cat's yowling sound pleasant, everyone burst into enthusiastic applause. It was the applause of the relieved, of the grateful, of those who embraced the end of their torture. Many a gentleman was tempted to drop on his knees to give thanks that this torment was finally over.

"My ears will need at least a fortnight to recover from this spectacle," Lady Beecham mentioned to Mrs Townsend as they moved to the adjoining salon to partake of refreshments. "I am surprised they let her sing in the first place."

"She is the sister of Lord Sackville, so naturally Lady Westington had to invite her to sing." Mrs Townsend drew her arm through Lady Beecham's and lowered her voice. "It is clear the poor woman has not had any musical instruction whatsoever. She has no ear at all for music. Rather difficult to believe she is his sister. Him being so handsome, young and all the crack. But like his sister, he's somewhat odd, don't you agree? There is an air of eccentricity about him."

Both heads turned toward Lord Sackville, a golden-headed Adonis belonging to the dandy set with his garish pink waistcoat, padded coat, and pinched waist, who lounged on the sofa by the window. His shoulders shook. It appeared he was laughing silently at a private joke, as there was no one else about to share the joke with.

"Eccentrics, both. Their cousin Millicent Sackville as well. One hears she is in London. She hasn't been seen in society in decades. One can't blame her in the least, for it is commonly known the women in that family are not favoured appearance-wise."

The heads of both women turned to take in the figure, dress, and hairstyle of Ava Sackville, who still sat by the pianoforte. She was a short, dumpy woman in a bulky, grey dress with a lace fichu draped about her neck that looked like its original function had been that of a crochet tablecloth. Her hair was greyish-brown and drawn back into a severe, tight bun. A pair of oversized spectacles perched on her nose. Everything about her screamed spinster.

"Poor woman," Mrs Townsend agreed. "It can't be easy looking like this. Especially with her brother being so very handsome!" An affected sigh. "I expect the baron will be looking for a bride, soon?"

"That is to be expected. Oh! But there are bigger fish to catch this season. Have you not heard? They say that Ravenscroft is looking for a bride!"

A gasp. "No. Really? That is news indeed."

"Yes, and they say he is in a hurry, yet quite unable to find anyone suitable!"

"Why would that be? Ravenscroft? He is plumper in the pocket than Croesus, with that father of his."

"That appears to be precisely the problem. Living-stone is bound to live for several decades, still, and he is said to be terribly tight with his purse strings. Also, with the fast life Ravenscroft's led so far, he isn't too appealing to some of the more respectable families."

"Some will find it easy to overlook his lifestyle if one considers what he is to inherit one day." There was a gleam in Mrs Townsend's eyes.

Lady Beecham giggled. "Don't tell me you are about to set your cap at him..." The ladies moved into the other room and out of Ava's earshot.

Ava bit on her lip as she collected her sheets of music, pretending she hadn't overheard the exchange of the two women.

So far, so good. She would never be asked again by anyone to sing again, ever. That had been precisely her objective. From now on, for the rest of the season, she could sit in a corner of the room and observe, rather than be the one being observed...

Kit made his way across the room to her side with an exaggerated swagger. He bowed to one lady in the passing as he did so and flashed a smile at another before he reached her side.

"Congratulations. You have outdone yourself. That has been a perfectly hideous spectacle." He took the sheaves of music from her and stacked them up on the piano.

Ava pushed the spectacles up her nose. "Thank you. Let us hope it need not be repeated."

"No fear," he replied cheerfully, "I see an invisible bubble of social ostracism engulf us as we speak. No one dares approach us lest you burst into song again." He lowered his voice. "Are you certain this was such a good idea?"

"They will do their best to avoid me from now on, but certainly not you. You seem to have roused considerable interest amongst the ladies."

Kit arranged the tulip in his pocket hole. "Of course. My charm is irresistible to the female sex."

"Oh, hush Kit. Naturally you would arouse interest; after all, the last baron, Uncle Richard, was said to be an old, cantankerous bat. May he rest in peace. That aside, you are still in Society's good graces, freshly arrived from the Continent, with an air of mystery about you. It helps that you look the part, despite that awful pink waistcoat. And do stop using that lorgnette; you don't need it in the least, and it merely looks ridiculous."

"What, this?" He lifted a lorgnette from the previous century that was attached to his waistcoat and looked through it haughtily. "Only if you drop those hideous spectacles of yours. Makes your eyes look owlish. And don't overdo the squinting. I had Lord Montagu ask me whether an eye disease runs in our family, I tell you."

"I can't see without them." Ava pushed her spectacles up further on her nose. "Did you notice? I learned to speak without a lisp." She bared her teeth to reveal her buck teeth. "It took much practice, indeed."

Kit snorted.

"Smile," Ava hissed. "That woman with the hideous purple turban by the fireplace is assessing you."

Kit turned around and bowed ostentatiously in the direction of the lady, who simpered back at him. "That was Lady I-forgot-her-name. Dashed impossible to remember them all. Said she sent us an invitation to a masked ball. We seem to have received several verbal invitations already. Balls and picnics and the like. And more balls. It looks like this season is bound to be dreadfully dull with only dancing and concerts by amateurs. Do we really have to suffer through it all?"

"Expect more cards to come flooding in tomorrow," Ava prophesied. "And yes, we ought to go to the most important ones. It is the only way to get a firm footing in English society."

Kit cleaned the lorgnette with his handkerchief and

looked at her through it. "I don't know. Life in Vienna somehow seemed to be easier. Fewer rules and all that."

"It is just that everyone knew us in Vienna. No one knows us here. But this will change soon."

Ava noticed a tall gentleman standing by the French windows. He had a strong profile and piercing eyes that assessed her broodingly. He was tall and athletic, and his well-cut coat strained against his arm muscles. He had a stern jut of the chin that seemed at odds with the thick, dark-brown curls that tumbled playfully over his high forehead.

Their eyes met.

Something flipped in her chest, and Ava blushed hotly. She tore her eyes away and tugged at her pashmina shawl.

"Who is that man by the window?" she hissed at Kit.

"That? That is the famous Ravenscroft. There is some scandal attached to him, but other than that, he is being skirt-chased by all and sundry; I fail to see why everyone is so in awe of him."

"He's been observing me the entire evening."

"He's no doubt taken by your beauty." Kit yawned. "Or your singing. Or both."

"I very much doubt that," Ava said dryly.

"I behold a woman with sheets under her arms bearing down on us. It appears there is to be more singing, and I have had my share. A man can take only so much crooked singing in one evening."

As Ava followed her brother out of the room, she felt Ravenscroft's stare between her shoulder blades.

There had been a brooding, inquisitive look on his

face, as though he pondered on a weighty question that somehow involved her.

Why would someone like him notice a spinster like her? She was invisible to everyone else.

He was dangerous, her instincts told her. Very dangerous.

Chapter Seven

Tristan, Earl of Ravenscroft, was not having any luck finding a wife. Two weeks after his father had pronounced the momentous decision that would change his life forever, Tristan's list of marriageable ladies had shrunk dramatically.

Even though most ladies would marry him in the blink of an eyelash, they were not what he was looking for. Doxies, ballet dancers, widows with dubious pasts, and beautiful fortune hunters. Flighty, frisky, flirty beauties who were unashamedly after his fortune. It was sobering that this was the only sort of women he seemed to attract.

He needed someone respectable and plain.

There was only one insurmountable problem: the respectable, virtuous, plain old maids seemed to hold him in dislike.

It was confounding.

Lady Evelyn Mountbatten, for example. A stick of a

woman with straw-coloured hair and a pointy nose, ugly as Medusa. She'd had three unsuccessful seasons before her parents had wisely withdrawn her from society. She had, at first, accepted his proposal, only to burst into tears a minute after, and to reveal she would rather die than marry him.

Tristan had blinked. "I beg your pardon?"

Lady Evelyn had buried her face in her handkerchief, and, in-between violent sobs, revealed that her heart had been given to someone else already, and that marrying Tristan would kill her. Tristan, relieved, had taken his hat and withdrawn.

He had never even seen the second person on his list, Miss Georgiana Harrington, so he could not ascertain whether the rumours of her having a hunchback were true. He supposed not. For that lady had scrambled deftly out of her window and fled as soon as he'd been announced. Her parents had apologised profusely, asking whether his lordship wouldn't mind waiting an hour or two until she returned. After half an hour of torturous conversation and glasses of cloying lemonade, Tristan had mumbled that he had a pressing appointment and left, only too glad that this cup, too, had passed.

Then there was Miss Esther Dorington. By George! That lady had been outright cross with him, calling him a useless philanderer and scolding him for "attempting to make her the butt of a joke by ridiculing her unfortunate situation in life."

"I assure you, Miss, this sentiment is farthest from my mind—"

"Begone, scoundrel, and look for thy next prank elsewhere!" She'd lifted the poker to bash him over the head.

He'd fled.

Three proposals.

Three rejections.

By Jove, that was humiliating.

The entire experience had left him with a vague feeling of unease. Was the prospect of being married to him so revolting that the well-bred, respectable ladies preferred to flee through the window and bash him over the head with a poker?

Tristan sighed at the irony of it all. He, who could have any beauty at a snap of a finger, considered it a chore to find a plain, respectable wife.

Not that the beauties were any easier to converse with. The last time he'd conversed with a Rum Doxy, it had gone thus:

"My lord! Vauxhall was so pretty last night! The lampions! And the fireworks! And the pretty music! Wouldn't you agree?"

"Hm."

"I must say, I enjoyed the fireworks the most. I haven't seen anything more beautiful. Not even the ladies, and there were such lovely ladies in attendance, wouldn't you agree?" (Batting eyelashes, waving fan.)

"Ah." (Fan falls.)

"La, I had this dress made especially for Vauxhall. It was a gorgeous confection of fuchsia silk. Although the trimming was more orange and cornelian." (Her fan had lightly touched his sleeve.)

He'd perked up. "You mean like the stone?"

"My lord?"

"You know. Stone. Carnelian." If there was something he understood in this world, it was stones. "It is a chalcedony variant, reddish-brown, slightly translucent."

"My lord!" (Gasp.) "Are you implying my dress was translucent? How shockingly vulgar!"

"Oh! No, no, no. I meant because you mentioned carnelian."

"Coornelian. My dressmaker uses the word. The colour is all the crack."

"Yes, well, a carnelian has a red-brown colour—"

"But my dress was orange. Then you insisted it was translucent." (Blush.)

"No, I meant the stone, or a variant thereof, is slightly translucent."

"Rest assured, my lord, my dress was neither like a rock, nor was it translucent." With her nose in the air, she'd sailed away.

She would do her best to spread that it was all too true: silent and brooding Ravenscroft was a shocking rake who liked women with translucent dresses...

Tristan looked at his list with foreboding.

Now there were only the Sackvilles left. There were two, apparently.

He'd happened to hear one of them sing the other evening. The entire performance had left him physically ill. Not only had his ears hurt, but his eyes as well. The hags of Macbeth appeared comely compared to Ava Sackville. Tristan had grappled with himself the entire evening, but in the end, he could not bring up the courage to seek introductions with her brother, Lord Sackville, who'd appeared to be quite the dandy.

Tristan sighed. It was not to be helped. Word had gone out that Millicent Sackville, who had not been seen in society for decades, had joined her family in town. He would have to call on them and to propose to whatever Sackville creature happened to be at home.

Chapter Eight

Miss Ava Sackville and her brother had returned from visiting their cousin in Berkshire the day before. They had stayed in the country at Sackville Hall for only two days, for a pressing engagement had required them to return to town—with their cousin in tow. That was worth a good gossip, for Miss Millicent Sackville had not been seen in society for more than twenty years. One wondered what she looked like after all this time.

When Tristan arrived at their residence on Bruton Street, the butler immediately announced that Lord Sackville was not at home. A nuisance, but Tristan wasn't here to see his lordship, but his sister. Or cousin. Or was it aunt? He could not remember the precise family relationship. Too late, Tristan remembered Miles had mentioned the word "grandmother" in reference to one of the Sackville women. He felt a flight of panic overcome him.

The butler took his greatcoat, beaver hat, and stick and showed him into the drawing room.

The windows were swathed in heavy, brown brocade curtains, which shut out the daylight. He took a turn about and leaned against the mantle of the fireplace. Above it hung a painting of a Siamese cat.

There was something odd about the room, he decided, but could not pinpoint it. He was certain that he was alone in the room. Then why did he feel as if someone was watching him?

He turned and looked over his shoulder.

No one was there.

He glanced towards the closed door.

Wait. Was that a pair of eyes gleaming in that dark corner? And under the desk, something moved.

He turned to the other side and— "Aah!"—a screeching, hissing furball hurtled itself right at his face.

He stumbled backwards, over a footstool, and came crashing to the ground.

Just at that moment, the door opened, and Miss Millicent Sackville entered the room.

"Satinpaws!"

The cat miraculously let go of chewing his left ear and ambled towards the woman with a raised tail.

Tristan scrambled up, pulled down his waistcoat, and bowed.

Miss Millicent Sackville was a spinster as one expected them to be, with greyish hair drawn back in a strict bun, a plain brown dress, a thin, erect figure. Everything about her was faded.

She looked at him with wide, terrified eyes and clutched her cat in front of her. "The Earl of Ravenscroft," she whispered, as if he were Beelzebub personified.

He shifted and cleared his throat. "Miss Sackville."

"Are you hurt?"

He touched the scratch on his cheek. "Other than a scratch on my cheek, I seem to be fine."

"Christopher is not here," she said in a barely audible voice.

"I have come to call on you, actually."

"Me!" she exclaimed. "Oh dear. Would you, er, that is, *must* you have some tea?"

When he affirmed, she looked like she was about to burst into tears.

"Very well, if you would have a seat." She pointed to a chair. "If you please."

He would. The problem was that it was already occupied; there was a cat in it.

He sat on the sofa instead.

Come to think of it, now that his eyes had adjusted to the lighting of the place, he could see that there were several cats. Not counting the one in the portrait. One, two, three... was there a fourth behind the curtain?

"How many cats have you got?"

Her face brightened. "Seven."

"Good Lord."

"Satinpaws had a litter of five kittens, you see. I could not bear to give any of them away, and she is very protective of them. Do you, do you, do you not like cats, my lord?" Her voice quavered.

"I do not," he replied tersely, as he brushed some cat's hair off his precious pantaloons.

She seemed to crumple in her chair, and he cursed inwardly, wishing he'd responded differently.

"Cats are so—so—hairy," he tagged on lamely.

"They are, are they not? I have to brush Satinpaws three times a day." The white cat was thin, with black pointy ears, and looked at him malevolently. She'd be better named Scratchyclaws, it occurred to Tristan, as he rubbed the scratch on his cheek.

He stared at the woman, who sat stiffly in her chair, too terrified to look at him. Now was his moment: he would have to propose.

He cleared his throat. He opened his mouth. The vision of being married to her with seven cats flashed through his mind.

The cat narrowed her eyes at him and hissed.

The woman looked at him with frightened eyes.

He snapped his mouth shut.

He couldn't do it, by Jove. He simply couldn't.

The silence was so thick you could cut through it with a butter knife. He stared at her helplessly and wondered whether it would be unpardonably rude of him to jump up and run.

Just then, the door opened, and the butler brought in a tray, and Tristan exhaled with relief. Even more cats entered the room, all the same colour, with the same glassy eyes, and he swore they all hated him on sight.

The woman poured tea, and he racked his brain for something to say.

Miss Millicent spoke first. "Is Lord Livingstone well?" There were flecks of red on her cheeks.

He shrugged. "Well enough, aside from the usual afflictions one has when one grows older, I suppose."

"I see." She looked up to meet his eyes. "I used to know your father once. A long time ago."

"Did you, indeed?"

"Yes. When I was considerably younger, of course; barely seventeen, and had my first season." Her eyes glazed over in memory. "How long ago that was."

Tristan could not imagine her ever being young and having a season, but he nodded.

"He... your father had the reputation of being very charming."

Tristan nearly spat out his tea. His father and charming! Hah! The old devil was as charming as a chunk of granite, and equally hard in terms of stubbornness.

"I remember well when he got engaged." Miss Millicent finally loosened up as some memories surfaced. "Your mother, Marianne, was a diamond of the first water. It was a match made in heaven."

"You knew my mother?"

Millicent nodded. "We were friends before she married. She left this earth too early. It was so tragic. It—it broke him, didn't it?" She fiddled with the fringe of the tablecloth.

Tristan scowled. "Did it? I always thought their marriage was more of a marriage of convenience. A man like Livingstone is not capable of loving much."

Millicent stared at him with wide eyes. "I think you might be wrong there."

Tristan shrugged. "He is a cold, emotionless man who lives a calculated life down to the tiniest detail. All he cares about is family honour."

"You do not seem to get along very well with him?"

He laughed harshly. "He is a miser, and I hold him directly responsible for my mother's death. So no, we do not get along well."

Millicent's hands went up to her cheeks. "Oh, no."

"It is as it is." He found himself talking against his will. Maybe because he'd never talked about it with anyone. "My mother died miserably after having spent a winter in an institution because my father was too miserly to fund the heating of the place. She caught an inflammation of the lungs because there wasn't enough coal to heat the house."

"I don't understand. She was in an institution? But why?"

"To prevent some misunderstanding, it was because—"

Just at that moment, the door opened. He shut his mouth in time before he spewed forth more about a topic that he actually never wanted to talk about.

A melodious voice said, "Millicent, I found him! The little one was hiding under the stairs."

Tristan looked up, interested.

Then his jaw sagged.

Ava Sackville had grown even more hideous since he'd last seen her. Maybe that was because he hadn't seen her up close that evening when she'd sung. He'd been skulking by the windows and had seen her only from across the room, in safe distance from her screeching.

Tristan shuddered at the memory.

Miss Sackville was a little, shy woman, barely reaching his shoulders, plump, dressed in what appeared to his eyes to be a grey potato sack. Her hair was brown streaked with grey, tied up in a bun. Her face was round and pasty, and there were one, two, three, if not more moles on it. And was that a wart on her nose? In her hands, she held another hissing cat.

"Oh." She stopped in her tracks and stared at him with wide eyes. "I did not know you had a visitor." She tugged on her fichu.

Millicent smiled at her, evidently relieved she had arrived. "Ava, this is the Earl of Ravenscroft. My lord, this is my cousin, Miss Ava Sackville."

The hag dropped into a crooked curtsy.

He tore his eyes away from her buck teeth, remembered his manners, and bowed.

"Lord Ravenscroft." There was a gleam of wariness in Miss Ava's eyes. "Would you like some tea?"

"I already had some. Thank you."

Both women stared at him.

Silence again.

Dash it all, this was awkward. He could not remember ever being in a situation that was as uncomfortable as this.

"Well. I'll be going, then. Thank you for the tea, Miss Sackville." He bowed again and was relieved to find that the butler was waiting for him with his hat and cape. He put both on and turned to flee.

"One moment, my lord." Miss Ava followed him out into the hallway.

"Miss?"

She drew her thick eyebrows together. "What exactly was it you wanted from my cousin?" To say that Ava Sackville was blunt was an understatement.

He bristled. "To call on her, of course. Not that this is any business of yours."

She pulled herself up stiffly. "Surely you must have known that my cousin has not been out in society for the last twenty years. Normally she doesn't receive any callers. It is not a secret. What is it you wanted of her?"

He would die three times and roll over in his grave rather than admit he'd considered for longer than a second that he'd intended to propose either to Millicent, or to her, Ava.

He put on a cold, derogatory smile. "Miss. I need not explain my actions to anyone, particularly if they are motivated by mere social courtesy."

"Social courtesy? Really?" She crossed her arms. "It would have made more sense to me if you'd called on Kit."

"Kit?"

"Ah. So, you haven't even been introduced. Which makes this even more curious. Kit is my brother. So, you don't even know him. You wanted to call on Millicent, whom you don't know, either. I daresay you have never even met her before today."

He was losing his patience with the woman. "And if I did not?" he snapped. "What is it to you?"

"I have heard everything about you, my lord," she hissed, and suddenly she not only sounded but also looked like a cat, her eyes narrowed to green slits. He took an involuntary step back. "I have seen the caricatures." He had no idea where she'd suddenly pulled it from, but she lifted an umbrella and pointed it at his chest, like a foil. "They say you are always dragging people into all sorts of pranks. Let us be clear, my lord, my cousin Millicent is a spinster, but she is the sweetest, kindest, gentlest creature that lives on this planet. If you dare slander her, or drag her into one of your pranks, or cause people to laugh at her; if her name is ever uttered in a derogatory fashion in the clubs because of you—I shall come after you." She jabbed the tip of the umbrella into his chest.

"Ow."

"And my brother personally will call you out." She paused, before adding ominously, "As will I."

"With an umbrella?" He *had* to ask.

She glared.

He was being assaulted in a dark hallway of a house full of cats by a spinster. With an umbrella. Protecting her older cousin's virtue. Inconceivable how he could have ever thought of her as shy. Suddenly, the ridiculousness of the situation overcame him.

"Bested in a duel with an umbrella. I can just see it." He lifted both hands in surrender. "Peace, Miss Ava, I meant no harm. Pray drop your weapon. 'Tis dangerous indeed. I daresay my waistcoat has a hole in it already. You will draw blood momentarily. Rest assured that this really was merely a courtesy call. My mother was acquainted with your cousin once. She also knows my father. Since she hasn't been in town the last twenty or so years, he suggested I call on her since he himself is indisposed." That was a half-lie, but it sounded good.

After a moment's hesitation, she dropped her umbrella. A rueful look crossed her face. "If that is true, I apologise. You must think me inordinately uncivil. I am very protective of my cousin, you see. She is the only family I have left. Aside from my brother." A hint of a dimple appeared in her cheek, but disappeared before he could fully take it in.

What was it about the creature that was somewhat strange? He couldn't quite pinpoint it. What an odd creature she was. She would be a perfect bride in terms of ugliness—he shuddered—but no, no and no! Miles was right. He couldn't sink that low. He had enough of Sackvilles. He'd cross all Sackvilles off his list, forever and always.

With a curt bow, he stepped out of the door and into his carriage.

The woman remained standing outside, looking after him with a puzzled air.

"Deuced strange women, both of them," Tristan muttered as he sat down in the upholstered seat of his carriage.

Something mewled.

He jumped. What was that? There, it mewled again.

He patted his pocket and pulled out a ginger kitten, which promptly bit into his thumb.

"Fred!" he roared as he grappled with the hissing thing. The carriage stopped. "We are being invaded by cats. Pray, take this—this—*thing* back to their house."

"Yes, my lord." Fred took the hissing, spitting kitten with equanimity and carried it back.

He returned shortly after. "She said you are to keep it." Fred dropped the kitten into Tristan's lap.

"I beg your pardon?" Tristan stared at it with hostility.

"A present, the younger Miss Sackville said. In terms of apology. They have six others, after all."

"Is this a joke?"

"No, my lord."

"Take it off me. Carry it on your own lap."

"With all due respect, my lord, I have to drive this carriage. Having a feline on my lap might distract me so much I might cause an accident. Not to mention the horses, who might get nervous." Fred looked apologetic and not in the least inclined to pick up the kitten, who found his lordship's lap very comfortable, as it had made a couple of turns, dug its claws into his woollen trousers as if to test the material, decided it would do, and then curled up and settled down between his thighs.

"The devil! What's it doing now?"

"Looks fairly comfortable and about to fall asleep, I'd say," Fred said. "Miss Ava Sackville said that if you throw it out into the streets, she will find out and be very displeased and come after you. With her umbrella." Fred did not pull a muscle in his face as he said so.

"She would," Tristan said, with feeling. "By George, she would! It seems, Fred, we are to be saddled with this feline thing." He looked distastefully down at his lap. His pair of trousers would be ruined for good. "Go on, then, we'd best head home before she saddles us with another one."

As his carriage pulled into Pall Mall, he looked down

on the ginger ball of fur. "I suppose you need a name," Tristan mused loudly. "Greek Fire or Flamethrower would be quite apt. I suppose it will have to be something more conventional. Achilles it is."

Achilles purred contently.

"WHAT WAS THAT ALL ABOUT, MILLICENT?" AVA inquired after the earl had left. "You seemed upset when conversing with his lordship."

Millicent needed to recover from Ravenscroft's visit and fanned her face. "The fright he gave me! I was having such a peaceful morning, reading about Ravenscroft's scandal in the papers. When Bentley announced him, I thought he was mistaken. But there he was! As though I'd somehow conjured up his presence by merely thinking about him. Then Satinpaws, naughty, naughty Satinpaws, thought she had to protect me and her kittens from him."

"What did she do?"

"She jumped into his face."

Ava uttered a bright peal of laughter.

Millicent covered her face, mortified. "It was humiliating! He was on the floor, grappling with the cat."

Ava laughed so hard tears streamed down her face. "Don't tell me Satinpaws managed to bring his lordship to fall!"

"He was thrashing about, and I believe he hurt himself. Oh, Ava, it is *not* funny! And then he insisted on staying for tea! And he was sitting there, large and disapproving and so well dressed like he was about to go to a ball, and he insisted on talking to me and all these awkward silences! I couldn't bear it! Oh Ava!" She jumped up, agitated, and fanned herself harder. "If I hadn't known better, I would have thought he was about to-to-to *propose*. To me. Lord Livingstone's son." Millicent burst into tears.

Ava jumped up in alarm. "Millicent, oh no. You are not crying, are you?" She patted Millicent's arm. "But proposing? Are you certain?"

Millicent dug out a handkerchief and wiped her nose. "Of course not, since he never actually uttered the words."

"But... why you?"

"I haven't got the faintest idea, Ava." Millicent looked at her worriedly. "I fear he is up to no good."

Ava scowled. "I knew it. He told me he was here because you were acquainted with his mother. So, he lied about that after all."

"Oh, no, that is true all right." Millicent crumpled the handkerchief in her hand. "His father is Lord Livingstone." She stared down at her hands. "And I did know him. Once. And I was friends with his wife before they married."

Ava looked confused. "So, he told the truth, and this might have been a mere social call?"

"I am not certain. It is odd since he never called on me before. The things he said!"

"What did he say?"

"That he and his father do not get along at all. That Livingstone is a miser and a murderer! That his mother died in an institution because of him."

"Oh dear. Can it be true?"

"I don't know. I daresay she died under some mysterious circumstances. She'd disappeared entirely for a year, then I read about her death in the papers. I was so sad, for she'd been a dear friend, but after she married Livingstone, we lost touch."

Ava furrowed her eyebrows. "There is a rumour going around that it is his father who insists that he gets married. I am not surprised if their relationship has gone sour."

"I have read about it, too, which is why the silly notion popped into my mind that he wanted to propose to me." She waved it away. "It is all fudge and nonsense. I am not good at social interactions anymore. I must have misconstrued his intentions entirely. Let us speak of it no more."

"Rather sad if one is forced into marriage like that," Ava mused. "So entirely without affection for one another."

"I quite agree." Millicent grasped Ava's hands. "I say that one ought not to marry but for love."

"Have you ever been in love?"

Millicent looked at Ava with widened eyes. "In love? Me?" Her eyes dropped. "Oh, my."

Ava took that as a negative. "I haven't been in love either. It isn't in our stars, it seems."

"I have once loved a man," Millicent said in a low voice. She was talking more to the cat on her lap than to Ava. "He was tall and beautiful, and ten years older than me. He was also a rake."

Ava dropped the spoon with a clank. "Who was he?"

Millicent continued as if she had not heard her. "It is difficult to believe now, but when I was younger, I was rather pretty. He told me so countless times. He brought me flowers every day and wrote me love sonnets. I was terribly in love with him. We were to be married."

"And?" Ava waited breathlessly.

Millicent's fingers flitted nervously from plucking at the crocheted tablecloth to the sugar bowl, to the lid of the teapot, and back again to plucking at the tablecloth. "He wanted me to live in a grand mansion. Bigger than Sackville Hall. Bigger than anything I've ever seen before."

"Goodness, Millicent. Who was he?"

She looked up, and her brown eyes filled with tears. "You see, I would have had to leave my cats."

Ava registered the full import of what she said. "You turned down a gentleman's suit because you could not bear to leave your cats?"

"He did not like cats. Said he abhorred them. And then, my mother was an invalid and needed me to take care of her. I couldn't bear the thought of her being all alone in Sackville Hall. My father—may he rest in peace—was not a bad sort of man, but he could be rather cold at times. And then there was everything else. The house to manage. The gardens."

"In other words, you could not bear to leave your home."

Millicent looked up; relieved Ava understood. "Yes. I could not bear to leave my home. But, Ava, I used to think home was a place like Sackville Hall. But now, I think home is the people you love."

Ava chewed on her lower lip as she considered the notion. Her entire life she'd searched for home, thinking it was a geographical place. Could Millicent be right, and she'd looked in the wrong place for home?

She cuddled the little kitten on her lap, which had begun to purr. This reminded her of Ravenscroft. Her forehead darkened. "Oh! I gave Ravenscroft one of Satinpaw's kittens! Maybe that was a mistake."

"He clearly doesn't like cats." Millicent sniffed. "A person who doesn't like cats has no heart."

"We will have to keep an eye on him. I'll ask Bentley to ask in his household whether he treats the little one well. In secret. Servants tend to talk to each other and be an enormous source of information."

"I must ask Bentley to bring my hartshorn salt, for my nerves are quite upset." Millicent still needed some time to recover from Ravenscroft's near-proposal.

"How excessively odd, this entire episode," Ava said thoughtfully.

Chapter Nine

He'd had a narrow escape, indeed! For Millicent Sackville could have been his mother, and this Miss Ava was not only ugly, but ill-mannered and disagreeable. Unfathomable to be married to either of them.

Tristan had deposited Achilles in the hands of his housekeeper, with strict instructions to keep the creature out of his sight.

What he needed now was a glass of good, strong whiskey.

As he downed his drink, the butler announced Miles, who promptly came sauntering into the room.

"In the doldrums, I see?" He clapped Tristan on the shoulders. "I would be, too, in your stead."

"Helpful and cheerful as always, Miles," Tristan replied testily.

"Never fear. I have just the solution to your conundrum." Miles fumbled around and pulled out a bill.

"What is this?" Tristan unfolded the bill. It was from

the Opera House, the King's Theatre in the Haymarket. "*Don Giovanni?*"

"This, my dear boy, is the solution to all your problems. The cure to your malaise. The elixir of life."

"I read the premiere was utter chaos. The pit overflowed to such an extent, people swung fists and duelled over seats."

Miles dropped into a chair. "It is true. I was there. They shamefully overbooked the house. But it was worth every minute. Come with me to the opera tonight and let us languish over Violetta Winter's beauty."

"I don't know, Miles. I am indifferent to opera and don't have a box. The noise is intolerable; one can barely hear the music." Tristan had once reprimanded two gentlemen who were heatedly debating about the corn laws while the opera was in full swing. The gentlemen had ignored him, and Tristan had left in the middle of the first act after a drunken dandy had thrown tomatoes at him by accident. They'd been for the singer who'd begun singing an aria that was from another opera entirely, just because he'd wanted to. Tristan would have called the dandy out, but one did not call out drunken fools.

"You will stay in my box, of course." Miles placed a hand over his heart and bowed. "I'll accompany you. I go only to hear Violetta Winter. And, by the by, there is absolute silence when she sings. From the very first tune of the overture to the very last until the curtain falls. You can hear a feather drop. I tell you, Tristan, I've never experienced anything like it. They say it is because the diva refuses to perform unless there is silence during the entire duration of the opera. Apparently, it's part of her contract. Refuses to put a foot on stage otherwise. They say she once let the audience wait for a full three hours until it dawned on them they had to shut up before she showed up to sing. Says it's barbarically bad-mannered to talk during a performance, that it's not done on the Continent. Can you believe the gall of it? Insists that we, the crème de la crème of the English *ton*, are to listen to the music quietly. The notion is so very bourgeois. If it weren't Violetta Winter, she'd find herself singing to an empty house. Everyone knows we are there to socialise and show off our newest waistcoats, not to appreciate music." He flicked at his cravat, tied in the Oriental style.

Tristan had to admit he was getting curious. "Sounds like she is quite a personality if she manages to keep an entire theatre of three thousand people under control."

"Thus is the power of a diva. She reigns over our hearts." Miles was in raptures again. "Oh, do come. You must see this. I promise you will not regret it."

"Very well. Since I have no plans for tonight, I might as well accompany you. But I warn you, Miles, if I fall asleep during the first act, I'll leave during the interval and not stay for the second act."

Miles' eyes gleamed. "Want to bet you won't?" He extended his hand.

Tristan hesitated, then shook his hand. "Done."

Chapter Ten

THAT NIGHT, TRISTAN, EARL OF RAVENSCROFT, stumbled along Haymarket in a dazed stupor. Rain drizzled onto his top hat, and he ruined his buckled shoes as he stepped into a puddle, but he barely noticed the cold water seeping up his stockings.

What in holy thunder had he just experienced? He could barely put it in words. His eyes were glazed over in memory, his ears—by George—what had he just heard?

He'd never heard such music in his entire life.

That voice!

And—*her*!

Sweet, merciful heavens. That woman!

She was—there was but one word—divine. He stopped to ruminate on the divine angel, the ethereal beauty of the goddess he'd just seen.

It had started just as he'd feared. It was a squeeze of immense proportions long before they'd even entered the vestibule. There was shoving and arguing, and a lady had fainted. Tristan would have turned around and gone home there and then if Miles hadn't pulled him along, and with the help of his footman, elbowed their way through the crowd. Things had eased up somewhat when they'd reached the staircase to the boxes. The director had stepped on stage and regretted to announce that there was to be a delay of about an hour because Violetta Winter had not yet arrived; in the meantime, the audience was to enjoy a performance of country dances. As soon as he'd uttered those words, he'd rushed off stage as the audience had pelted the poor man with orange peels.

"We want Violetta Winter! Not dolts performing country dances," Miles had shouted down from his box.

They had to sweep the stage first to remove the orange peels before the dancers could perform. As soon as the dances began, everyone settled into their seats to discuss the latest on-dits.

Tristan drummed his fingers against the balustrade of the box.

Miles chattered about the latest wager in White's, and what horse he intended to buy at Tattersall's later this week.

Tristan had no mind for wagers, White's, or horses, for he espied Mrs Townsend in the box across, slowly waving her fan in front of her face. She batted her eyelashes. This reminded him he had not yet solved his problem regarding his marriage. Less than a week was left. He groaned.

"Ladies and gentlemen, I have good news. Mlle Winter has arrived," the theatre manager announced.

The audience cheered.

"However, she will only consent to perform if there is silence."

To Tristan's astonishment, the chatter tuned down. The violins tuned their strings, and the maestro stepped into the orchestra pit.

Miles had been entirely right. There was such revered silence, one could hear a feather drop.

She was slighter, slimmer than he'd imagined. Somehow, he'd thought she'd be a tall, heavy-bosomed Valkyrie, not this dainty slip of a girl. She wore a splendid silken white taffeta robe a la française; her auburn red curls tumbled over her shoulders, unpowdered. She had a slim neck and a pleasing turn of the ankle.

Then she opened her mouth to sing.

Her light, lyric coloratura soprano was sweet, yet of immense power; it rang easily over the orchestra, penetrated to the farthest crevice of the theatre, rising into the domed ceiling, where it lingered. The crystal chandeliers chinked and clinked as the glorious tunes reverberated against it and returned to penetrate his soul.

Her voice was pure, innocent—and full of pain. There was revenge in it, too, and fire, oh, such fire. Then, a few moments later, she was in another role, that of the peasant girl, Zerlina, playful, loving, and seductive.

He'd never seen, nor heard, anything like it.

Tristan was lost, lost, lost.

During the interval between the acts, when the curtain had barely fallen, Tristan shot out of his chair into the corridor, and stumbled down the stairs.

Miles went after him. "No chance, old chap. They won't give anyone access to the green room. New rule."

"Since when?" Tristan shoved aside the people who were on the way to the refreshment room. It was customary for gentlemen to visit the green room behind the stage in between the acts to flirt a little with the dancers, maybe more.

"Since Violetta Winter." Miles elbowed his way through the crowd of men that had gathered in front of a closed door. "See?"

Miles was right. The door leading to the stage was firmly closed and a giant of a man stood in front of it with crossed arms.

"Good heavens. That fellow looks like he's a Viking about to lop our heads off." Indeed, the blond hulk grasped a scimitar that was attached to his belt. The group of hopeful gentlemen that had already gathered in front of the door was outraged that they were denied access.

"Stand back," the Viking's voice boomed. "No green room visits allowed tonight. She will not see anyone."

"But, my dear fellow, how can that be?" The nasal voice of the Duke of Cumberland sounded plaintive. "I have always paid homage to the divas and dancers during the intervals. Is this pleasure to be denied to me?"

The giant remained unmoved.

"Do you know who I am?" boomed another voice belonging to the Viscount of Malvich. He held a squashed bouquet of red roses.

"I must see her," shouted another.

For one moment, Tristan considered showing off his aristocratic privilege as well, then realised it was futile.

"There's no point," Miles confirmed. "Believe me,

I've tried every single night. She won't see anyone. It is quite unnatural. Breaking with a very serious tradition. She won't have a patron. She's even turned down Prinny, can you imagine? We are not pleased."

The previous diva, Angelica Catalani, had set up court in her dressing room and invited those lords and titled ones with particularly heavy pockets. It was common for the divas to supplement their coffers with the lavish payments of their patrons. It was also commonly known she'd had more than one lover at a time.

Was this tradition to be broken?

"But she has to choose at least one of us," protested Cumberland. He was quite old, and his teeth were yellow.

"Oy, the duke thinks she will choose him," sniggered a dandy in front of him. He smelled overpoweringly of perfume and sweat.

"It's his bloody title. Don't underestimate that," replied his crony, a fellow in a purple waistcoat. "I would place a wager she will choose him over one of us younger dandies."

"That's a good one. How much?" As the two dandies were busily arranging their wager, Tristan plucked a pencil out of one fellow's hand, scribbled an IOU on the back of his theatre bill, and handed it over to Miles.

"For a wager well won."

Miles grinned. "I told you so. I should have wagered more. You are smitten. Like the rest of us poor sods." He folded and pocketed the bill.

"It is a fact I don't have luck either on the gaming

table or with bets. Fortuna has forsaken me. Come, let's go." Tristan refused to stand at the end of a long line of lovelorn gentlemen, of which he now could count himself in the ranks. Besides, he could not wait to see her again, for the Second Act was about to commence.

At the end of the opera, they showered Violetta Winter with flowers. The squashed bouquet of the Viscount landed on some unfortunate musician's head. She gracefully picked up several violets from the ground and pressed her other hand against her chest in humble thanks. She liked the simple, smaller flowers, Tristan noted. He would send her a bouquet of violets the very next night. Her eyes rose to the boxes, to him—by George —she saw him!—her dainty lips tilted up in a smile—his chest squeezed—ice and heat trickled down his back— then her eyes moved on.

"Did you see that?" Miles turned to Tristan.

"She saw me," Tristan said stupidly, leaning out of the box to get a final glimpse of her, but she had disappeared in the side wing.

"Nonsense. It was me! She saw me." Miles puffed out his chest with pride. "Amidst an entire house full of people, she singled me out! And smiled."

Tristan turned to him in outrage. "Balderdash. She looked at me and our eyes met. Then she smiled."

They nearly came to fisticuffs in the middle of the theatre.

Miles patted him on the shoulder. "Calm down, dear fellow, calm down. Both of us. She singled out both of us."

Tristan grumbled but accepted his compromise,

while being certain it was him, she had seen. Fighting with Miles was the last thing he wanted.

"Well, that was that. Another failure," Miles grumbled as he squashed his hat on his head and headed towards his carriage, which waited in front of the theatre.

"Failure? How so? The music was divine. She was divine."

"Make no mistake, she was divine. But I came here like everyone else, for the sole purpose of seeing her. Might need a protector, you know. Who better than me? But the Viking once more crossed my plans. Saturday is another night and another attempt."

"You want to be her protector?" Tristan looked at him in disbelief.

"Shh. Not so loud." Miles looked around shiftily. "As does everyone else, of course. As I said, she must choose one of us."

"Must she?"

"Of course! It's the tradition."

"But with that Viking as a door guard..."

"That, indeed, is a conundrum. Shall we?"

Tristan shook his head. "I prefer to walk home."

He badly needed to clear his head.

Thus, it came that he was wandering about Haymarket, lost in the fog that had begun to seep out of the ground. At one point it started to rain. More than one hackney sprayed him with puddle water, and his coat was entirely drenched.

His mind was with the vision he had seen on stage.

His entire being, his body and soul, was on fire.

If he could, he'd drop to his knees right now, right in

the middle of this puddle, and worship her, burst into song. Never mind that he couldn't hold a tune.

Three and a half hours of opera and he'd turned into an even greater sop-wit than Miles.

Tristan lifted his eyes and saw the stars above—a miracle in and of itself, for the London fog had lifted.

He was besotted.

Chapter Eleven

"You did well." Phileas Whistlefritz slouched in another corner of the carriage. "The house was raving."

"I know. It was frightening. Especially when that fellow attempted to climb over the orchestra pit right over the musicians' heads to get on stage." Violetta Winter—also known as Ava Sackville—shuddered.

She had not expected the masses of people who'd pushed to the stage, the thunderous applause, the demands for encores, the adulation that almost frightened her. Certainly, she'd experienced much recognition when she sang elsewhere in Vienna or Paris. But she'd not expected the English to be so overwhelmingly enthusiastic. She had been lucky that no one had discovered her identity—so far.

When her mother was still alive, she and Kit had been allowed to attend the opera every Saturday night. One could say that Ava and her brother had grown up in theatre and opera houses.

Not only had her mother been a fine singer herself in her day, but her father had also been very musical. Not to speak of Kit, who sang a very fine baritone. Until his voice broke and he turned to acting, he'd even sung female roles. When her mother had gone on tour, her doting husband had accompanied her, and the children, naturally, had come along. It had been a restless life; an active, adventurous, and at times dangerous life, with the war on the Continent. They'd lived in palaces and palazzos, villas, and farmhouses. One summer long, they'd even joined a gypsy caravan and had slept on the floor in tents. She hadn't enjoyed that at all.

On her tour to France, Napoleon was enraptured with her and had insisted on offering her the position of court singer, which she'd tactfully refused. That same night, she'd packed up and left rather hastily to Vienna, where she'd settled down. Vienna, city of music. This is where they'd stayed while war had raged through Europe.

It had been an easy, comfortable life.

Until they'd received the notification that the last Lord Sackville had died, and Kit had not only inherited an estate with a manor but also a title, provided he returned to England.

She'd always yearned for a stable home. For a normal life. Even though she'd never known, really, what exactly that was: normal.

"I told you, didn't I, that you would take London by storm?" Phileas pulled up the lapels of his burgundy-coloured coat and looked pleased. "Only good that we have Hagen guarding the door, otherwise your admirers would have tramped it down. Every buck, dandy, and pink of the *ton* was in attendance. I heard the line of gentlemen lining up for an audience with you reached the vestibule. Alas, how disappointed they were when they could not meet you."

Ava plucked at the feather adornment of her reticule with a frown. "They are so very insistent."

"You kept the Duke of Cumberland waiting outside with the rest! The audacity! You know it is tradition here that the lords have access to the diva during intervals? You are denying them this."

Ava sat up straight. "Miss Violetta Winter is not like the other divas. She is not at anyone's disposal when she is in her room. She needs quiet and rest to prepare for the next act."

"Yes, yes, I know. Thing is, that the others don't know. Can't you make an exception, at least for the Duke of Cumberland?"

"No."

"For our national hero, Wellington?"

"No."

"His Royal Highness?"

"No!"

"Divas," grumbled Whistlefritz. "Dash it. For whom will you make an exception?"

"The agreement was for me to sing 'a tiny, wee opera,' as you told me, if you recall. That resulted in you booking me for nine, I repeat, nine operas. The audacity! Why am I even speaking to you, still? Why haven't I already dismissed you?"

He looked sheepish. "Because, ultimately, I only want what is best for you?"

She snorted.

"Because the pay is good?"

"That is more like it."

"Because... we are friends?"

"Don't look at me with those puppy eyes, Phileas." But he'd said the truth. Phileas, despite his foppish appearance, which Kit liked to emulate, was, next to her brother, the only person she trusted. He did have her best intentions at heart. He was cast in the odd position of protector. He was the one who'd organised Hagen the Viking as her personal guard at the opera. And yes, they were friends.

"Ultimately, Phileas, I cannot recall ever having agreed to having my personal time during the intervals at the disposal of those gentlemen, as you call them. They are merely on the lookout for a new mistress, and I am not available."

"Yes. But if Angelica Catalani did not mind—"

"I am not Catalani!"

"Thank the heavens you aren't." Phileas shuddered. "That woman nearly bankrupted the Opera House in her time. A nightmare." He wrung his hands. "If you could consent to seeing one, only one admirer, that would help tremendously in maintaining your reputation."

"My reputation?"

"As a diva, of course. There isn't a single diva at the opera who didn't hold court. A lady and her knights, just like in mediaeval times."

The carriage arrived. Phileas opened the door and jumped out.

"Hold court..." Ava mumbled. She sat up straight. "Hold court? A lady and her knights... just like in mediaeval times. Phileas, I have an idea."

Chapter Twelve

THE NEXT MORNING, TRISTAN FOUND HIS CLUB WAS abuzz with the latest news that their beloved opera diva had changed her mind.

"She has consented to grant access to any worthy suitor," Miles read aloud at a breakfast table in the morning room.

Tristan took a sip of bitter black coffee and cursed as he burned his tongue. "Read that again."

"It says, 'Our beautiful, talented Violetta Winter has announced she has consented to grant access to her humble company any worthy suitor willing to pay court to her in the mediaeval courtly tradition.'"

"The deuce? What does that mean?"

Miles raised a hand. "Listen on. 'The invitation is extended to gentlemen only, on Wednesday at eight o'clock in the evening, to drop off their cards in the box provided at the opera." He dropped the newspaper. "I can't believe it. She is going from 'no one enters my fortress' to 'come all and sundry'? What can be the meaning of this?"

Tristan picked up the paper and read it. It was true. The woman had put an invitation in the newspaper for the entire world to see. It couldn't be any more vulgar and indiscreet. He shook his head. "That's in three days. But you did not read on. It says in small print underneath: fifty gentlemen will be chosen to take part in a 'tournament'. So not 'all and sundry' after all. She will pick her swain."

"I take it you will drop off your card." Miles plucked a crumb from his sleeve to feign disinterest.

"Naturally. As will you?"

"Of course. I wouldn't miss this for the world."

"Tournament." Tristan frowned. "A melee? Jousting? It sounds bloody. Is this how we are to court women these days? Is it a fashion I somehow missed?"

"Wouldn't be surprised if it is. Let us find out."

"Zeus' beard, I nearly forgot. We have the Westington supper and musicale that night." Tristan groaned.

"Ah yes, it is your birthday, is it not? The ultimatum looms. I wonder whether your old man really meant it?"

"I don't dare to find out."

"Let us drop off our cards and then proceed to the supper, then. It'll be a fine evening to find a bride." Miles grinned. "Until then, we spend the afternoon at Watier's?"

Tristan grumbled, then shook his head. "I have some things to do. We meet in the evening."

AVA WENT TO OXFORD STREET SHOPPING. SHE TOOK the carriage and footman John with her to the clockmakers to have Kit's pocket watch fixed. She also wanted to buy a birthday present for Millicent. Sometime earlier, she'd seen that the clockmaker sold the prettiest music boxes she'd ever seen. There was one in particular that had taken her fancy. When one opened the lid, it played a pretty melody, and three little kittens, white, black, and brown, popped up and danced on their hind paws. It was the most adorable thing, especially since the white one looked exactly like Satinpaws. The shopkeeper had told her with some pride that it was a unique box and the only one of its kind in all of England. She'd asked Mr Grant, the shop owner, to set it aside for her. Millicent would love it, and she would love seeing a smile on the woman's face.

A bell dangled when she pushed the door open.

"Good afternoon. I would like to pick up my watch and the music box, if you please," she said when the shop assistant approached her.

"What music box?" he looked at her, bewildered.

"The one with the kittens?" Ava raised an eyebrow. Where was Mr Grant, with whom she'd conversed? He was further inside, at the counter, talking to a gentleman. "Never mind, I shall talk to Mr Grant directly."

She stepped up to the two gentlemen, both who bowed over something on the table. Ava narrowed her eyes and saw that it was a music box. Mr Grant took it, stuck a key into it, and wound it up. Then it played its melody, an enchanting tune.

"There it is, my box," Ava said, satisfied she'd made such a good choice.

"Your box?" the gentleman asked in a frosty tone as he turned.

"You!" Her heart gave a funny lurch as she acknowledged the Earl of Ravenscroft. She'd not recognised him immediately. He wore a black greatcoat and a hat pulled low over his face.

"Miss Sackville." His gaze lighted on her warily. "We meet again. Without kittens this time, I hope?" He looked behind her as if afraid he'd be assaulted by cats.

"How is the little one I gave you? I trust he is well?" She was certain he'd thrown it out into the street.

"Terrorising the entire household, but otherwise thriving."

She hadn't expected that answer.

"You choose this box, yes, your lordship?" Mr Grant rubbed his hands. "It is an enchanting little thing, made in Switzerland by the famous Jaquet-Droz brothers. There is only one like it in the entire world, I guarantee it."

Ava frowned at the box. "But this is my box, if you remember, Mr Grant? I particularly asked you to set it aside for me because I intended to purchase it."

"Eh—" Mr Grant's gaze slid away to his lordship "—I cannot recall having made such a promise. My lordship here is willing to pay twice the amount of its original price."

"Is he?" Ava set her hands on her hips. How dare the man disregard her merely because an earl turned up in his shop and wanted something? Did he think she had no money? "I will pay thrice the price."

"Really. Is this to be an auction?" Ravenscroft sounded bored. "I said I would buy it and there it is."

"I have the entire amount right here with me. I'll pay immediately. And you?" Ha. She got him there! It was well-known the nobility never paid for anything. Mr Grant would have to run after his money if he sold the box to Ravenscroft. If he was lucky, he'd get paid in three years' time.

But the earl remained unimpressed. "Mr Grant it is, yes? Pray wrap it up nicely."

"Of course, my lord." Mr Grant hesitated. "I take it is to be a present for a lady. Just so that I can choose the correct colour for the wrapping tissue."

"Indeed. She prefers pink."

Ava wrinkled her nose. No doubt he wanted the music box—her music box—for one of his many mistresses.

She smiled at him. She must have revealed her buck teeth because both Mr Grant and the earl both took an involuntary step back.

She pulled out her last weapon. "True gentlemen give precedence to the lady. A true gentleman—" she emphasised the 'true'—would withdraw and allow the lady to purchase the music box."

She gripped her umbrella tightly. If he dared to respond, "Lady? I see no lady," or something similar, she would impale him on the spot.

"True," he drawled. "Except..." he shrugged. She clenched her fingers around her umbrella. "I am so very sorry. But it appears I am no gentleman." He looked so apologetic, yet boyishly impudent that she felt a strange sensation in the pit of her stomach. It rendered her speechless.

"Miss Sackville, I need this box more than you do." Turning to the man, he said, "Send the bill to the usual address, will you, Grant?" He took the parcel the man handed to him, tipped his hat, and stepped past her out of the door.

The bell jangled.

He left.

"Impossible man!" Ava seethed.

"He is a lord, Miss," Mr Grant muttered. "What should I have done? Can't make yourself an enemy of his kind."

She pointed her umbrella at Mr Grant. "You have no backbone whatsoever."

"See here. I shall give you a discount on the watch. And I'll add on this here, as a small present, yes?" It was a dainty little porcelain pocket watch painted with flowers.

Ava sniffed. "It is pretty, but not what I wanted. But very well. Pack it up."

"Yes, Miss." He hurried to do so and then ran to the door to open it for her. "Come visit us again soon," he fawned and bowed her out.

"Not in your lifetime," Ava muttered.

"He is hateful, odious, and altogether impossible," Ava raged at Millicent later that afternoon.

She meant Ravenscroft, not the shopkeeper, though he had been odious, too.

Millicent pulled a needle with sage green thread through her embroidery. "Yet he is also charming and most wonderful to look at. They say he is a terrible rake."

"Millicent! You haven't lost your heart, have you? Ever since he called on you, you've been terribly dreamy."

Two specks of red appeared on her face. "Oh no! No, no, no. How can you even think that? Lord Livingstone's son!" She placed her hands on her cheeks. "It is only because it has been so long since I last had a gentleman converse with me. Aside from Kit, that is. But one hardly sees him, does one?"

Kit was very busy in the clubs, indeed.

"He doesn't like cats," Ava said darkly. She meant Ravenscroft, not Kit. "He barely tolerates the kitten we gave him."

"That is certainly a mar on his character. Cats know immediately who is trustworthy and who is not. On the other hand, he hasn't thrown the little one out into the streets either, so that improves his character somewhat."

The butler brought a package with a note. "It is for Miss Sackville."

Millicent took it, read the note, and gasped. "It is for you, Ava. It is from Ravenscroft."

"Speaking of the devil," Ava mumbled. She unwrapped the coarse paper, which revealed a box that was wrapped in delicate satin paper. She opened it.

It was a musical box, not exactly like the one she'd wanted, but very similar.

He'd written: "*Miss Sackville, Mr Grant told a fib today when he said it was the only box of its kind in all of England. I found this piece, which I hope you will enjoy. Pray accept this little box with my utmost apologies for my uncouth behaviour this afternoon. Your servant, Ravenscroft.*"

Ava's hand fluttered to her mouth. "Oh, my!"

"How prettily written!" Millicent beamed. "See? What did I say? He isn't as terrible as you make him out to be. What a charming little box this is!" Millicent took it from her hand and admired it.

This little music box was like the one with the cats, except in its centre was a colourful little bird that opened its wings and pirouetted to the lovely tunes. It was a Jaquet-Droz box in blue enamel and gold, the top encased with a ring of half-pearls. It looked more beautiful and also considerably more expensive than the one with the kitten, which had been more plain.

"I can't possibly accept this," Ava stammered.

"Of course you can." Millicent wound up the box with a little golden key and clapped her hands in delight when the bird flapped its wings and sang.

"It was actually meant to be for you, Millicent," Ava finally admitted. "As a birthday present. Now you have seen it, you decide what to do with it. Should I return it to Ravenscroft, or would you like to keep it?"

"Oh Ava, how lovely of you! I would very much like to keep it. I have never had anything like it. His lordship has an excellent taste."

Seeing her cousin's delight with the box, Ava relented.

What a strange man this Ravenscroft was! She found him deeply unsettling. But what unsettled her more was her reaction to him every time they met. This fluttering in her heart region. This humming in her body.

It bothered her excessively.

Chapter Thirteen

Tristan had exactly an hour left to find a wife. He would have to inform his father by midnight who his bride was to be. What on earth was he supposed to do?

His eyes drifted over the room where everyone had assembled for the musical presentation. There was to be some singing, a piano, and a harpsichord recital. With a squeeze in his chest, he remembered Violetta Winter the previous evening and sighed. After her divine voice, he simply couldn't bear to listen to any amateurish performance. No one compared to her. There was not a single woman in the room he felt like marrying.

Someone tapped his arm. Lady Erskine. She was a flirtatious widow, and for one mad second, he'd considered proposing to her. His reasonable mind told him she was an unsuitable match. Everyone knew she was a fortune hunter. Lady Erskine was notorious for having had three marriages, and each of her previous husbands had died under mysterious circumstances. His father would never countenance it.

What was she chatting about now? Something about the new milliner who'd opened a shop on Oxford Street, and whether he preferred caps, bonnets or turbans on a woman's head, and what colour did he think suited women the best? She fluttered her lashes.

"Carnelian," he replied absent-mindedly. "The colour, not the stone. And to prevent any misunderstandings, I don't mean any translucent gowns, either."

Her round pink lips formed a shocked O. "My lord!"

Thankfully, performances were about to begin.

He removed himself from the woman's grasp on his arm.

The planking of the harp gave him a headache. When a strained, whiney soprano began singing, Tristan fled.

The double doors of the music room were open and led to an anteroom, which was of equal splendour. He closed the door behind him.

On a side table were refreshments and drinks, and he stepped toward it and poured himself some Madeira from a decanter and downed it in one go. In the background, the infernal twanging and singing, albeit muted, continued.

He turned, wondering whether he should just throw his pride into the wind, go to his father, and beg for an extension.

It galled him to no end.

But his father had been so unyielding. Knowing him, he would not grant it.

He pulled out his pocket watch.

He broke out in a sweat.

What a quagmire. How, within the next hour, was he to get a wife? Not to mention that he would need another fifteen minutes for the footman to deliver the notice to Livingstone, who lived across the other side of the Square.

Tristan set down his glass, stepped to the window, pulled both his hands through his hair, threw back his head, and groaned.

Click.

His hand froze in his hair.

Click, it sounded again.

He whirled around.

The room was empty, as everyone had flocked to the adjoining music room. The settees and sofas along the wall were unoccupied.

But wait. There, in that corner, in the shadow, next to the palm tree.

He narrowed his eyes.

Ava Sackville.

Chapter Fourteen

AVA HAD NEVER AMUSED HERSELF AS MUCH AS THE night of the Westington supper and musical presentations.

It was the food, she decided, as she bit with gusto into another apricot and almond tartlet. Everyone had flocked into the music room to listen to Miss Harriet's screeching, so Ava found herself alone in the anteroom with a table full of sweets, puddings, and comfits. That, Ava decided, as she loaded her plate, was already well worth the evening.

She had never attended a supper and musicale where she was a spectator. In her early days as a performer, she was never offered any food or drink. After her performances, she left those venues tired, drained, and light-headed with hunger. This had improved little after she became famous, for, in the excitement of having Violetta Winter amongst their midst, the hosts might press a glass of champagne into her hand, but they usually forgot to offer her food.

Goddesses didn't need to eat, apparently.

Well, this one did.

And how she ate!

Ava selected a piece of puffy meringue and crossed her eyes in bliss as she bit into the sugary shell. She took her plate in one hand, a glass of champagne in another, and sat down in a comfortable armchair in the corner of the room. The door was half shut, so she was not overly bothered by the musical strains that drifted into the room.

Here she would stay for the rest of the evening and practise her knitting.

Ava, who was used to being the centre of attention at each social function, found her position to be unique. How different her perspective was when one was a wall-flower, forevermore looking in from the margins, yet never being a part of it. She found the experience curious and humbling, but also amusing.

Never again, she swore to herself, would she mock spinsters, those single ladies who, for no fault of their own, were unable to haul in a husband. It was not a position to be envied. Or the opposite: how some people met them with pity and overexerted kindness. That was equally bad.

Ava had been ignored from the very moment she'd stepped into the house. Lady Westington had given her a fleeting nod when she'd entered, but her eyes had already wandered on to her dashing brother, who looked like Adonis this evening, with his blond curls and tightly fitting coat.

There was no head turning towards her. No one had

nodded a greeting. No one had rushed over to kiss her hand. No one had glanced twice at her.

It was as if she was invisible.

It was wonderful!

Quite possibly, it had to do with her outfit.

She'd stroked a hand over her stiff, grey brocade, which she'd dug out from the bottom of the theatre trunk. The dress was hopelessly out of fashion, with a waist that was too low, and a material that was too heavy. The derisive line of Lady Brockmore's lips as she'd passed her told her she'd succeeded.

The advantage of being invisible, she found, was that it gave her something which she was hitherto unfamiliar with: freedom.

She could do whatever she wanted—read a book, knit a shawl, poke a finger in her nose—and no one would notice. No one cared what Miss Ava Sackville, spinster, was up to, as long as she sat prim and proper in her corner.

She could observe the lords and ladies as they peacocked around the room and amused herself by guessing who was who.

Her host, Lord Westington, was a portly man with a booming voice, dreadfully vulgar as he flirted with the ladies.

Lady Westington wore a plume that was altogether too big for her head, and she flirted with Lord Buckville, who was a dandy and evidently in love with Lady Erskine, the beauty of the evening with dark, corkscrew curls and a very good figure in cerulean blue. Lady Erskine in turn seemed to be more interested in flirting with Ravenscroft, who stood tall and aloof by the windows, not making any attempt at all to socialise.

Ava found she could not tear her eyes away from him. He was impeccably clad in a dark-blue swallowtail tail-coat, silken waistcoat, and breeches. The simple elegance of his outfit stood in stark contrast to the flamboyance of many other gentlemen. He had his hands clasped on his back and his profile was sharp, classical. His chin was firm, his lips almost stern, his forehead high, and his nose narrow. A strong profile, Ava thought; not exactly hand-some, but arresting. She observed him with interest. Did she imagine it, or did he not feel entirely at ease talking to Lady Erskine? He clutched his fingers in his back rather tightly, stepped backwards when she stepped forward, and he did not smile even once. When the lady batted her eyelashes at him, he seemed at a loss.

Interesting.

"Ladies and gentlemen, we will proceed with the performances. Miss Murray will commence with a harp piece," Lady Westington had announced.

Time to disappear. Ava had slipped through a half-open door and found herself in the room with the sweet buffet. After she'd finished eating to her heart's content, she sat in a shadowy corner to practise her knitting.

To her surprise, not ten minutes after the perfor-mance had begun, the door opened, and a man entered stealthily, shutting the door behind him.

Ravenscroft.

Her heart hammered in her chest. She froze in her chair and held her breath. He evidently did not see her, for he stepped up to the table, poured himself a glass of Madeira and downed it in one go.

There was something erratic about that movement.

He stepped to the window and pulled his hand through his thick, dark brown mane once, twice.

He tugged at his cravat and rubbed his neck.

It was an impatient move that expressed agitation.

About what?

And why?

Ava bent forward. Was that a groan?

There, again.

He pulled out a pocket watch, shook his head, and sighed.

He was clearly suffering.

A gamut of emotions ran through her. Ravenscroft had annoyed her, infuriated her, even. Then he had baffled her by his unexpected generosity, and now she felt an unexpected twinge of sympathy for the man. Underneath it all was that perplexing fluttering in her stomach every time his gaze met hers.

She was *not* attracted to him, she told herself.

Besides, it wasn't as though this had happened too often when they'd met in the past, and he hadn't even noticed her presence tonight.

She picked up her knitting needles and proceeded to knit as loudly as possible, which wasn't easy because her needles slid in her moist hands.

Click.

He whirled around. His eyes fell on her.

Mud-brown eyes with amber flecks. Dark, deep pools

of soulful eyes with a hint of melancholy—her stomach flipped.

Ava nearly dropped her knitting needles.

"Good evening, my lord," she stuttered.

He stared.

Well. What would he see? A spinster. It was quite illogical of her, but suddenly she wished she had worn a prettier dress. She was aware of her gauche dress, her wig, which she hoped wasn't crooked, her pasty face and her awful spectacles. He'd see an old maid hunching over her knitting work.

"Miss Sackville." He took several steps towards her, towered over her, and frowned down on her ferociously. "Miss Sackville," he repeated, then cleared his throat. "We meet again."

"Yes."

His eyes fell on the bundle of wool in her lap. "What are you knitting?"

"I am not certain." She lifted the misshapen thing. "It might be a shawl for my brother."

"I see." He drew his thick eyebrows together as if trying to see a shawl in there somewhere. "May I ask why you are knitting a shawl here instead of attending the performance?"

"Because it amuses me more." Ava continued knitting.

The last time they'd seen each other they'd quarrelled, and she'd been very cross with him. Then he'd pulled the rug from under her feet by unexpectedly sending her a music box. She'd intended to send him a thank you note but had found that inexplicably difficult to write. She cleared her throat. "I have not yet thanked you for the pretty box you've sent me. It is exquisite and worth far more than the other box with the kitten. I would have sent it back, but Millicent insisted on keeping it. It gives her great joy. Thank you."

He gave a curt nod. "It is a trifle. I finally found it in an obscure little shop at the edge of the city, after having visited every other clockmaker in Jermyn Street, Bond Street and Piccadilly."

Ava blinked. "Are you saying you were specifically looking for this box after you've purchased the kitten one?"

He shifted from one foot to the other. "Well, yes. I must have spent an entire afternoon scouring half of London to find another one."

Ava digested that piece of information. "It was kind of you to do so. It wasn't necessary, but it did bring great joy to Millicent. Knowing you went through such great pains to obtain it will make her appreciate it even more."

"Is Miss Sackville well?"

"Yes, thank you. She prefers to be at home with her cats, naturally."

"Naturally," he echoed.

"How is your cat?" she asked.

He blinked. "Achilles?"

She smiled. "Is that how you call him?"

"I must call him something. He sleeps and eats and scratches me." He lifted his hand to reveal some scratches on its back. "He never wants to be petted when I want to pet him. Infuriatingly so. He managed to get the cook to prepare him the finest fillets of chicken and give him the creamiest of milk. He has taken possession of my bed, and my armchair, and the drawer with my stockings. He thinks he is the king of my household as everyone scrambles to do his bidding whenever he as much as meows."

Ava looked at him with a curious little smile on her lips. "My. It sounds like the Earl of Ravenscroft likes cats, after all."

He widened his eyes in horror. "Me, like cats? Never!"

He'd stepped up closer to her as he talked, and she caught a whiff of his cologne. Cedarwood and musk. Crisp, clean, and male.

Ava looked away and stoically continued to knit, even though she'd dropped a stitch. The entire thing was going to unravel, thanks to him.

He stepped from one foot to another, clasped his hands on his back, glanced at the door, back again, and shuffled again. He looked at the ormolu clock on the mantlepiece, frowned, and looked back at her again.

"Miss Sackville."

A pause.

"Yes?" Ava peeped up at him through her lashes, wondering why he suddenly appeared so nervous.

"Would you—could you—imagine—I mean—would it be possible for you—dash it all, by George, how difficult can this be!" He made an agitated turn about the room, walked up and down several times, then returned and dropped to his knees in front of her. "I know this is unorthodox, but my intentions are honourable. Miss Sackville." He took a big breath. "Would you do me the great honour of bestowing me your hand in matrimony?"

Ava's jaw dropped.

It's a joke, was the first thought that flashed through her mind. Her first instinct was to brush him off with a laugh.

Then she saw the pleading look in his eyes. A dull red had crept up his cheeks. He was still on his knees in front of her. A vein pulsed in his left temple.

Goodness gracious, he was sincere! She dropped her knitting.

So, this was it, her very first marriage proposal; it shot through Ava's shocked mind, from the man she'd least expected to propose.

Oh, she'd received proposals a-plenty. Every lord and dandy made her a proposal—daily—for her to become his mistress. They would promise to shower her with jewels and silks, set her up in grand mansions, and palaces—but marry her?

That they would never do.

She knew the earl needed to marry. Everyone knew.

So why was she surprised he proposed to her? Why did her mouth dry up and her heart hammer, as though it mattered?

As though he might mean it.

"But...why me?" It burst from her lips.

He pressed his lips so firmly together they appeared white. He closed his eyes. When he opened them, there was a defeated look in them. "Because no one else will have me."

"No one else?" she echoed dumbly.

"No respectable, honourable, kind-hearted woman."

He paused to think before adding, "Who is as true and loyal to her family as you are."

Ava's mouth had dropped open. He thought her all that?

But surely, surely, he did not know who she really was?

He was proposing to Ava Sackville, an ageing spinster.

On his knees.

He seemed ridiculously nervous about it.

He looked like he desperately wanted her to say yes.

She felt deeply touched.

She therefore did something which she'd never thought she'd do in a million years.

"Very well, my lord," she replied breathlessly. "I'll marry you."

Chapter Fifteen

THE DOOR BURST OPEN. THE PARTY SPILLED INTO the room and fell silent as they beheld the spectacle in front of them.

"What is the meaning of this?" Lady Erskine's shrill voice broke the silence.

Ravenscroft scrambled up. "Miss Sackville has just given me the great honour of agreeing to become my wife."

Stunned silence.

Then everyone talked at the same time.

"Well, I never!"

"You what?"

"Her?"

"Surely, he must be joking?" Lady Erskine tottered as if about to faint, but since there was no gentleman behind her who would catch her if she toppled on the parquet, she caught herself and looked shocked.

"Er, yes. I mean no. It is no joke. I am indeed a fortunate man. I am—quite happy, actually." Then he did something unexpected: he smiled.

It was like a lazy ray of sunshine breaking through the clouds and lightning up an austere landscape. It softened his features and brought a twinkle to his eyes that was at once charming, enchanting—and seductive.

Ava gaped.

This is why he attracted women like bees to the honeypot.

This was no awkward, bumbling schoolboy.

This was a stalking panther, a lone wolf.

He would pounce when one least expected it.

He was very, very dangerous.

What on earth had she done?

Miles stepped up to him and slapped him on his shoulders. "Lucky dog, you."

"I suppose no one need ask my permission," Kit proclaimed to no one in particular. "Thought there was something of a custom involving the bridegroom first asking the head of the family for permission—etcetera etcetera—especially since one was never even introduced, but at this point this seems to be redundant, and the observing of customs and etiquette a rather dull affair. Imagine this—" he changed his voice to Ravenscroft's drawl, "'Sackville, may I marry your sister?'"

Then Kit switched positions, lifted two fingers, and waved them in the air. "'By all means, Ravenscroft, get my sister off my hands—for at this point it is unlikely I would say no, correct? So, we might as well skip all that faradiddle and proceed to the celebrations. Where is the champagne?"

"My apologies, Sackville. Of course, I should have sought introductions first." A flush of red crept up Ravenscroft's neck.

"Yes, yes. You will make up for it by coming to tea tomorrow afternoon. Especially since I missed your memorable first visit. It is expected." There was an imp sparkling in Kit's eyes.

"Oh yes, my lord," Ava declared in a voice he dared not contradict. "It is expected."

"Well then, tea it is," the clearly overwhelmed earl said.

After Kit pumped his hand heartily, the crowd began murmuring again. Lord Westington, the host, passed around champagne, and a footman was sent speedily to Lord Livingstone with the news. Miss Sackville and her brother left soon after with the agreement that they were to meet again for tea tomorrow afternoon.

It was done.

He was betrothed.

He felt like a load of granite was lifted off his shoulders. No, not granite but iron meteorite, for it had a greater density than granite and were therefore heavier.

His bride looked sensible enough; she was certainly homely looking and on the chubby side of things. Under her unshapely dress, she clearly had curves.

Her hair was a drab brown, and she had several moles on her face, and buck teeth, which she flashed at him every time she smiled. Her hands were small and dainty, as they flitted about busily knitting this indefinable rag she insisted was a shawl. And her eyes were pretty, too. A blend of molten green and sage, like jadeite or prehnite. He wasn't certain which mineral was more apt. He would have to look at his stones later to decide. Her smile wasn't half-bad either. A sweet smile, a bit shy. For one confounding moment he'd felt a squeeze in his chest, followed by a rush of—protectiveness?

That made no sense at all. He thought of how, when he'd called on her cousin, she'd pressed the tip of her umbrella against his chest and his lips involuntarily quirked upwards. And later, in the shop, how her eyes had flashed when they had argued about the music box. She certainly had spirit. She was fierce, deeply compassionate, warm, and kind. His words describing her had been sincere.

Something told him that depositing her at Ravenscroft Hall and forgetting all about her might not be as easy as he'd imagined, and for some reason that thought confused him. He brushed it away.

His father ought to have nothing to complain about, after all, she was a most respectable Sackville. The main thing, for now, was that his father was apprised of the news before midnight. Tristan whipped out his pocket watch. It was ten minutes past midnight.

The footman appeared, breathless and sweating, and bowed.

"Well?"

"Two minutes before midnight," the footman gasped. "I personally handed his lordship the missive two minutes before midnight." He mopped his brow.

"How did he take it?"

"He appeared in his nightgown and nightcap, my lord. He was very much displeased to be roused from his slumber."

"Yes, yes, the old man goes to bed early. But what did he say?"

"I handed him the note, sir, and he sat down in his armchair and opened it grumbling and growling, and then he slapped his thigh and proceeded to shout with laughter."

"He laughed?" That old devil. Of course, he'd amuse himself at his expense.

"Yes, my lord. A frightening sound. I nearly jumped out of my boots. He asked me whether it was true that you, my lord, were betrothed to a Sackville, and I said yes."

"And?"

"And then he continued laughing, sir."

Tristan grunted.

"And then, sir, he seemed to get all silent and lost in thought. I remained standing there, not knowing whether I could leave. Then he suddenly looked up and said, 'Remains to be seen whether he can hold her.' 'Excuse me, my lord?' I said. 'I never had any doubt the boy would come to his senses in time,' he said. He also said that he regrets he won't be able to meet your bride immediately because he is departing for Bath early tomorrow morning to take the waters. He expects to be introduced to her first thing upon his return. Then he gave me a coin and dismissed me," the footman added pointedly.

Miles, who stood next to them, roared with laughter.

"Blast the old man," Tristan growled. "It is just a

game to him." He fished a coin out of his pocket and gave it to the footman, who took it happily. It was good his father was leaving for Bath, which bought him some time to get to know his bride.

"A good night's work. I see. What now?" Miles asked.

"Watier's," Tristan replied curtly.

"What. More gambling? Is this wise? Oh. I see. To tease the old man. He never said you had to change your ways *before* you get married."

A slow, sinister smile crossed Tristan's face. "Precisely. He may think he is pulling the strings, but this marionette has control over his own destiny. Care to join me?"

"Any time, old friend. Any time. Your unmarried days are counted, after all. Must take advantage of it and throw yourself into debauchery, dissipation, and degeneracy for as long as you can."

Chapter Sixteen

"DID YOU KNOW YOUR BETROTHED IS ALSO YOUR most ardent admirer?" Kit asked with a raised eyebrow, lifting a card between two fingers. It was the day after the betrothal. They were in the drawing room of their townhouse and Ava rested on the sofa with a damp cloth with lavender essence over her forehead. After all this excitement with her engagement, she had a raging headache.

"Oh? How so?"

Kit handed her a card.

The Earl of Ravenscroft, it said in stately, golden letters underneath the crest of an eagle.

"It was in the box." Kit was in the process of emptying the box with the calling cards, reading off each name, and making a list of fifty gentlemen that would be invited next.

Ava forgot her headache and sat up so abruptly the cloth fell to the ground.

"And you know what he wrote on it?"

"Read."

"*Mlle Winter, I have greatly enjoyed your performances. It would be with utmost delight to make your personal acquaintance to discuss a certain matter. Your humble servant and most ardent admirer, Ravenscroft.*"

"No," Ava breathed.

"'Certain matter,' eh? What a rascal. 'Utmost delight', he writes, haha, and not just 'ardent admirer', but '*most* ardent admirer.' Other than that, I must say, his competitors are trying harder." Kit rummaged among the mountain of calling cards and fished out several others. "Some of them managed to write verses of love sonnets on their cards; however, one needs a magnifying glass to read them. And here, several verses comparing you to the fairy queen Titania. In comparison, his lines are rather prosaic and, I hate to say it, dull?"

Ava took the calling card and inspected the barely legible scribble in black ink. His handwriting was messy, but his signature was a strong, bold stroke. Ravenscroft it was, undeniably.

"I had no idea he was interested in opera."

"Believe me, sister dear, ever since you are singing on England's shores, every single gentleman on this island has developed an inexplicable passion for opera," Kit replied with irony.

"Who would've known? Still waters run deep, and all that, don't they? How long have you been engaged? Midnight last night, and now it is—" he pulled out his pocket watch "—barely noontime. So barely twelve hours. Not a day engaged, and your bridegroom's already fishing in other waters. Naughty, naughty."

Her brother was entirely right. Ravenscroft was proposing to one woman and courting another at the same time. Even if she was one and the same person, he couldn't know that.

Ava identified the sinking feeling in her stomach as disappointment.

She thought he'd be different. It turned out he wasn't any different from any of the other men.

"What a shame," she whispered.

"What do you want me to do? Left, or right?" Left stood a bin, where the majority of the calling cards landed. The housemaid would burn them in the fire-place afterwards. Right meant the list that Kit was penning. There wasn't a single name on it yet. "You have to say 'yes' to some of those chaps, you know. We're at one-hundred-and-thirty-six, now, and you've rejected them all. Not that it matters, because we seem to have at least a thousand cards left." He scratched his head.

"I don't happen to like any of those names," she replied, crossly. "Besides, my head is hurting, and it is difficult to concentrate when one has a raging headache."

Kit picked the next card from the pile. "The Marquess of Barham."

"No."

"Why? May I ask, just out of curiosity? You don't even know the chap. Why not give him a chance?"

"He sounds fat."

Kit laughed. "Fair enough. What about Lord Fitzfritzian?"

"No. He sounds silly."

"You're behaving like that princess," Kit grumbled. "In that fairy tale *König Drosselbart*."

"King Thrushbeard. It was my favourite tale. Papa used to read it to us all the time."

"I remember. The princess there did not end up well, if you recall. She declined all her admirers, just like you. The king lost his patience and married her off to the next-best beggar who happened to pass by. Let it be a warning to you."

"The beggar was a king in disguise, if you remember? So, you see, a happy end after all."

"The point of it being that she could've had that king all the time to begin with. She was just too stubborn and too arrogant to accept his suit. Had to go through all sorts of suffering before she found her true love. Don't follow in her footsteps, sister." Kit was unusually serious.

Ava huffed. "Nonsense, Kit. This is no fairy tale. This is harsh reality. Trust me to know the difference."

"Sometimes, sis, I am not sure you do," her brother muttered.

And now, it seemed Ravenscroft had joined the group of contenders. It was such a shame.

Kit drummed his fingers onto the tabletop. He was still waiting for her verdict. "What is it to be? Left, or right? Bin or list? I recommend the bin; t'would save you endless trouble."

She could end it all right now. End the silly engagement, burn his card. Never see him again. It would be better for her peace of mind.

"Right," she said curtly.

Kit scribbled his name on the list. "What game are you playing?"

"None." She picked up the cloth and placed it over her eyes. Very well, so maybe she'd just lied. Kit was right and this was a double game of some sort, where the heroine was hiding, and the hero did not exactly know what he was looking for.

Kit put down his pen and watched her with a troubled look on his face. "Are you certain you want to marry him, sis? No one says you have to; you know."

Ava felt a little foolish because she did not entirely know herself what she wanted.

"I am merely amusing myself, of course." She pulled at the strings on her misshapen shawl.

"How so?"

She decided to evade the question by posing another question. "Why do you think he proposed? A man who can have any diamond of the first water wants to marry plain Miss Ava Sackville, spinster. Why do you think that is?"

Kit thought. "He evidently needs you to secure his inheritance. I suppose his father is pressuring him. There are fortune hunters a-plenty out there."

"Precisely. He wants a plain, biddable, virtuous old maid. One who would not cause him any trouble, one who would walk in his shadow and say yes and amen to everything he said. With the intent of installing her in some sort of mansion in the deepest countryside and then forgetting about her."

"That sounds positively mediaeval!"

"It is. A man like him deserves to be taught a lesson, don't you think?"

Kit whistled.

Ava Sackville was not yet ready to admit to herself that if she'd scrutinised her soul, there lurked yet another reason why she had accepted his proposal.

She would rather die than admit it.

He'd looked so vulnerable, lost, and very alone when he'd thought himself unobserved in the room.

His shoulders had been hunched, and he'd looked defeated.

There'd been a moment when she'd wanted to reach out and—do what?

Maybe brush away that brown lock that had tumbled over his forehead. Maybe take his hand and tell him everything would be all right.

She'd wanted him to notice her, that was clear.

Then he had, and he'd surprised her once more. He'd been so awkward in her presence; her, a spinster.

He'd been *kind*.

Then he'd proposed, more helpless and bumbling than a schoolboy.

All those dandies who'd delivered bouquets bigger than her dining table, the missives they'd sent with poetry clearly written by someone else, the glib words that had fallen from their lips, the flattery, the compliments... she was so tired of them.

None of it was real, no one was authentic.

No one had ever bumbled his way through a marriage proposal.

She'd been charmed.

That was it.

And that was why she'd accepted.

Ava absent-mindedly plucked on a loose bit of woollen yarn and undid an entire row of her knitting.

What would she do now?

How long would she play this game?

Or would she just do the outrageous thing and actually marry the man?

Become the Countess Ravenscroft.

Who knew? It might be rather nice to be married to him for real.

THAT EVENING, WHEN 'THE INFAMOUS LIST' WAS published in the *Evening Times*, many a gentleman was said to have thrown himself into the Thames out of pure despair. Some others drowned their sorrows in alcohol and bemoaned their ill-luck, for they had been cruelly declined by this season's Incomparable.

Only a small group of fifty men were the lucky ones who made it.

And Tristan was amongst them.

He nearly spat out his brandy when he spied his name on the list.

He rubbed his eyes and looked again.

There he was, undeniably: The Earl of Ravenscroft, in firm, black print.

He would meet Violetta Winter!

As soon as the papers were distributed in the club that evening, there had been a minute of absolute silence.

Only the rustling of paper was heard as each gentleman hastily perused the list.

Then a collective moan had rent through the air.

In the entire club, only he and the Duke of Cumberland had made it on the list. And Miles, of course, but that was a given since he always won everything.

"We sure are lucky devils! We have drawn the grand prize." Miles rubbed his hands.

"Not yet. Keep in mind there are forty-eight others."

"Have you read the small print?" Miles lifted his quizzing glass and read, *"This is to be a poetry tournament. The quest of the fifty selected knights is to present their best poem in the tradition of courtly love. The winner is the one who pleases Mlle Winter the most and a boon shall be granted to him thereof*—I am now of the frame of mind to call it off. I thought a mediaeval tournament was all about slaughter, bloodshed, and mayhem, which would have been child's play and just to my taste. But a poetry tournament? Write a poem of courtly love?" Miles shuddered. "Makes me want to run screaming into the other direction."

"Excellent. Do us all a favour and call it off."

"You would like that, wouldn't you?" Miles polished his quizzing glass with a napkin. "You are still determined to participate?"

"Of course I am. Why wouldn't I be?"

Miles cleared his throat to make a point. "You already forgot?"

Tristan frowned. "I haven't the vaguest notion what you are talking about."

"Your bri-ide," Miles sang.

Oh.

He was to be married, wasn't he? He apparently had a bride. Since yesterday.

Dash it if he hadn't forgotten in all the excitement.

"Never mind, never mind—" Miles waved his hand about "—one thing need not interfere with another. You simply need to be very organised and keep both worlds apart. Trust me, I have ample experience in that." Miles crossed his legs.

"You do?" This really shouldn't surprise him, but it did.

"Well, yes. I once courted two females simultaneously. Somewhat tricky, but doable. Thing is not to mix up both, or else there will be a devil of a pickle. Make sure to keep both names apart. Easy to mix them up, you see. Results in an angry bride, and an angry mistress. Lose both. Not good." Miles evidently knew what he was talking about.

"So, this is how you lost Miss Leigh." Miles had been engaged once, but the woman dissolved the engagement soon after. Tristan had never known what exactly had happened, as Miles never talked about it.

Miles found his brandy glass intently interesting. "Yes. Well. Mistakes happen." He suddenly looked up. "Look. The truth is, I was an idiot. As a good friend, let me say this. Learn from my mistakes. Just don't do it."

Tristan sighed. "Do what? Not marry Ava Sackville? You know I can't do that. And not accept the invitation I have just won when hundreds of others were declined? It would be folly." Besides, he had to quench that fire in him that she had started. He could barely sleep at night because of her. The only thing that would put it out was to see her. He was convinced of it.

He had no other choice left.

He had to juggle both.

Miles raised his glass. "If so, then good luck, my friend. You will need it."

Chapter Seventeen

After three days, Tristan called on Ava to take her out on a ride.

She sat next to him stiffly and clutched the side of her seat as the curricle sped down the lane. He was a fast coachman.

A good ten minutes had passed, and they had not exchanged a word.

He threw her a sideways look. Her face was shadowed by her bonnet, a misshapen thing that seemed to have seen better days. He directed the curricle into Hyde Park, where the horses settled into a steady trot.

After a while, it behoved him he had to try harder.

He cleared his throat once, twice.

She squinted at him.

He fiddled with his whip.

She tilted her head sideways and waited.

"Pleasant weather today," he finally said.

Ava looked at the overcast sky, where the clouds hung low. "Yes, if one likes the rain." She'd brought an umbrella, of course, which she clasped between her hands.

"Rain. I like rain." A thick drop splashed on his gloved hands, and he brushed it away. "Do you?"

"Not particularly." She snapped her umbrella open so suddenly he jerked his head back to prevent a pointy tip from gouging his eye out. She, however, seemed oblivious to his discomfort. The seat was narrow and tight, and he could not move aside to avoid her pointy umbrella, which she held too low. He lifted a hand to move it aside.

"I find it rains too much in England, and I don't like getting wet."

Come to think of it, neither did he. There was nothing more to be added to the former bit of observation. It was a fact. It did rain considerably in England. It had been a wet year overall, with sudden, unexpected snow in October, followed by a cold and wet November. The upcoming winter promised to be severe.

As if to prove her point, another raindrop landed on his nose.

The sound of the carriage wheels grinding into the pebbled ground, the hooves of the horses clapping, and their steaming breathing was the only sounds heard for a good while.

Tristan swore to himself. This wasn't going well at all. "It is your turn to say something."

"Very well. More on the weather, then. The rain here is particularly cold and sharp like little pebbles." She whisked the raindrops from the sleeve of her pelisse.

"Pebbles. Do you like rocks?" he asked abruptly.

"Rocks?" She looked at him as though he were a dull-witted horse that raced against the racetrack at Ascot.

"Yes." He stared with concentration at the road ahead. "Rocks."

"Why would anyone like rocks?" She spun her umbrella in such a manner it upset his beaver hat in addition to poking out his other eye.

"Believe me, madam, some people do like rocks."

"Do they? They are ugly, grey, sharp little things that always end up in one's shoes."

She had just given an apt description of herself. Ugly, grey, and sharp little thing was exactly what she was.

"Either that," she continued, "or one stubs one's toes against them. A stubbed toe hurts massively." She turned to him, and he backed away from being impaled. "Didn't you ever stub your toe?"

"Well..." Come to think of it, he had. Only this morning, he'd stubbed his naked toe against his walnut dresser, and he'd hopped around on one foot, howling. His valet had stormed into the room, asking whether his lordship was having a seizure. So yes, he knew very well that something as minor as a stubbed toe could hurt insanely as if someone had smashed a glowing pitchfork into it. "I suppose everyone stubs their toes at one point," he grudgingly acceded.

"So there. Rocks are most definitely painful, annoying, and dull."

"Not at all. Rocks are immensely fascinating. They come in many shapes, forms, and sizes. Like... like..." His glance fell on her lumpy bosom. "Like, uh..." He narrowed his eyes. Did he imagine it, or was one bosom higher than the other? "Like... Like... er, you." Realising his *faux pas*, he talked on swiftly. "I mean, er, women. I mean, of course, what I meant to say was that women are also interesting. As are you. As are people in general. Like rocks."

Good heavens. How could he be so crude? Now he'd gone and offended her. She would probably take that pike masked as an umbrella and impale him on the spot.

Instead, she regarded him thoughtfully. "I have been called all sorts of things. A hag, a dry stick, an ape-leader. But never a rock."

He started to sweat. "I mean that, of course, as a generalisation. I sincerely apologise if I have offended you."

"That, I must say, is a rather unique comparison. I am wondering whether that isn't a compliment."

"I meant, of course, people. I am as fascinated by rocks as I am by people. People are interesting." That was a blatant lie, but one had to say something, anything, to cover up one's gaffes.

Miss Sackville, however, had grown still. "Are they really?"

"Pardon me?"

"Interesting, I mean. People. I find them mostly frightful. Especially crowds," she said, so quietly he thought he must have misheard. Then, as if waking from a trance, she shook herself. "It is really raining terribly now, and I am quite drenched. I suggest we return?"

They were indeed wet. During the heat of their discussion, she'd lowered her umbrella in front so she could see his face, and the rain had drizzled down on their heads with a regular rhythmic pattern.

He turned the curricle, and they returned to Bruton Street in silence.

He hopped down, immensely relieved that this agonising ride was over, straight into an immense puddle. Splash! He repressed a groan. Not only would his valet kill him for having ruined his boots for the second time this month, but now he was also obliged to lift the woman out of the curricle. She would weigh a ton. It wasn't to be helped. He was a gentleman, and a gentleman helped his betrothed out of the carriage, so she did not have to step into the puddle. Never mind that this meant he'd have to dwell longer in the cold, murky puddle and he already felt the water seeping up his trousers.

"There is literally the red sea spread out in front of your house, Miss Sackville. Let me assist you to prevent your feet from getting wet."

He held out his hand, but she did not take it.

"Why do you want to marry me?" she suddenly asked, an odd look in her eyes.

He clenched his hand. "As I told you before—"

"Don't repeat that talk about me being respectable and kind and what not, and that you couldn't find anyone else. I believe that to be a half-truth," she interrupted.

"Because my father will otherwise cut off his purse strings." He snapped his mouth shut, horrified that he'd uttered those words. Was he mad? Even if it was common knowledge, this was not something one told the woman one intended to marry. Not in such blunt words.

She nodded slowly. "And there was no one else you

could ask. Not that there aren't enough beautiful ladies around. You could have asked Mrs Townsend, for example. Or Lady Erskine. But—" she tilted her head with the odd hat sideways to look at him "—neither of them will do, will they? One is commonly known to be a fortune hunter. The other does not have a respectable background. A doting father would make sure his scion will marry into a good family." She paused. "Like the Sackvilles. You would have never offered for someone like me if it hadn't been for your father forcing your hand."

He stared at her, horrified she'd so accurately analysed his situation.

"Something tells me you would get along brilliantly with my father," he mumbled.

"You must be wondering why I have decided to marry you," she said.

Not really, he was tempted to answer. It was his inheritance, what else? Plus, a title, an estate... he was the catch of the season.

"I don't need your money," she suddenly said, taking the wind out of his sails. "I am financially independent and do whatever I want. I don't need to marry. A married woman is a kept woman; you lose your freedom and all your possessions at once. Spinsterhood isn't all that bad when you are relatively well-off financially."

The pride in her voice made him listen up.

"Then why would you give it all up?" he couldn't help but ask. Especially to someone like him.

She looked up at him suddenly. "You have been honest with me, so I'll be honest as well. The reason is that I would very much like to have a home. Possibly, children," she added.

He scratched his neck and looked away. "Ah. Well, that is a natural enough sentiment."

"I have travelled extensively with my brother. We have scoured the entire Continent, braving wars. I have never felt I belonged anywhere." She stared into the distance. Raindrops slid down her cheek like tears and he resisted the sudden urge to wipe it away. "I have always wanted a home."

"Ravenscroft Hall shall be your home, then." *Deposit her at Ravenscroft Hall and forget about her...*

Tristan swallowed. He doubted it would be that easy.

He held out his hand, and she placed hers, as wet and slippery as a herring, into his. He helped her up, grabbed her by the waist, which felt oddly quaggy and soft, and he fleetingly wondered how many petticoats that woman was wearing. Then, realising he'd needed his entire strength to lift her, he let go of her hand and placed his other hand on the thickened waist, and, bracing himself— lifted her in a sweeping arc over the puddle.

She was so light he barely felt her weight. He set her down. Before he could ponder on this, she lifted her umbrella again, and this time, she did poke him with it.

"Ouff."

"Oh dear. I am so sorry—"

He lifted his hand and rubbed his temple. Glaring at her, he said, "You carry a dangerous weapon there, madam."

"Are you hurt?"

"No. But it missed my eye by a hair's breadth."

129

"I am terribly sorry. Let me make up for it. Would you like some more tea?"

Another round with two eccentric spinsters and the mocking brother? He'd already suffered through that ordeal earlier.

"No, thank you. I have some appointments, so I shall be returning to my home."

"Then I shall see you..." Her voice petered away uneasily.

Rain dribbled on her mangled bonnet and as she stood there, she looked wet and drab and dowdy and somehow—forlorn. Like an anxious little child.

Without thinking, he bent down and pressed his lips on hers. Her soft, sweet lips quivered underneath his.

Something stirred deep within him.

He pulled away. She hadn't moved, but stood still, frozen, with wide eyes.

Dash it all. A man was allowed to kiss his betrothed, wasn't he?

"Before I forget." He fumbled around in his pocket and retrieved a small package. "I have something for you," he said gruffly. "A small present."

No doubt she expected a ring or some other jewellery. He dropped the package in her extended hand, and she unwrapped it with unsteady fingers.

"A—stone?"

He cleared his throat. "It is a prehnite." He took it from her hand and held it up between two fingers. "It is a mineral. If you hold it against the light, you can see it is translucent, but not transparent." He emphasised the word "not." "I chose it because of all the stones, it is closest to your eye colour, though it doesn't catch the precise shade."

She looked at the stone on her hand.

"Thank you," she whispered. She looked dazed.

"You're welcome," he said gruffly. "I shall call on you in the next few days."

As he directed his horses home, he sighed. What an afternoon. They'd discussed the weather, rocks and stubbed toes. And then he'd kissed her.

Was he mad? How could he have kissed her already? Judging from her expression, she'd enjoyed it as much as licking one of Elgin's marbles at the British Museum. As for him... it left him wanting more. And that was profoundly disturbing.

Chapter Eighteen

Sweet heavens, he'd kissed her!

Surely, it hadn't meant anything, merely a polite, swift peck on the lips, but it had left her feverish, restless, and oddly dissatisfied. His lips had been so soft and gentle, but a sudden warmth had pooled in her stomach like hot, oozing honey, and she'd just wanted to forget everything around her and melt into him.

She'd wanted more.

She must break off the engagement at the next available opportunity.

She would tell him it was a mistake.

It would never work.

She had not considered the full implications of what a union between them would bring, she would tell him. But she knew now they would never suit.

Fact was that she did not need a rake.

She needed someone loyal.

Someone who saw her for who she really was.

She had accepted his proposal at the whim of the

moment because she had allowed herself to be swept away by dreams of normalcy. Getting married, having children. Belonging to someone. Belonging somewhere. To love and be loved. What would that be like?

Her life was the stage. She was an opera singer, not a spinster. Men were lying at her feet, worshipping her. She could have any lover and however many she wanted.

Was that to be her life forevermore?

Why this yearning deep down, for something else entirely?

Ava stared at the lovely rock he'd given her. The colour of her eyes, he'd said.

She shook herself and tucked the stone into her jewellery case. This farce was leading nowhere, only to heartbreak and sorrow.

After two days of brooding over the kiss and analysing every aspect of what he might have meant by giving her the stone, Ava had enough.

She needed to get out.

Out, and away, clear out her muddled, overheated mind.

Shopping! That was the thing that would distract her.

She'd tried to persuade Millicent to accompany her, but to no avail. "Oh, no, Ava. I can't possibly! All those people!" Millicent had shuddered. "I haven't been shopping in over twenty years."

Ava paused in the motion of tying her bonnet under her chin to stare at her cousin. "Twenty years! My dear Millicent! I am speechless! Is there never anything you want to buy for yourself?"

Millicent shook her head. "It really isn't necessary. I have Mary to do the errands, you see. And John, the footman, to take my mail. And Mrs Phillibert, my housekeeper, likes to do all the remaining shopping, which is fine with me. Really, it is. Don't look so horrified, Ava. I really haven't missed going out all these years." Millicent picked up Satinpaws and buried her face in her fur.

"But you *must* go out. If it is not shopping, come at least with me in the afternoon for a short walk. To the park."

"But the cold air... the rain...it might even snow... what if we catch a cold?" Millicent balked at putting even one foot outside the house when it rained.

"Nonsense. It is sunny today and a brisk walk in the fresh air will do us both good."

"I am not certain..."

Ava lifted her chin stubbornly. "Either you come shopping with me now, or you accompany me to the Menagerie later this afternoon. Either of the two it must be, for you are spending far too much time indoors. I'll not leave you in peace until you make your decision."

Millicent groaned. "How cruel you are. But very well. Since I cannot bear seeing animals in cages, let us go shopping. But we will only go to one shop and not one step further!"

Ava hoped that once Millicent was out in the streets, she would begin enjoying herself. It worked. To Ava's surprise, Millicent was fascinated by the Burlington Arcade, and when she stopped short in front of a jewellery shop, it was impossible to get her to move on.

"Do you see this brooch?" Millicent pointed at an

exquisite flower-shaped brooch, its leaves made of gold and the petals of sapphire. "I rather like it."

"It is very pretty." Ava would never have thought that Millicent was the type of woman to take fancy to jewellery, but she must have been wrong, because Millicent went into the shop and bought the brooch without blinking. She left the shop, beaming. "My first purchase in over twenty years. It has to be something special."

"Congratulations." Ava was happy for her cousin. "What would you like to see next? Books, maybe?" Hatchards was not far across the street.

"Oooh," Millicent exclaimed as she saw the pretty tomes of leather books displayed. "Do you suppose we would find a copy of Blainville's *Travels through Holland, Germany, Switzerland, and Italy*? I left my copy at Sackville Hall and miss it sorely."

"Let us find out," Ava said. "Maybe you could find even more travel books there?"

"Do you think so, Ava? That would be splendid, indeed."

As they stepped into the shop, Ava looked up and saw a familiar male figure stride toward the shop next to Hatchards. He was tall, powerfully built, and well dressed. Without looking left or right, he entered the shop.

Ava shoved Millicent in front of a table with the newest books. "Why don't you look at these books here? I shall join you momentarily." She left the bookshop, ambling by the store next to Hatchards. Pretending to study the display, she peeked through the window to seek out the tall man inside. She had not imagined it. It was

Ravenscroft. He was talking to a shopkeeper behind the counter, who fawned over him. He pulled out several items and laid them out in front of Ravenscroft, who nodded.

Ava stretched her neck and stood on tiptoe, but she could not see what he bought.

There were long, white items hanging down in front of her that blocked her vision. If she could only brush them aside... With a jolt, she registered what they were.

Stockings.

The entire window display was full of stockings. Plain, ribbed, in black, white, and a range of other colours, with matching garters and ribbons.

Her dazed mind took a minute to process that the Earl of Ravenscroft was in a hosiery, purchasing stockings. Not just any stockings. *Female* stockings!

The shopkeeper handed him an oblong box, which Ravenscroft clamped under his arm.

He turned and headed toward the door.

Ava pirouetted on her heel like a ballet dancer and charged down the street to merge with the crowd. She looked down, praying the bonnet hid her face. With some luck, he would turn the other way and not see her...

After a while, she cast a surreptitious look behind her and saw how he climbed on his curricle and drove away. He hadn't seen her.

Ava returned to the shop and pushed the door open. A little bell rang.

"Good afternoon, ma'am, how may I help you?" The shopkeeper rubbed his hands.

"The gentleman who was here just now is a friend of

mine. I would love to buy the same thing he bought just now. I trust in his excellent taste." She smiled angelically at him.

"A pair of the finest silken lady stockings in pale pink, with matching ribbons. If you would care to have a look, here." He pulled out a pair. "Are they not a work of art?"

Ava barely glanced at them. "I'll take them."

"Would you like a buckled garter or a ribbon with them? His lordship chose the finest ribbon. This one, here."

Ava touched it. It was indeed fine. "I'll take it. Tell me, does he come here often, buying stockings?"

The shopkeeper did not think her question odd. "Oh yes, he is one of our most cherished customers. He has been buying with us for years." He placed the stockings in a pale blue box and tied a ribbon around it.

"And he always buys the same stockings?"

"Oh no, ma'am. We have such a variety here. He has bought all the colours except for black. But his lady prefers pastels, with ribbons, never garters. We make sure to have a selection of the finest pastel-coloured stockings with matching ribbons just for his lordship."

"I see," Ava said tonelessly. She paid, took the package, and nodded at the shopkeeper.

The man held the door open for her. "Do honour us again soon, ma'am."

Back on the street, she stood for one moment to regain her composure. She inhaled a shaky breath.

Why this surprise? Why this sense of disappointment oozing at the bottom of her stomach like black tar?

First the music box, then stockings. Presents for his

138

ladylove. Of course, he would have a mistress. Many men did. Why had she expected him not to? Why had she hoped that, regardless of his reputation, he would be different from all the other men? She was angry with herself for having believed that even for a moment.

Ava marched up to the girl that stood by the lamp pole, selling biscuits.

"For you." She handed her the box. The stunned girl took it.

With a steaming mind, Ava returned to Hatchards, where she found Millicent happily immersed in her books. She'd barely even noticed Ava's absence.

"Is it time to go, yet? Look, Ava, I have found three books and I simply cannot decide which of the three to buy!" Millicent looked flushed.

"Why don't you buy all three?" It was good to see Millicent excited; good to see her enthusiastic about something.

"Do you think I should?"

"Yes, and what's more, we can always return for more. Millicent, would you mind very much if we walked for a bit? Look, the street seems to be terribly congested, and I can't bear to be trapped in a stuffy carriage that won't move. My head is exploding, and I need to get some fresh air lest I go out of my mind."

"Oh dear, you are not falling ill, are you?" Millicent touched Ava's forehead. "You are quite warm."

Ava shook her head. "No. I just need to think, that is all. Walking helps me think. Let us walk to Green Park and we can meet John with the carriage there."

"Very well, my dear. Although I think, if one is about

to fall ill, that a poultice with linseed and mustard together with a drop of Dr Redfern's elixir works wonders." Millicent caught up with Ava's rapid stride.

"No poultice will fix this muddle," Ava muttered, as she walked down Duke Street.

"Won't you tell me what is the matter? You seem out of sorts."

"I just think this will never work."

"What?"

"This engagement. He is a terrible rake, isn't he?" She understood now she had to interpret the kiss in this light. It had been meaningless, for surely, he was used to stealing kisses from all sorts of ladies, maybe even maids...

Millicent knew immediately who she meant. "Oh. Yes. Everyone says so, at least." She sounded thoughtful. "However, I always wondered how much of it is true. One ought to keep in mind most of it is just gossip and rumours."

"I am convinced it is true," Ava replied darkly.

"Regardless of those rumours, I must say, Ava, I am so happy you are marrying him. It was the best news ever. I understand now that it was you he'd intended to propose to that day he came unexpectedly for tea. He will make a wonderful husband. He certainly is most wonderful to look at." Millicent's voice sounded dreamy.

Ava stopped short. "Millicent! You haven't lost your heart, have you?"

Two specks of red appeared on her face. "Oh, no! No no no. At my age? How can you even think that! Lord Livingstone's son!" She placed her hands on her cheeks.

"He doesn't like cats," Ava muttered darkly.

"No, he does not. That is definitely a mar on his character." Millicent stopped in her tracks. "Oh! Ava! Did you hear that?"

"What?"

Millicent grabbed her by the arm. "There! Again!"

There was a quiet mewling coming forth from the basement of a house. "If I am not mistaken, it sounds like a kitten in distress."

Before Ava could prevent her, Millicent headed doggedly towards the house.

Ava rushed after her.

Tristan had to take a different route to his club because the main road was congested due to a carriage accident. He took the side streets that were narrower and directed his curricle through the streets with ease. Coming up to a halt to let a woman pass who was carrying a basket full of fruit clamped under her arm, he chanced to look sideways into a narrow alley.

He blinked. Did his mind play tricks on him, or was that the tall, slim figure of Millicent Sackville? She stood with her back to him. Surely, he was imagining things. It couldn't be her. Tristan raised his ribbons to move on, when he saw another figure appear between the grid iron bars that fenced off the basement of the house. And since she was standing upright with her face turned toward the light, he could clearly see that this was his fiancée, Ava Sackville.

What was odd was that she was on the wrong side of the fence. Millicent reached with her hands through the iron bars, intertwining her fingers, as if making a stirrup for Ava to step on—to aid her over the fence.

What in blazes?

He jumped off his curricle and headed towards them. "What in Zeus', Hera's and Apollo's names are you doing?"

Ava looked up and glared at him. "You. What are you doing here? Go away, we don't need you."

That unexpected outburst of hostility stopped him in his tracks.

Millicent waved at him. "Well met, my lord, just in time to save us like a true gentleman. You see, Ava climbed over the fence and sprained her ankle. Now she has problems making it back."

"Nonsense, Millicent, of course I can make it back. I don't need anyone to save me. Hold on tight. I'll place my foot here and try to pull myself over. I did this once; I can do it again—owww." She hopped on one leg.

Tristan interrupted, "What are you doing on the other side to begin with?"

"Saving cats," Millicent explained. "Can you hear it?"

A heart-rendering mewling sound emerged somewhere from the basement.

"There must be little baby kittens down there trapped and they need to be saved," Millicent said. "I suspect the coal cellar under the pavement. Except there is no one in the house, for we knocked. The gate to the basement is locked and so Ava climbed over. Except then she fell down the stairs and nearly broke her foot." She wrung her hands. "I daresay she could have broken her neck and died."

"Nonsense, it's a light sprain," Ava said with a grimace.

"Anyhow, the cellar door is locked with a heavy bar that is jammed, so there is no way to get inside. We decided to get some help. And now she can't get back over the fence. But here you are, so everything will be fine." She beamed at him. "How are we to do this?"

"I see." Tristan thought swiftly.

"Oh, for heaven's sake." Ava, clearly impatient, placed her uninjured foot on the lower horizontal bar of the fence, pulled herself up, and placed the second foot on the upper horizontal bar, using it like a ladder, and swung herself over the top. But she hadn't counted on her petticoats, which entangled themselves hopelessly with the iron pikes hitching her skirts up. Tristan had the view of a small foot in a half-boot showing off a trim ankle with a finely-formed calf, a shapely knee and part of a *very* shapely thigh encased in plain white stockings. There was a glimpse of a garter.

He swallowed and cleared his throat, which suddenly felt tight.

Miss Ava Sackville had unexpectedly fetching legs. Who would have known?

A sound of pain tore him out of his reveries. She'd placed her weight on her injured ankle. And then things happened as they must: she windmilled her arms in the air, and fell, tearing her skirt.

Tristan rushed forward, catching her before she crashed to the ground.

"Oomph." The impact knocked the wind out of his sails.

Millicent clapped. "Well caught, my lord!"

He held her in his arms, once more surprised at her lightness. He instantly became aware that half of his bundle consisted of petticoats, and that the actual person was underneath layers of soft, mushy padding that was pressed against his breast. A strand of fine hair blew into his face. A fleeting whiff of a sweet, enticing scent filled his nose. Was that violets? Or was it honeysuckle? He wasn't overly good at identifying flowers. An overpowering desire to kiss her again overcame him.

She clung to him, groaning, and he snapped out of the fog that had momentarily overtaken his senses.

"Ava, for heaven's sake, say something. Are you hurt?" Millicent immediately began fussing.

"It's just my foot," she said through clenched teeth. But her hands were at her head, clutching her bonnet, which had become askew. Tristan imagined glimpsing some copper in her hair, but surely, he must be mistaken.

"Your ankle is swollen. You need a poultice with garlic, onion, and castor oil," Millicent prescribed.

"That sounds positively horrid!"

"Nonsense, it'll reduce the swelling in a jiffy."

"Let me carry her to my vehicle." Tristan set her down gently in his vehicle. He pulled out a blanket and draped it over her.

She looked up at him with round eyes. "Thank you," she whispered.

"You're welcome," he said gruffly.

Millicent wrung her hands. "Alas, we are far from

done! We require your knight in shining armour services once more. What about those poor babies?"

"Babies? What babies?"

"The baby kittens! We can't leave them here to die! Can't you hear them? Abandoned in the coal vault under the pavement."

Tristan scratched the back of his head. "Kittens!"

"Poor little mites, they're likely without their mother and they will die unless someone saves them. You must save them!"

Tristan groaned. "Aren't there enough cats in this world already?"

"My lord!" Millicent pulled herself up and glared at him ferociously. "If you leave those poor, poor babies to die, not only will the heavens weep over your cold, cruel, unfeeling character, but I'll curse the day I ever set my eyes on you and pray for all things unfortunate to come hailing down on you 'til the day you die. Regardless of whether you marry Ava," she added with a sniff.

Tristan shrank. "Good heavens, Miss Millicent, you are spitting fire. One would think that you had suddenly turned into a dragon."

She sniffed. If it had been any colder, he would have seen the steam emerge from her nostrils. "I save cats and give them a home. It is what I do. No cat deserves to roam the streets homeless and abandoned. In ancient Egypt, cats were revered as gods!"

"Indeed." Tristan scratched his neck. "Well, in this case, I had better save those dratted cats, had I not? Lest I fall out of your good graces." He rattled at the gate. He could climb over it, as Ava had done, but he had a better idea. "Come here, James."

His tiger descended from his seat.

"Your lockpicking skills are required."

James studied the lock with a frown. "Begging your pardon, my lord. But I require an instrument."

"I see." Tristan thought one moment, then his eyes fell on Ava. "Would you take off your bonnet, please."

"I—what?"

"Please take off your bonnet."

"Very well. This is becoming more and more curious by the minute. I would very much like to see James pick a lock with my bonnet. So here you are." Ava untied her bonnet, took it off and held it out to him.

But Tristan ignored it. Instead, he lifted his hand to her head, causing Ava to move her head back to evade it.

"Keep still," he growled. "I won't hurt you."

His fingers brushed her temple.

Their eyes met.

She held her breath and shivered.

As expected, she had at least a dozen hairpins on her head. He pulled at one of them, and a strand of her hair came loose. It was fine and soft and decidedly auburn, not brown.

Her hands flew up immediately to arrange her hair.

Interesting.

"Will this do?" He handed a hair pin to James.

"Excellent, my lord." James took it and set to work. He unlocked the gate in a second and opened it with a creak, revealing a flight of narrow stairs leading to the vault.

"James?"

James paled and took a step back. "I have a terrible fright of crowded, dark, spaces, my lord. I'll expire on the spot, and then you will have to go in and save me, too. Guaranteed!"

Three pairs of eyes were on him. A pitiful sound emerged from the vault, the mewling of a litter of baby kittens, about to die.

Tristan pulled off his beaver hat, cursing all Sackvilles, cats, and coal vaults. He whipped his hat at James, who caught it expertly. Then he shrugged out of his coat. The boy took that, too.

Sizing up the narrow wooden door, he calculated that he could fit through, but barely. With some effort, he lifted the heavy wooden bar out of the rusty latch and attempted to open the door, but it jammed. With one perfectly aimed kick, he slammed his boot against it.

"Take care not to hurt yourself, my lord," James advised. "May I advise to kick more to the left side."

Tristan threw him a deathly look. "Any more advice from you, and you will find yourself climbing in there, retrieving kittens."

James paled and stepped out of his reach.

A second kick, and the door hung on its hinges.

Tristan pried it open.

The coal cellar was narrow, dark and, as expected, full of coal.

The crying sounds were louder. It was definitely animals in distress. Miss Millicent's face crumpled up in pain. "Oh, those poor, poor things! Rescue is at hand!"

But where were they? As luck would have it, they

were placed behind a massive coal pile. It couldn't be helped. He had to climb over that pile of coal. He slid down the hill and sneezed. Coal dust everywhere. The sweet, rank smell of decay mingled with the smell of coal. James, who peered through the door, asked every two seconds whether his lordship was still alive.

"Yes, blast it, James," Tristan eventually shouted.

Once his eyes had accustomed themselves to the darkness, he saw a bag in one corner of the vault. He untied the bag and out tumbled a litter of those little creatures. He put them back, scrambled out of the vault, and handed the bag to James, who took it to Millicent.

"Five of them, poor, poor babies, they haven't even opened their eyes yet. They need milk immediately, or else they'll die," she said.

Tristan dusted his hands off. They were black. He was probably looking a fright, like a chimney sweep. "We had best get you home quickly. And I had best get myself cleaned up."

"You are a hero, Ravenscroft," Miss Millicent declared. "Except..." her face fell. "We already have six cats, since we gave one to you, did we not? I would love to pamper those kittens until they are well and plump, but in a house with six other cats..."

Tristan looked at her, horrified. "Oh no, no, no, one is quite enough—" he lifted his black hands to ward her off "—I wouldn't know what to do with all these others."

"Cats are companionable creatures. They also need each other, otherwise they'll be lonely," Millicent lectured.

Heaven help him if she saddled him with more of

those little monsters. There was cat hair everywhere, and every time he attempted to pet him, Achilles hissed and scratched him. And every time Tristan was busy and did not feel like petting him, Achilles sidled up to him and rubbed his head against his hand, purring. He was a contrary creature.

"One could take them to Ravenscroft Hall," James intervened. "I daresay they'd thrive in the stables."

He would throttle James once they reached home.

Ava looked at him with a raised eyebrow. "Ravenscroft Hall? Surely there is enough space there?"

"Oh yes, that would be the thing, indeed!" Millicent said.

Three pairs of eyes were on him.

Accursed creatures! And now they would saddle him with five more of those things.

"Confound it." He drew his hands through his hair, probably drawing a streak of soot with it. "Very well. If that is what will make you happy."

"It would make me very happy, indeed." Miss Millicent beamed.

He lifted a tiny kitten and carefully petted its head with his thumb. It mewled.

Miss Ava merely regarded him with an odd look in her eyes. "Thank you, my lord," she said quietly.

He cleared his throat. "Well. James will take you home. It will be tight, but my curricle can accommodate the two of you."

"Our John is waiting for us with the carriage at Green Park. He will wonder what happened to us," Millicent said.

He nodded. "I'll find him anon."

Miss Millicent beamed at him. "Such a gentleman. A true knight in shining armour!"

He cared little for the look of hero-worship in her eyes.

The soft, dewy look in Miss Ava's eyes he cared for even less, mainly because he did not understand it.

"Well, there it is, then." James flicked the whip, and the curricle left with the women and kittens. Tristan left to find the Sackville carriage. That he would have to pass through St James' Street by his club, for everyone to see, looking like a chimney sweep, would crown his day.

Miles would lie on the floor, howling. Tristan sighed. What a day.

Then his rare smile flitted over his blackened face. He started whistling a happy tune. Those legs! That had been a spectacular sight, indeed.

Chapter Nineteen

"It was rather... curious," Ava told her brother later, still bemused by the entire experience. She lay on a sofa, with a blanket about her. A doctor had looked at her ankle and proclaimed the injury was minor. Still, she would have to cancel her opera performance that night, and possibly the one after that, too. Her manager would not be pleased, not to mention all the people who expected her to sing, but it was not to be helped.

"I wouldn't have expected it of him. I must say, it shook my image of him rather badly."

Kit leaned against the fireplace in the blue salon of their townhouse and looked down on his sister with a grin on his face. "Bowled you over, didn't he? Thought you had him all figured out, and then he turns out to be a blasted knight."

Millicent had used similar terminology. Ava brushed it away. "It's just cats. But I must say, it was very nice of him to take those kittens."

"Since you are going to languish on that sofa for the

next few days, I have brought something to entertain you." He handed her a roll of sheets.

"What is that?" She took the roll and unfolded several sheets with colourful prints. "Oh! Caricatures. How droll!"

"There's one of you, here." Kit pointed at a sheet. It depicted a lady on stage, wearing a white robe, her hair piled up on her head, her mouth open, her hands beseeching the skies.

"I don't really look like that, do I?" She pulled a face.

"Worse. Look at the pile of gentlemen languishing at your feet."

Ava inspected the picture. What she'd thought was a mountain consisted of a pile of writhing male bodies. Underneath, it said, "Our new diva slaughters men with her voice".

"Goodness, how awful."

Kit grinned. "There's one of your husband-to-be as well. Several, in fact. Looks like he's a prime favourite with the artists."

Ava shuffled through the sheets and pulled out the one where Tristan lay on the park bench, empty bottles at his feet, surrounded by a group of dubious women. "Marry me," the sign around his neck said.

Ava snorted. "I have seen it before. I wonder how much truth there is to this."

"There is always a kernel of truth in every rumour. Why don't you ask him the next time you meet?" Kit donned his coat and hat. "I am off to the club." He twirled his stick, paused, set his stick back on the table and took off his hat again. He looked unusually grim.

Ava looked up. "What is the matter, Kit? I thought you were leaving?"

"I just thought you should know this." Kit took a turn about the room, then stopped in front of her. "At the club last night."

"And?"

"And. Saw Miles Davenport there. As well as Ormsby, Willsbury, Mountbatten."

Ava shrugged. "Except for Miles, I don't know any of them."

"Precisely. Yet they seemed to have a definite opinion of you."

"Of Violetta Winter, you mean."

"No. Of Ava Sackville."

Ava frowned. "And?"

Kit traced the marble pattern of the fireplace with one finger. "And what they said wasn't very pleasant. How Ava Sackville was the ugliest hag in all of England, how her thighs were no doubt as big as a whale's. And how Ravenscroft was a fool to be shackling himself to her. You get the gist of it. Lewd, indecent talk. And what's worse, they started on Cousin Millicent as well. How she wasn't as innocent as she appeared, for there was a scandal apparently, ages ago, involving her and some rake."

Ava, who'd been taking a sip of her tea, started coughing.

"Well, I couldn't let that pass, could I?"

"For heaven's sake, Kit. What did you do?" Ava would have jumped up, but her foot prevented her.

"Calm down, sis. Let me tell you the rest. So, with

our family honour impugned, I saw myself facing the three of them at Hyde Park tomorrow, pistols at dawn."

Ava gasped.

"Before I could charge down on them, wrathfully, demanding satisfaction, *he* suddenly stood there, for it turns out he'd been sitting in that armchair in the corner, entirely unnoticed, listening to everything they said. Ravenscroft can be rather terrifying when he's really angry, did you know? But what's odd, he did not demand satisfaction at all." Kit shook his head in bemusement as he recalled the past events.

"Thank goodness."

"No. He went about it in a more direct manner." Kit flexed his fingers. "He smashed his fist into Davenport's face, then into Ormsby's chin, and no doubt would have blackened Willsbury's eye as well, if that fellow hadn't backed off in terror, begging his apology. The other two did, as well. 'Didn't know you were there listening,' Miles Davenport said. 'My apologies, did not mean to offend your betrothed.' I tell you, Ava, I don't like the man. Fishy, slimy type."

"Yes, he is, but pray tell, what happened then?" Ava listened breathlessly.

"Ravenscroft growled no one was to impugn your honour, or Miss Millicent's honour, or any of our family's honour, not even when he was not there. For he would find out. And come after them. Their knees were knocking together, one could almost hear it. Turns out he's a prime boxer, you know, boxes with Gentleman Jackson himself, and they say he's not half bad with pistols, either." Kit's eyes shone. "You have betrothed yourself to quite the champion, I must say. Not half bad at all."

"Did he, now?"

"The only thing I regret is that I didn't even get a chance to slam my fist into any of their faces, for as your twin, that ought to have been my prerogative. Then they saw me, and would you know, they fawned and grovelled like I was Prinny himself, and all three of them apologised to me without a peep, and Ravenscroft promised me afterwards he would teach me boxing." He cracked his knuckles in delight at the prospect.

"Goodness." Her hand fluttered to her throat.

"Yes. But I am not to tell you any of this, of course. So, feign ignorance when he comes around." With those words, he popped on his hat, grabbed his stick and with a whistle on his lips, left Ava to ponder on the episode.

THE EARL CALLED ON AVA THE NEXT DAY. SHE WAS lying on the sofa in the salon; her foot was better, but she kept it elevated, and packed in one of Millicent's poultices. Her cheeks were flushed, and Tristan thought she did not look quite so hideous in the wood-green shawl that brought out the colour of her eyes.

"The doctor says it is just a mild sprain. I am to rest my foot for several days and then I may resume walking again."

He handed her a bouquet with pansies and violets. She buried her face in it. "How charming. Thank you." She studied the bouquet. "A fitting combination. Pansies for thoughtfulness. Violets for faithfulness." She uttered a sudden peal of a laugh. "That means you are thinking about being faithful."

"See, this is why I prefer stones. I know nothing about flowers or symbolism or any of that." Tristan shifted the weight on his legs. "I just bought flowers I thought you might enjoy."

"Hm. Yes." She threw him a look through her lashes that Tristan thought was quite arch, if not flirtatious. "Pansies can also mean love, you know. Love and faithfulness. I would certainly accept that."

He thought the room was becoming too stuffy.

She pulled out the violets, collected them in a little bundle and brought them to her face. "I love violets."

Something stirred in his memory, almost rose to the surface, then sank again and disappeared. He shook it away. "I am glad that I chose the right flowers, then."

To shake off the awkwardness that befell him, he picked up one of the sheets on the table. "A caricature. Is this how you entertain yourself?"

"Kit brought them. I find them amusing. Especially the one about you."

He groaned. "This incident will haunt me for the rest of my days. Had I known that my prank would lead to this, I'd have thought twice before hiring that actress."

"Tell me about it." Ava leaned back.

He did. To his surprise and gratification, she threw her head back and laughed. It was a light, pleasant sound that woke the desire in him to hear it again, and again.

"And have you thought of a way to get back at Miles?"

"No. Beyond the basic schoolboy hoaxes, I have all but run out of ideas."

"Let's see. He left you in the park all alone for an entire night, so it must be equally severe. How about luring him to the tower and getting him to save a damsel in distress in the menagerie, and getting himself locked in, preferably in the grizzly bear's cage?" She mused. "It could also be the lion's cage, or that of some other beast."

"Good heavens, what imagination. He'd never come out alive. Yet how excellent!"

"Isn't it? You could also ask one of the tower guards to pretend he is a long-sought criminal and throw him into the dungeon, only for a night or so. The guards would have to be bribed; I suppose."

"Why not have him locked up in Marshalsea or Bedlam, while you're at it? Only as a joke, of course."

She brushed it away. "Not nearly as romantic. One supposes that the old tower dungeons still have medieval torture devices. If one could lock him into the old torture room, with an iron maiden, rack, and thumbscrew, that would teach him a lesson, don't you think?"

Tristan looked at her with awe.

"I heard all about it, you know," she added softly. "About what happened at the club. And I want to thank you. Not because these men are idiots and deserved to be punched, but for stepping in before Kit could. He would have called them out all at once and met them at a duel. He could be dead now."

"Nonsense." Tristan frowned. "I would never have allowed that. And Miles Davenport is an idiot and a fool, but ultimately, he means no harm. Sometimes the only way to get a message across with him is through fisticuffs. This is why I have a friendly boxing match arranged with him in a few days, where I have the opportunity to pummel him once more. Your brother is invited, too."

Ava shook her head. "Boxing. Fisticuffs. Duels. I find my methods of punishment more creative."

"Maybe you are right, and we ought to clap him into the tower for a night only."

"Yes, the one that is haunted by the white lady. The white tower, I believe. To teach him that he is to leave all ladies forevermore alone."

A laugh escaped him. "Miss Sackville. You surprise me. You surprise me greatly."

She looked so ridiculously pleased that he suddenly felt the desire to hold her again. Like yesterday. Smell the violets in her hair. He resisted the urge.

"I would like it if you could call me Ava. And—" suddenly she looked bashful "—I have a present for you." She picked up a small package wrapped in silken paper from the table next to her and handed it to him.

He took it and unwrapped it. "A shawl."

A purple, misshapen, shawl. It looked so miserable that a laugh escaped him. At the same time, it touched him in an odd way. "I beg your pardon. It is lovely. I thought you meant this for your brother?"

She shook her head. "I have decided that it is for you. It is my first completed piece of knitting, ever."

"Then I shall wear it with honour." He wound it about his neck, bravely.

Her cheeks flushed.

Something rushed through him that felt like... tenderness.

He bent forward, and the kiss he brushed over her forehead was as light as butterflies. Her skin felt soft and warm under his lips. He jumped up. "I must be going. If the doctor agrees, I would very much like to take you on a ride in three days. Provided your foot feels better, of course."

"That would be agreeable." She smiled.

As he left the house, he realised that he very much looked forward to that ride.

LATER THAT AFTERNOON, THE VISCOUNT MILES Davenport arrived at the Sackville townhouse with a tremendous bouquet of pink roses. He walked into the salon, his hat under his arm, and bowed with a flourishing motion. He had a blue bruise under his right eye.

"Lord Davenport." Ava's voice was frosty.

"I am here to present my respects, with all due apologies for certain, er, incidents that may have come to your ears, regarding your person. I would like to express my sincere apologies for my part in them. The only excuse I have is that, when I am foxed, I turn into a sorry numbskull, though Ravenscroft would argue that I am a sorry numbskull in my sober moments anyhow. If you can find it in you to forgive me, you would make me the happiest of men. There, I said it."

Ava narrowed her eyes. She did not like Miles overly much, but he seemed to be sincere. "Yes, my brother told me about all this. I suppose Ravenscroft sent you here."

"With all due respect, Miss, he doesn't know I am here. This was my idea." He looked around where to put the flowers, and he placed them on the table in front of her. "Eh. This looks familiar. Violetta Winter."

Ava's head snapped up.

He lifted the caricature. "She hasn't been singing the last few days, and rumours say she's had an accident. The entire house nearly rioted when another singer stepped in instead. I don't even know her name. Poor woman, no one wanted to listen to her." He squinted at the picture. "Jolly good picture, this. I may be reading too much into it, but this fellow here could be me." He pointed to a man with a similar hair roll as he had. "And I daresay this is Ravenscroft." He pointed at the figure next to him, with a speech bubble 'Won't you be my light-o'-love?'

Ava regarded the picture. "Why do you think that is Ravenscroft? In all truth, it could be anyone."

"The waistcoat. There is only one man who wears such a sober-coloured waistcoat." He tilted his head aside. "It is of course a mystery why that woman only exists in the theatre. She seems to disappear into thin air as soon as she leaves the stage. No one has ever seen her arrive or leave. It is as if she is a ghost..."

"What a bag of moonshine." Ava laughed uneasily. This Miles, fool that he pretended to be, was more sharp-minded than she cared for.

He tilted his head to the other side, still pondering. "If she is not a ghost, then she must still be a person... hiding, in all likelihood. In disguise, maybe? I wouldn't be surprised if she were in our midst, in a completely different role. She is a consummate actress, after all..."

His speech petered off as his glance fell on her.

Silence.

Ava cleared her throat.

Miles blinked. "I beg your pardon. I have just had the most fantastical notion. It is all nonsense, of course... Tristan is right, I ought to have my brains investigated. It isn't normal how my brain functions sometimes. I believe my parents dropped me on my head when I was an infant. Yes, that must be it. Never mind my ramblings, ma'am, they are the figments of an overly imaginative mutton-headed mind."

He withdrew with another lavish bow, leaving Ava behind, feeling ill at ease.

What on earth had that been about?

Surely, he hadn't recognised her, had he?

Chapter Twenty

Ava wondered whether the idea of the tournament hadn't been a colossally bad idea after all. Because now, all London was talking of nothing else. Wagers were placed in all the clubs with astronomical amounts, and even many women took part. It was the first thing they talked of when she entered a salon, and the last thing she heard when she left.

Even in the theatre, they were whispering about it behind her back.

The theatre director had invited her for tea on more than one occasion, with the sole purpose of discovering who she favoured, so he could place his bets accordingly.

"I do not know, I cannot know, and I will not know until the actual contest!" she'd insisted.

"But surely you must have some sort of idea—"

She'd given him a withering stare. "Do not talk to me about this ever again." Which had left him spluttering.

What disturbed her the most, however, were the names that were bandied about in connection with those wagers. The Viscount Ormsby, the Duke of Cumberland, and.... the Earl of Ravenscroft.

She felt downcast that Tristan doggedly took part in the bets.

All for what?

A night with Violetta Winter?

Disappointment churned bitterly at the pit of her stomach. That, and a gnawing, growing sense of worry.

What if, with all this preoccupation over Mlle Winter, he discovered her real identity?

The scandal would be insurmountable.

She ought to break the engagement as soon as possible.

She'd never ought to have allowed it to happen in the first place, for it was only a matter of time until her disguise unravelled. If she allowed this marriage to take place, he would inevitably discover who she was on their wedding night.

She swallowed at the thought.

Yet she'd allowed this farce to go on for weeks. One last time, she'd told herself every time before they met. One last walk, one last meeting, one last ride in the park, pretending she truly was affianced to him. Then she would break it off.

It was a shame, really, for they had finally developed a sense of comfortable companionship. She looked forward to those outings.

Sometimes they talked, sometimes they did not, sometimes they merely sat side by side with each other, each following their own thoughts.

When he talked, it was usually interesting. He

always listened to her with his head tilted to the side, a cocked eyebrow, a thoughtful frown. He listened to her like he really heard her.

"You are concerned about something," he said now. They were driving along Rotten Row and emerged onto the Serpentine, which had frozen over.

She lifted her head and turned her face towards the weak winter sun that had broken through the clouds.

"I heard you are participating in that poetry contest of that opera singer," she said softly.

The knuckles on his reins tightened. "Did you, now?"

"Is it true?" Silly thing to ask when she very well knew it was true; she'd seen his card with her own eyes.

But she wanted to see his reaction.

"Yes."

"May I ask why?"

A muscle in his jaw flexed. "Because. Why not?"

"That isn't a proper answer."

He turned to her side and scowled. "Maybe it is an improper question that does not deserve a proper answer."

Her patience snapped. "It is a question that any woman would ask of her betrothed, especially when she finds that his name is bandied about in every drawing room, salon and club, together with that woman's."

He regarded her with a lifted eyebrow. Usually, she liked that eyebrow. But now it just infuriated her.

"If I didn't know otherwise, I'd say you sounded jealous."

Ava nearly fell off her seat. "Jealous? Me?" Jealous of herself? That was so ridiculous that she laughed. "No, I am not jealous. I would simply like to ask you not to participate in the poetry contest," she replied softly.

He looked at her with narrowed eyes. "You want me to withdraw?"

"Yes."

He seemed to consider the matter.

Ava gripped her reticule tightly on her lap.

"No," he replied eventually and lifted his ribbons to speed up the horse.

"I ask you as your future wife."

"Still, no." He did not even consider what she'd said.

"Why not?"

"Because." He shrugged again. "Ultimately, it is harmless. A spot of fun."

It is not, she wanted to scream. "You are allowing yourself to be seduced by that woman," she said flatly.

He threw her a startled look. "What nonsense. It is a game. There are some stakes to be played and I am playing. I would like to win. That is all."

She took a big breath. "They say the winner can ask of her anything he wants. What would you ask for if you won?"

"You should not be concerned about this." His jaw was set in a stubborn line.

What an infuriating answer! "Of course, I am concerned! I am very much concerned that I am about to marry someone whose definition of fidelity differs from my own."

"Fidelity." His jaw worked. "As in, loyalty, faithfulness, constancy."

"Yes. Precisely. Do you not believe in those virtues?"

"Of course, I believe in them." He shrugged. "Whether it is realistic to believe in them is another matter."

Ava's stomach tumbled to the ground. He was one of those men who would not think twice to keep a mistress while he was married. Why did it matter so much to her? She'd intended to break off the engagement anyhow. Yet she could not help but pursue this topic.

"Most people do not find it possible to live up to such high virtues," he added.

"What about love?" she whispered.

Ravenscroft did not reply.

He drove around a curve, then he uttered an oath and pulled the curricle to a sharp halt.

Before she could ask what the matter was, he jumped off the seat and lunged towards a small group of half-grown lads who had gathered around something on the ground. The ensuing melee unfolded so fast; she could barely follow what happened. He knocked the heads of two boys together, drew the third one back by the scruff of his neck, and pulled back a fourth. The boys, frightened out of their wits to be accosted by a fine gentleman, ran off in all directions. The object around which they had gathered seemed, at first sight, to be a mere bundle of rags, until one looked closer, and it turned out that it was a child, a beggar child who was crawling on the ground. Ravenscroft knelt next to him. He was crying.

Ava scrambled off the curricle and knelt next to them. "Poor child! Are you hurt?"

"They pelted stones at him," Ravenscroft answered

tersely. "Scum." He turned to a passer-by, who'd stopped to watch the drama unfold. "Call a hackney."

The man nodded and did so.

"What is your name?" he asked.

"Mick," the boy whispered.

The child was bones and rags. His twisted, thin limbs stuck out in all directions, and it was clear he would never be able to walk. Without much ado, Ravenscroft bent down, picked up the child, and placed him into the hackney.

"Mick. You are going to a children's hospital where they will take care of you. Will that be all right with you?"

The child nodded.

Turning to the coachman, Tristan said, "I want you to take the child to the Children's Hospital in Gower Street. Deliver him directly to Dr John Allan, who is a good friend of mine. Tell him Ravenscroft sends the child. Ask for a note with his signature on it and deliver it to me as proof." He took out a purse and handed it to the coachman. "If you do as I say, you will receive more of this." He shook the purse and the coins inside clinked.

The coachman, who'd torn off his hat, having recognised quality, said, "Yes, my lord."

Ravenscroft stayed to see the coachman get back on his seat and drive the coach off.

Then he returned to his curricle and helped Ava back into her seat.

They drove on in silence.

"It is not the child's fault." His voice was grim. "He

will have a hard enough life as it is, never being able to walk, having to crawl on the ground."

"No, my lord." Ava said softly. She could barely process what she had just witnessed.

"I don't like it when the strong throw themselves on the weak. It is intolerable. Whether that happens in the clubs or drawing salons, or at Eton, or in the gutters."

"It is very unjust," she agreed. "By the by, I read about this children's hospital in the paper the other day. It has been founded by a Dr John Allan, with the help of a generous anonymous patron. How do you know this Dr John Allan?"

At first it appeared he would not reply. "He has been instrumental in the establishment of the hospital," he eventually said. "He would work on finding a cure to this disease that leaves children crippled after a fever."

"That is what I assumed. And?" Ava prompted.

He shrugged.

"You are that anonymous patron," Ava stated.

"It is not something I generally want people to know," he muttered.

She turned to him with wide eyes. "Good gracious. I am correct? It was a wild guess."

"After my mother died, I donated part of what I inherited from her to that institution." He looked straight ahead, deep in thought. "She never said so, but I know she would have expected me to do so."

"In other words, the Earl of Ravenscroft is a secret philanthropist." Ava leaned forward and narrowed her eyes. "Are you, by chance, embarrassed to admit it?"

"Nonsense," he grumbled.

"Of course, you wouldn't want people to know. It is very much out of character, is it not? It quite ruins the carefully cultivated rakish reputation."

"My mother died in an institution very much like this one after having spent a winter there. Do you know why she died?"

Ava shook her head.

"Because they didn't have enough coal to heat the rooms. She died because of a cold that developed into an inflammation of the lungs. She died because my father refused to donate coal. So, I swore that whenever I would come into a fortune, I would do things differently. I would do what he had neglected to do. So, you see, there isn't anything philanthropic about this sentiment at all. It is about the childish, revengeful desire of getting back at my father."

"I am terribly sorry about your mother," Ava said softly. "I heard she was a lovely woman."

"She was. She left us too early." There was a grave expression on his face. "Miss Sackville. Ava. Could we come to the agreement that what you have witnessed today stays between us?"

Her eyes sparkled. "I'll think about it, Tristan. Anonymous patron, cat saver, spinster defender, and philanthropist."

"You forgot amateur boxer, mineralogist and opera aficionado," he grumbled, and she laughed delightedly.

What a complex man he was! Never in a million years would she have thought that within the span of a few minutes only, she would see him in an entirely different light.

Chapter Twenty-One

His fiancée was peeling back layer after layer of his identity. She wasn't entirely wrong when she'd mocked him about him carefully cultivating the reputation of a rake. What bothered him more, however, was the conversation they'd had earlier. When she'd spouted all that nonsense about fidelity and love. And when she'd asked him to desist from participating in the poetry tournament. Tristan had to admit the conversation with Ava had hit a sore spot, and he'd snapped at her.

She had every right to ask him to desist, and if he were a good fiancé, he would. But he wasn't, and they were not yet married, and there was too much at stake for him.

And lastly, he wanted to get a closer glimpse of Mlle Winter.

It was his only chance.

The poetry tournament was tomorrow night, and he was not getting any wiser about what poem to present.

What was it she'd wanted again?

A poem on mediaeval courtly love.

Where did one find such a poem?

He'd scoured his entire library and hadn't found a thing. He sat down on his desk, pulled out a sheet of paper and a pen, and stared at the blank page.

Love poem.

He cracked his knuckles.

This ought not be so difficult.

My love is like a red, red rose.

Wait. Those weren't his words. They were by this Burns fellow.

He crumpled up the paper, threw it into the fireplace and began again.

Your eyes are like—

He had no blasted idea. He'd never actually seen her eyes.

He crumpled up the paper with a growl of irritation. How could one write a love poem to someone one didn't know?

She had green eyes. His bride-to-be, that is.

Not entirely green, no. That was too mundane. They were molten green-grey, with little glints of orange light. And her pupil was black.

They were dashedly pretty eyes that changed colours depending on her mood. For when she frowned, they turned hazel. And when she was angry, fiery sparks glinted up from their depths...

Thus inspired, he set pen to paper.

Your eyes are like grapes...

"Bah." He tore the paper into tiny pieces.

He pushed his chair back.

He needed help.

And he knew just who to ask.

THE NEXT DAY, MILES STROLLED INTO HIS STUDY, grinning. "How's your poem getting along?"

"Wipe the smirk off your face. My poem is fine. What about yours?" Tristan's poem lay on top of his desk, neatly scribed and ready to be presented.

"Fine, fine. Easiest thing in the world to write love poems. I do it all the time." Miles strolled over to the desk and leaned against it. He was wearing a burgundy tail-coat with an elaborately tied cravat, and his hair was carefully arranged in a windswept fashion.

Tristan wore black, as always, and he wondered whether that was too funereal for an occasion like this. He didn't know that his stark black-white outfit made him look saturnine, which distinguished him from the rest. "Do you? How fascinating. I seem to recall that you said earlier that poetry made you want to run screaming into the other direction."

"Did I?" Miles busily cleaned his quizzing glass, which he rarely used but carried around with him anyhow because it was en vogue. "How things change, for I have discovered a hidden talent for poetry. Besides, my ladybirds love love poems. Tell me about yours."

Tristan laughed. "Not a chance."

"Is it a true poem on courtly love?"

"I suppose it is. Yes."

"So tight-lipped about your presentation. Are you

afraid I'll steal it?" Miles lifted the quill and dropped it back into the inkstand.

"Touch anything on my desk and I'll call you out," Tristan growled.

Miles lifted both hands. "Sorry. Very touchy about this, aren't you?"

"This is very important to me."

"It is important to me, too."

The men stared at each other.

"Confident of winning?" There was something in Miles' smile that told Tristan he was up to something.

"Of course. And are you?"

"Naturally, my friend, naturally. I shall eclipse you all with my particular work."

"That remains to be seen. For I very much want to win," Tristan growled.

"So do I." Miles chuckled. "Are we to call each other out over this?"

"If it comes down to it: yes."

"This is nonsense. Mlle Winter will decide who the winner is. There is no need for us to bash each other's heads in. The better poet will win." Miles grinned like a cat who was about to pounce on a hapless sparrow. Experience told Tristan that this meant he was up to one of his pranks. He'd better be on guard.

"You are correct. Who says that either of us will be chosen?" Tristan retorted. "This is all nonsense anyhow."

The butler came and handed Tristan his coat, hat, and gloves. After a moment's hesitation, he grabbed Ava's knitted shawl and wrapped it about his neck. Maybe it would bring him luck. He certainly would need it.

"Precisely. It's nonsense. And on this note, I suggest we go to the club and afterwards go to the tournament in brotherly companionship." Miles clapped Tristan on the shoulder. "We can always bash each other's heads in afterwards."

Tristan thought it was a fine notion.

Chapter Twenty-Two

THE FIFTY CHOSEN ONES WERE GATHERED IN A ballroom that looked like a mediaeval hall. The hall was grand, with marble pillars and marble floors. At the front, several stairs led up to a raised platform with a baldachin of heavy velvet brocade that framed an elaborately gilded chair.

Tristan blinked. If he was not mistaken, it looked very much like a throne.

Only a few torches were lit, casting a semi-dusky, mysterious atmosphere over the hall.

A general murmuring rose when the double doors opened in the back. The crowd parted and Mlle Winter glided past, flanked by Viking Hagen and Phileas Whistlefritz. She was dressed in a mediaeval-style dark-blue gown with gold trimming, and an elaborately embroidered belt cinched her tiny waist. Her hair cascaded down her back in a wave of fiery auburn. She wore a black velvet mask that hid most of her face. Only her strawberry-shaped mouth was visible.

"I wonder why she's hiding behind a mask," Miles mumbled. "It's not as though the entire world hasn't already seen her on stage."

Tristan agreed. He watched how the three stepped up the platform, Mlle Winter sat down, and the two men stood by her side. The canopy cast a shadow over her so even though she literally sat on a pedestal, it was difficult to see her. Tristan found it interesting that he wasn't as thrilled to see her as he'd expected. His heart did not pound, his breath did not quicken. What he felt instead was a vague sense of annoyance. The woman was celebrating herself as if she were Queen Guinevere herself. All because some fools like him lay at her feet, worshipping her.

It couldn't be helped. He had to proceed with his plan.

Phileas Whistlefritz stepped forward and spoke. "Gentlemen. You are the lucky chosen ones. You are here tonight because you have been selected to take part in this tournament of Wit and Courtly Love. Imagine that this is a mediaeval court like King Arthur's, and you are here to pay court to our lady." He made a flourishing bow to Mlle Winter, who nodded regally. "Each of you will present your poem and Mlle Winter will choose the winner. She will choose the one who pleases her most. I herewith call our first knight, the Duke of Cumberland."

"Tournament of Wit? No one ever said anything about anyone having to be witty," Miles complained as Cumberland stepped forward, pushing out his chest in self-importance.

"This is going to be a very long evening," Tristan groaned. He felt his pocket for his paper, which rustled as he patted it. He'd managed to get a very fine poem, and all he had to do was read it, and it would be done. But listening to everyone else reciting their poems was tedious, to say the least. The Duke of Cumberland, for example. He went first. He stepped forward, pushed his chest out and recited.

"My love is like a red, red rose..." His voice boomed.

"Stop. This is neither a poem written in the tradition of courtly love, nor has it been written by you. It's been written by Robert Burns." Mlle Winter cut into his recital sharply.

"But my poem is my personal interpretation of Burns—"

The Viking Hagen stepped forward, his hand on his sword, and scowled. Cumberland scrambled away.

"Next."

Whistlefritz read the names.

More than half of the contestants had plagiarised their poems and were immediately disqualified. Tristan squinted his eyes. Did he imagine it, or did Violetta appear bored? It was difficult to say, but the way she clenched her jaw appeared as if she repressed a yawn. She was clearly not impressed by her swains.

Then it was Miles' turn.

He stepped forward, bowed lavishly, and pulled out a piece of paper.

"My Lady, this is a poem written in the true tradition of mediaeval courtly love. The words are simple and meant to be sung in accompaniment of a lute." He cleared his throat.

> *"Lady of the Winds*
> *I saw at first a flicker of her dress*
> *Beneath the gloomy shadows of the trees*
> *And then a silver sheen*
> *Her silken hair spread wide*
> *A soft translucent net which flows*
> *In subtle waves..."*

Wait. Those lines sounded deucedly familiar. Didn't his poem start in the same way? Tristan hastily dug out the sheet of paper and unfolded it.

It was blank.

Confused, he turned it around, but the paper was empty on both sides.

The cur had stolen his poem and exchanged it for an empty sheet of paper.

He had no idea how it had happened, but his poem was gone, and here was Miles, reciting it as though he'd composed it himself.

And it seemed to be working, because for the first time this evening, Violetta looked interested.

> *Her icy pouting lips with hesitancy*
> *Brushed my cheeks—I felt*
> *The warmness drain from them*
> *Paralysing coldness swept through the*
> *Chambers of my heart – what immortality!*
> *I longed to be with her, the silver maid*

To fly with her and caress all the trees
The hills the plains and tempt the
Tranquil waters to rebel...
I looked into her face—and then
I stood alone beneath the trees."

Tristan took big breaths in and out. He repressed the anger that threatened to burst forth. He glared daggers at Miles, who, unimpressed, finished reciting the poem and bowed to a smattering of applause.

"That was original, indeed." Violetta's melodious voice rang through the room. "Though I would disagree that this is a song written in the style of mediaeval courtly love. It seems to be a modern poem about a woman's loneliness and the yearning for freedom, not love." She bowed her head to Miles. "Did you write it yourself?"

Miles cleared his throat. "Naturally. I am delighted, my lady, if it gives you joy."

She weighed her head. "Not joy, exactly, since the poem is rather sad. But it is interesting, I grant you that."

Certain that he had won already, Miles strutted to the other side of the room and smirked at Tristan.

Tristan growled. If they weren't in the company of others, he would throw himself at him and fight dirty like a pair of street boys.

Then everyone looked at him.

It was his turn.

Only now it occurred to him that he had nothing at all to present.

What was he to do now?

"Well? Sir Knight? Would you like to present your

poem?" Did he imagine it, or was there a mocking look in her eyes?

He walked up to the front, his mind working feverishly.

He turned and faced the audience, whose faces blurred into a giant blob of colour. He stared frantically at the tip of his boots and felt both his palms grow moist. He opened and closed his fingers.

"Uh." He could confess that he had no poem. That's he'd lost it. But then he'd look like a fool.

Dash it all, how difficult could it be to improvise a poem? He took a big breath, stood up straight and pushed out his chest, cleared his throat and began.

To My Lady Love.

That was good.

In fact, that was very, very good. All he had to do was find rhymes. He could rhyme. Any child could rhyme.

> *My Love. So gentle and so, uh, fair.*
> *With pretty eyes and pretty—hair.*
> *Sitting upon a golden—chair.*

Would one look at that! It worked! He ignored the snickers and continued.

A figure so, uh, divine and slim.

Maybe he shouldn't have mentioned the figure, but there it was. Now he had to find a rhyme for 'slim'.

A foot so dainty and so trim.

He was a poet!

He'd covered her figure, eyes and feet, now he ought to say something more about her hair.

Her golden crown on her head sits,
And lovely, lovely are her —

His eyes fell on her well-proportioned chest.

He bit on his tongue so hard it nearly bled.

Don't say it, don't say it!

He'd nearly blurted it out without thinking.

He feverishly sought a suitable rhyme, but for the life of him, he couldn't think of another word.

Sweat pearls formed on his forehead.

The guffaws in the audience grew louder.

"Spit it out, man, spit it out! Lovely are her what?" shouted a voice. It was probably Miles.

Pull yourself together, Tristan, he scolded himself. You can do this!

"And lovely, lovely are her—curls."

The audience booed with disappointment.

He sighed with relief.

But now he was stuck with her blasted hair.

One couldn't compare that to anything. His mind drew a complete blank. What was her hair like?

Her fiery curls so, so, so — red and bright,

Are the colour of uh, er, ah—amarantite.

"It is a sulfide mineral, you see," he added. "It comes from the Greek word for 'amaranth.'"

Since she tilted her head in a confused way, he took it as a sign that maybe it wasn't a good simile. He would have to look for something else.

With a sigh, he repeated,

Her fiery curls like—

In desperation, his eyes swept the room for an idea.

Miles' grin stretched from ear to ear. He already saw himself as the winner.

Determined, Tristan looked on.

A liveried footman repressed a yawn. He held a tray with some sort of finger food. Something that looked like—

Round and oblong, like her hair.

"Sausage rolls," he blurted out.

Her fiery curls like sausage rolls,
Bounce up and down like pulley loads.

He finished in a rush.

Not the most romantic metaphor, granted, but at least it rhymed.

Mostly.

There was stunned silence.

Not even a snicker.

He slumped his shoulders. That was it, he supposed. The ultimate defeat, a terrible loss of face.

Humiliation by poetry. He had ruined his reputation forever.

Then she opened her mouth and—bright and clear peals of laughter filled the hall. She laughed! And how she laughed. She held her side and she wiped her cheeks as if tears streamed down her face. The gentlemen joined it. The hall rocked with laughter and applause.

Tristan sucked in a big breath.

He'd made a complete and utter ass of himself. Relieved it was over, he crept back and collapsed in his chair.

Miles fell out of his seat as he gasped with laughter. "That was brilliant. Sausage rolls?" He slapped Tristan on his shoulder.

Then Mlle Winter stood up. She looked regal in her simple, blue gown, like a queen, indeed.

"This is a difficult choice for me. Of all poems presented tonight, the one that is most interesting is the one by his lordship, Miles Davenport. There is truth in the poem. And pain. Existential pain."

Miles jumped up and bowed, ready to make the speech of the victor.

She raised a hand. "But—" She waited until Miles sat down again. "But it is not a love poem. It is not a song written in the style of courtly love as we requested. It reminded me of my own—loneliness." She swallowed. "To my great disappointment, none of you have been able to produce the kind of poem I would have wanted. That aside, the poem that I enjoyed the most, the one that gave me the most pleasure—" she made a dramatic pause "—was the one by Ravenscroft."

The others groaned and cheered.

"Mainly because it was the only poem presented tonight that was authentic."

Ravenscroft had buried his face in his hands, so he did not immediately hear what she'd said. Miles elbowed him. "Looks like you're the lucky devil."

He looked up, dazed.

Mlle Winter chuckled. "I haven't laughed like this in a long time. Pray, did you improvise it?"

Tristan jumped up. "Er. Yes. I must confess it is not the poem I originally intended to present." He glared at Miles, who met his stare with wide, innocent eyes. "My original poem got—lost."

He could have exposed Miles there and then, but he abhorred scenes. Besides, he did not have any proof that Miles' poem had been his to begin with.

Violetta's eyes danced merrily at him.

For one inkling of a second, he had the impression that there was something very familiar about her eyes. But then, of course, she would be familiar since he had attended every one of her performances.

"I declare you the winner, then," she said in her light, musical voice.

"What. Me?" He must have misheard.

The light of amusement in her eyes changed to something more cynical. "Yes, you. Lord Tristan Ravenscroft, you are the winner. You made me laugh. Your poem has pleased me. Now to the most important part, for this is why you are all here, is it not?" She looked

186

around and waited until the muttering ceased. "Your boon."

"My boon." It seemed he had lost all control over his mental faculty because all he was capable of was bleating the same words after her like a sheep.

"I shall keep my promise and grant any wish to the winner of this contest. Well? I await." Her lips were pulled into a cynical smile.

This was his moment. This is why he had gone through all this trouble to begin with. He moistened his lips. This was important, he had to get it right. "I would like a night with you."

The line of her mouth twisted into a slightly bitter line. "Naturally."

"At Ravenscroft Hall."

"So it shall be. One night, and one night alone, I shall be yours."

The men clapped and whistled. "Lucky devil," shouted one.

"No." He shook his head. "No. You misunderstand. I mean one night of your music. Of your performance. The longest of Mozart's operas. Is it *Figaro's Wedding*? Or *Magic Flute*? I want you to perform that. And I want it to be your best performance of all time."

There was a beat of a pause. "A personal opera performance?"

"Yes, but not to me. I have heard you sing countless times. You need not sing for me specifically. I mean, of course, I'll listen, too, if you don't mind. I would be happy to listen." For heaven's sake, stop blabbering and pull yourself together! He cleared his throat. "What I am meaning to say is that I want you to give your best performance to Miss Isolde Sydney."

"Dash it, Tris," Miles muttered next to him. "You make me weep."

"And who is this Miss Isolde Sydney?" She drew out the name.

"She is my younger sister."

There was a beat of a pause as Mlle Winter stared at him. "You have a sister."

"Yes, ma'am."

"You want me to sing for your sister."

"Yes, ma'am."

"You entered this poetry contest specifically for this reason."

"Yes, ma'am. It seemed to me to be the only recourse since you would not answer my missives."

"Your sister. Isolde Sydney. She has not, ever, attended any of my performances at the opera?"

"No, ma'am." Tristan shook his head. "She cannot. She is very ill." He looked down. "Begging your pardon, ma'am, but I do not want to expose her in public like this by expounding upon her illness. Let it suffice to say that it is not possible for her to go to the opera or the theatre. Ever since she heard that you were in England, her biggest wish has been to hear Mlle Winter, the legendary opera star, sing. She loves music but has little to no occasion to listen to an entire orchestra unless I hire them. She has never seen an opera, least of all set her foot in an opera house. She is, however, exceptionally well-versed, and well-read." He gave Miles a hard stare. "She enjoys writing poetry."

Miles looked away and shifted uncomfortably.

"I am using this wish to ask you to please sing for her. Personally. Let it be your best performance, ever. A real opera, with the entire cast and the scenery and costumes and whatever else you need. For one night. Maybe sometime in the summer when it is warmer. Outside. We have an amphitheatre in the park of Ravenscroft Hall. It would mean the world to her." After a beat of a pause, he tagged on, hastily, "And to me, too, of course."

Did he imagine it, or were the eyes behind the mask suddenly bright, as if glistening with tears?

"Of course," she said softly. "Of course, I shall sing for your sister."

AFTERWARDS, WHEN TRISTAN COULD BARELY believe he'd really done it, Miles cuffed him on the shoulder. "I nearly bawled my eyes out when you brought up Isolde. Dashed nice thing to do."

"Ah. Yes. Speaking of which—" Tristan stopped and narrowed his eyes "—stand still and move your head to the right. A little more. Hold." He took Miles' face and moved it to the desired angle.

Then he smashed his fist into his chin. "And that is for stealing Isolde's poem and saying it's your own." Tristan conveniently forgot that it had been his own plan as well, to pass off his sister's poem as his own.

Miles, who'd seen it coming, rubbed his smarting chin. "I suppose I deserved that. Dash it, Tris, it's the second time within a fortnight that you get to plant me a facer. Although you must admit it is thanks to me that you have won. If I hadn't borrowed the poem, you wouldn't have made such an ass of yourself and made Violetta laugh. Also, if you hadn't improvised your piece of ridiculousness, Isolde's poem would certainly have won. Have you considered that?"

"Yes, and what would you have wished for as a boon? Surely not an exclusive opera performance for Isolde at Ravenscroft Hall?"

Miles looked away, ashamed. "Caught me here. I am evidently not as big-hearted as you. We're even now, aren't we?" He rubbed his chin again.

Tristan grunted.

Miles slapped his shoulder. "Let's go to the club and get foxed, then. Got to celebrate your victory, after all."

Chapter Twenty-Three

It was a quiet, gentle, tender moment that tilted Ava's entire world askew. It left her breathless, hot, and disoriented, with her heart slamming against her ribcage. It was not a grand celebration, epic event or monumental gesture. It was a dawning realisation that she had fallen deeply in love.

The day after the tournament, Tristan drove to Ava's house and handed her a bouquet of violets.

She buried her face in the purple petals. "Do you feel guilty for having won the contest? And now you are trying to buy my goodwill with flowers?"

The papers were full of his victory. And in the clubs and drawing rooms, they spoke of nothing else.

"Guilty?" He thought. "Well. Maybe a little."

Ava lowered her flowers and looked at him with wide eyes. "I did not really expect an honest answer."

He shrugged, looking visibly uncomfortable. "I know you did not want me to take part in the tournament. For that I am sorry. Trust me when I say that it was one of the most uncomfortable, embarrassing moments I have ever suffered through in my entire life."

Ava bit on the inside of her cheek to suppress a smile. "Was it?"

Tristan shuddered. "I hope never to have to repeat the experience. However, fetch your bonnet. I would like to show you something." Those had been the words when Tristan arrived in Bruton Street. In the carriage, she found, to her surprise, a basket full of kittens.

"Are they the ones you have rescued?" she inquired and lifted a little black one onto her lap.

"Yes."

"But why are they here? And where are we going?"

"We are visiting Ravenscroft Hall in Wiltshire. We'd agreed to take the kittens there, did we not?"

They drove in his coach through the London streets, and out into the countryside. The weather had grown severely cold, and Ava was glad she'd donned her warm coat.

Tristan gently wrapped a woollen blanket about her and handed her a muff. His coachman had placed a warmed brick under her feet. She felt taken care of like never before in her life.

Now would be a good moment to tell him who she really was. Except when she looked sideways and saw the crisp clean cut of his jaw as he looked ahead, with the frown between his eyebrows, her heart made a small lurch, and she decided not to speak. Not yet. Let her bask in the illusion that she was truly marrying him a little while longer. There would be plenty of time on the way back.

They drove through a rolling parkland in Wiltshire. Ava leaned back and enjoyed the view. They emerged from a forest and in front of them stood a grand mansion with a Palladian front that appeared larger and more sombre than Sackville Hall.

"Does your father live here, too?" Ava asked.

"No. He and I prefer to keep our living arrangements separate. I reside in Ravenscroft Hall; he prefers to stay in Stoneway Abbey in Sussex, but it is too large and gloomy for my taste."

"How many houses have you got?"

He shrugged. "Several."

Ava leaned back, amused. "Several. You have lost count of them?"

"Four, to be exact. Wiltshire, Sussex, Yorkshire, and Shropshire."

"Good heavens," Ava murmured.

The carriage drove up to the entrance, and Tristan handed her down.

"Is she up?" he asked the housekeeper, who emerged from the house.

"Yes, my lord."

He nodded. Offering Ava his arm, he escorted her into the house.

Despite its grandiose external appearance, the interior of the house was light and airy.

Tristan led her up a gigantic marble staircase, and when Ava lifted her face, light shone through the domed ceiling.

On the second floor, Ava noted the exquisite carpets on the floors and walls.

"My father brought them from his travels," Tristan explained.

He knocked on a door and opened it.

The room was an oriental dream, with colourful murals, Turkish carpets, and silken pillows on the floor. A massive four-post bed with heavy curtains in forest-green brocade stood in the middle of the room.

A little pale face, barely visible amongst the pillows, turned and the brown eyes lit up. "Tristan!"

"Hello, pigeon," he said softly. He took two steps to reach the bedside and knelt to grab the hands that extended toward him. "Look who I've brought today. This is Miss Ava Sackville, my fiancée." Tristan turned to Ava, who hovered near the door and extended his hand. "Miss Sackville, my sister Isolde."

Ava took several steps into the room. "Isolde," she repeated. "I did not know you had a sister."

"Not many people do," he replied, softly.

Ava turned to her. "Miss Sydney."

A pair of huge, luminescent eyes were on her. "I am so glad to meet you, Miss Sackville. Finally! Finally, Tristan is doing the right thing."

"I should have brought her here earlier, I know." Tristan smiled down at her fondly. The smile softened his face. Ava looked at him in wonder.

"I didn't mean that." An impish smile flitted over Isolde's elfin face. "I meant that you are finally bringing a bride home." She held her hand out to Ava. "Welcome, Miss Sackville."

"Please call me Ava." She took the little hand that she had extended to her. "Isolde. What a pretty name."

"I don't care much for it, but my mother was very romantic. Tristan and Isolde. She read too much German mediaeval literature. Mother was half German, you know."

She hadn't known. She cast a quick look at Tristan, who lifted one shoulder.

"You must forgive me, but I cannot get up." Isolde attempted to lean on her elbows to pull herself up. Tristan propped up pillows on her back, then pulled up two chairs and indicated for Ava to sit.

"And you sit there," Isolde demanded, pointing at the other side. "But first you must draw aside the curtains so I can have a better look at Ava."

"My sister tends to be somewhat bossy, I'm afraid."

"It's a Sydney trait, as I am sure you've already noticed," Isolde said, grinning. Then she studied her. Ava was suddenly self-conscious when the sunlight fell on her face.

"Hm. You are not pretty."

"Isolde! I must apologise, Ava—"

"Nonsense."

"It is the truth. But it matters not." A smile lit up Isolde's face. "We need not have a beautiful appearance; it is entirely useless. Look at me, I am beautiful but entirely broken."

Ava groped for words.

"Vanity, vanity," Tristan grumbled.

"Be quiet and sit over there by the window. I daresay you talked to Ava the entire morning so now it is my turn." Turning to Ava, she said, "Tristan is my legs. I send him all over London to fetch me things. Books, shawls, stockings—"

"Silly toys," Tristan interjected. "Like music boxes. It had to be one with dancing cats." Their eyes met. He pulled his lips into a wry smile. The memory of the clock shop and how they'd argued over the box hovered between them. Why hadn't he told her earlier about his sister?

"Speaking of cats, we've brought you an entire litter to play with."

Isolde clapped her hands. "Oh, where are they?"

"In the stables. I'll tell John to bring them up later."

Isolde beamed at Ava. "Tristan always brings me things. Look what he bought me the other day." She lifted the little music box from her nightstand. "I love it beyond anything. Isn't it lovely?" She lifted the lid, and the little kittens danced to the tinkling music. When the blanket shifted aside, Ava could see that her thin, twisted legs were encased in pink stockings, the ones Tristan had bought for her the other day in the hosiery.

Ava felt a pang of remorse. She had judged his character too harshly.

Tristan sat by the window, picked up a newspaper and flipped through the leaves as though the conversation did not matter to him.

A dimple appeared on her right cheek. "Now he pretends to read but, in reality, he's following every single word we're exchanging. Where were we?" She clasped her hands in hers. "Oh, yes, I remember. I am so glad you are going to marry him even though you are not beautiful because I can clearly see you are beautiful inside. And that is what matters most."

"Thank you," Ava replied, touched.

Tristan shook his head and mumbled to himself.

Isolde leaned forward with an imp dancing in her eyes. "Be careful, because he has the reputation of a terrible rake, you know."

"I heard that."

Tristan did not raise his eyes from his paper.

"Be quiet and continue reading. I am talking with Ava now."

He raised an eyebrow and flipped the page.

"As I was saying. He has the most dreadful reputation!"

Ava leaned forward likewise. "Does he, now?"

"Oh yes," Isolde whispered loudly. "The women are scrambling all over him but none of the nice, marriage-able ones; only Drury Lane doxies and opera singers."

Ava winced.

"How does she even know all that?" Tristan muttered to himself.

"I read the papers too, you know." Isolde looked smug. "Likely I'm better informed than you on all matters politics and social issues. I've also seen all the caricatures! Ava." She leaned forward. "There is something you need to know about my brother and his dark, terrible secret."

"Oh my. I wonder what that could be? I am starting to feel some trepidation."

"It is an open secret. Do you want to know what it is?"

"I beg of it. But secretly, please." Both women glanced at Tristan, who seemed absorbed in his paper.

"He is spending every night at the opera."

"Not *every* night," he muttered. "Only twice a week."

"Do you know why?" Isolde's eyes glittered.

"Why?" Ava's voice was breathless.

"Because he is in love!" Isolde fell back into her pillow with a laugh.

"Oh!" Ava cast a sideways look at Tristan's immobile face, which seemed to have turned a shade red.

"He is awfully, terribly in love."

Ava sighed. She hadn't expected that violent punch of pain in her gut at this announcement.

"And you know who it is?"

Tristan put down the newspaper. "Really, Isolde. If you can't come up with a more edifying conversation, then I must whisk Ava away from here. You are teasing her terribly. What must she be thinking?"

"Be quiet, Tristan. This is important." Isolde crossed her arms. "I want Ava to know this. Then you can whisk her away all you want."

"You were telling me about who he was in love with," Ava reminded her.

The moment of truth had come. "Oh yes, you must know. He is in love with the Incomparable of the Season, of course."

Of course.

"La Violetta Winter." Isolde raised her hands as if to conduct some invisible music.

Ava blinked. "Who?"

"The greatest opera star who has ever sung on the British stage. The golden nightingale."

Ava was, for a moment, speechless. "The new diva at the opera house."

"Yes. He has completely, and utterly, lost his heart. Do you still want to marry Tristan now that you know this?"

"Isolde!" He was definitely blushing.

"Mind you, it is merely infatuation, not really love. For I doubt one could love someone one doesn't really know—"

"I-sol-de!"

An imp danced in her eyes. "Well?"

"Excellent question," Ava murmured. "That is setting up oneself for lifelong unhappiness, if one knows that one's husband-to-be has already given his heart away to such an unattainable object of affection, too. Unless, of course, one decides it is a passing fancy and attempts to put more value on what really matters."

"And what would that be, I wonder?" Tristan had long given up the pretence of not being interested.

Ava shrugged. "Friendship, maybe. The ability to trust in someone. Being able to talk and laugh with one another."

Their eyes met. There was an odd look in his.

"Ava." A smile broke over Isolde's solemn little face. "I like you tremendously. Tristan—" she turned to her brother "—she is a gem. You had better keep her and know you do not deserve her."

"Oh, I am aware of that."

"And do you deny anything I've said?"

"No." He came over to her bedside and frowned down. "Violetta Winter is divine. You are merely jealous because you haven't yet heard her sing. And here is where I've got some piece of good news. Two, actually. You do not know this yet because the newspaper you are reading is a day old. One, I won the poetry contest, and the diva has agreed to sing specifically for you."

Isolde clapped her hands. "Oh! How fabulous! Did she like my poem, then?"

"She certainly did." Tristan shifted in his chair. "For the sake of honesty, I must confess that it was Miles, the scoundrel, who presented it, claiming it as his."

Ava bent forward. "What?"

Isolde dropped her hands and drew her eyebrows together. They were thick, and dark, and gave her face an elfin look. "What do you mean? He said it was his? But I wrote it for you?"

Now Tristan shifted around in his chair. "He must've stolen it. Maybe when he came into the study before we left. He read it as his."

"So, what did you do when it was your turn?"

Tristan shrugged. "I had to invent something."

Ava bit on her lips.

"No! Did you? Can you recite it for me?"

Tristan looked horrified. "Again? Over my dead body."

"Please, Tristan, please, please, please!"

"I would very much like to hear it as well." Ava suppressed a grin.

Tristan groaned. "You insist on humiliating me. Oh, very well." He stood up, posed, and recited the poem again, changing some lines as he'd forgotten the precise words. It was as funny as it was the first time because this time, he attempted to act theatrically by making various ridiculous-looking poses.

Ava and Isolde laughed heartily and clapped.

"How very well done," Ava said. "You deserve this win. Amarantite! How on earth did you think of this?"

Tristan shrugged. "I like to collect stones."

"But I must say, it was right that your silly poem won, and not mine, for it was the more honest thing to do, is it not? Think of how you must feel if my poem had won, with the diva thinking you wrote it yourself. It would have been very dishonest."

"Indeed." Ava pursed her lips. "Fie on Miles. And on you too for having attempted to pass off your sister's poem as your own." She lifted an eyebrow.

Tristan had the grace to blush.

"She will really sing for me, yes?" There were stars in Isolde's eyes. Ava's heart squeezed.

"I think so, yes," Tristan replied. "We still need to arrange the details, however."

"I am beginning to like the diva. One has heard such things about her, but I think they can't all be true. I believe she has a big heart."

"That remains to be seen." Tristan crossed his arms. "She has to keep her promise, after all."

"What—what does one hear of her?" Ava pulled up her courage to ask.

"She is a diva. Difficult. Peculiar. That she won't see any of the gentlemen in the green room." There was a cheeky look on Isolde's face.

"And what do you know about these things, pigeon?"

"More than you think. Have you tried yourself, Tristan?" She threw an impish look at Ava. "I apologise for asking in your presence. I am too curious, and life is too short for maintaining conversation with propriety."

"Of course."

"And?" Isolde turned to Tristan.

"Like you say, she won't see anyone. Which is why I decided to take part in this infernal contest. I fear you will tease me about it for the rest of my days."

"Your entire motivation behind this was to get her to sing for Isolde? Truly?" She took a big breath.

Tristan shrugged. "What else could I have done when she didn't answer any of my letters?"

Isolde yawned. "She probably receives too many letters to bother to answer. It was good you did what you did, Tris. I am glad she is to sing for me, too." Her voice became thick with tiredness.

"All this excitement is tiring you and you're looking pale and exhausted. You need to rest." Tristan got up.

"I feel perfectly fine, Tristan. But you may be right, and I might be in need of a short nap before we have tea. Why don't you go and look at your precious stones in the meantime and take Ava with you. And Ava—" she caught Ava's hand "—I am glad! Glad that I am to have a sister!"

Ava was deeply touched.

After they left her room, Tristan led her to the library. It was an airy room with windows facing the garden, and bookshelves between them, as well as on the opposite wall. A fire was lit in the fireplace.

"You seem uncommonly thoughtful," he observed.

"There is much to think about," Ava responded.

"Isolde is an imp who takes delight in roasting both of us. I should have warned you she tends to do that. I humour her too much, I suppose. She has been dreadfully spoiled."

"But... is she right? Are you in love with that opera singer?"

Tristan didn't even seem to think before he replied. "Of course, I am."

Ava gasped.

"Every single man in England is. It is meaningless because she is a goddess with a divine voice. Unattainable, unreachable, only to be admired from afar." He shrugged. "I suppose that is all there is to it."

"A goddess with a divine voice, to be loved only from afar..." Ava murmured. "That is so very sad."

"There is some masculine pride involved as well. When every other gentleman in the club participates to woo the beautiful Violetta Winter, it doesn't look good to be the only one not to."

"Yet again, you surprise me with your honesty."

He flashed her a sudden smile. He had the same smile as Isolde. It made him look boyish, and her heart made a small but definite leap.

"Thank you."

"Yes? For what?" Tristan walked up to the fireplace and leaned against it. He looked very fine in his buff-coloured trousers, matching waistcoat, and dark-brown coat. A lock of brown hair fell onto his high forehead. He had the same eyes as his sister: inscrutable; inquiring; irresistible.

"For bringing me here. For introducing me to your sister. For—for telling the truth." She fiddled around with the tip of her shawl. "I wish you'd told me about her earlier. Why did you not mention her before?"

"Force of habit." He took a turn about the room, went to a shelf, and pulled out a random book. "Isolde is a recluse. The *ton* has all but forgotten about her and that was intentional. I won't have the name Isolde Sydney in everyone's mouths, asking who she is and why she isn't in society, and what illness, for heaven's sake, she is suffering from. And whether it is contagious." He slammed the book back into the shelf. "Although, of course, with that tournament it couldn't be helped, and I had to mention her. And now Isolde will be the object of much gossip." He sighed. "And before you ask, let me tell you, no, it is not contagious. When she was a child, she was taken by a violent fever, which we thought she would not survive. She did survive, but it left her numb and stiff, then paralysed from the waist down. Both her legs and feet are horribly twisted, and she is unable to stand, walk, or dance."

"Like that beggar child you saved the other day," Ava said softly. "Is it the same disease?"

"I am afraid so. It begins with a fever that leaves the children in this state. It is a terrible illness. There is no cure. She was ten when she fell ill. I was seventeen. My father—" he took an agitated turn about the room "—my father back then thought it was best to have her confined to an institution, where she would be surrounded by doctors. She was only a child, then. I was violently against it. But Father insisted. Mother then decided to move with Isolde into the institution..."

"... where she died," Ava said sadly.

Tristan nodded. "I have never forgiven Father. But, after mother's death, he relented and agreed to take Isolde out. I promised to take care of her for the rest of her life, so I brought her here to Ravenscroft Hall. Father visits regularly. The two get on well, interestingly enough. He is soft and gentle with her where he is hard and unyielding with me." He stared out of the window. "It doesn't matter what I do, I'll always be a scoundrel in my father's eyes," he muttered more to himself.

Ava stepped up to him and touched his arm. "You are a wonderful big brother."

"Oh, we fight more often than not," he said, attempting to lighten the mood. "She can be a brat, as you have witnessed. Her faculties are as sharp as can be. Isolde is an insatiable reader and a talented writer and poet."

"What a brave, strong woman she is."

"Given the cards life handed to her, she has no other choice but to be brave." He swallowed. "Her disease has taken a turn for the worse. She is easily fatigued and her muscles ache more than ever before. The doctors are baffled. They give her a few years at the most."

"Oh Tristan." Ava looked at him, stricken. "Can there be nothing done?"

"No. Except hoping and praying that the doctors are wrong. Her one and only current desire is to hear the Incomparable sing. I thought about arranging a private soiree with her. Hire her to sing only for my sister. I would spend my entire fortune on making this happen. But that is extremely difficult to accomplish because it is impossible to get access to the diva. I have written to her daily, with no response. That is why I decided to take part in that ridiculous tournament." Tristan made a throwaway motion.

Ava never read any of the many letters she received. Suddenly, she felt like weeping. "I am certain she will consider it an honour to sing only for Isolde."

Tristan stepped up to her and looked down thought-fully into her face. He touched her cheek lightly, and a shiver went through her. "Ava. Do you know what I like about you? Your optimism. Your purity of heart. Your sense of humour. Your loyalty towards Millicent and your brother. You only ever see the best in people. Do you know how rare that is? Isolde was right. You are a gem, and I am the luckiest of men to make you my wife. I admit that, back then at the musicale, I proposed on a whim. I confess I wanted to vex my father by marrying, let us say, not the bride he had in mind for me. I was a vain fool. I still am. But I am a devilish lucky chap that it was you sitting there, and not someone else. I humbly admit I don't deserve you."

Now her eyes really filled with tears. "No, Tristan. You have it all wrong. I am not who you think I am."

"I know you seek fidelity." He cupped her face in his hands. "I don't know how, but I want you to know that I shall try my best to make you happy."

"Tristan." A tear rolled down her cheeks. He wiped it away with his thumb, tenderly.

His kiss was a light brush across her lips, agonisingly

sweet.

She shivered, aching for more. Aching to be completely embraced by him, aching to tell him the truth. "Tristan, I need to tell you something."

The door opened, and the housekeeper entered. "My lord, tea is ready in the green salon."

The two jumped apart. Ava tugged on her wig.

"Is she awake yet?"

"Yes, my lord."

Tristan carried Isolde into the garden and set her down gently into a chair. And it was in that moment, when the afternoon sun played on the locks of his dark hair as he bent his head to tuck her blanket in, that Ava realised she'd tumbled hopelessly in love.

She stared at him, dumbfounded.

"Are you well, Ava? You are quite pale. Does your foot hurt?"

"No... no—" she shook her head "—I am fine."

"Play with me, Tristan," Isolde said. "And you too, Ava."

"What is it you would like to play?"

A dimple appeared on Isolde's face. "I usually play cribbage with Tristan, gambling with real money. I usually fleece him. But since it is the three of us now, how about we play vingt-et-un? But take care, Ava, Tristan cheats shamefully!"

"Fie, Isolde. If you were a man, I would have called you out for that." Tristan picked up a pack of cards and shuffled them.

"And I would have bested you in the duel." She laughed delightedly.

Ava felt humbled on their drive home. She peeked at the man who sat across from her in the corner of the carriage, with crossed arms. She studied his profile as he looked out of the window. They were sitting in comfortable silence. There was no need for small talk, no need for chatter to fill an awkward silence.

His devotion for his sister was deeply touching.

His kindness.

His humour.

His honesty.

She felt a golden warmth spread throughout her body. That surprised her.

He surprised her, too.

Ava tugged at her lower lip, deep in thought. More than once today, she'd felt prompted to end the charade she was playing. More than once she'd opened her mouth to confess who she was. And more than once she'd closed her mouth again without uttering the words.

When he looked at her, with his inscrutable eyes, she could barely withstand his gaze. She felt confusion wash over her, and guilt, and a terrible fear gripped her.

Fear of the consequences that her confession would bring.

Guilt at the deception.

If she were truly honest with herself, she'd have to admit this was only half of the reason. Part of her, deep down, felt afraid that he'd reject her once he learned of her true identity.

For she was no goddess.

She was plain Ava Sackville, who was good at slipping into various roles. And Violetta Winter was one of them.

She'd entered this engagement because it had been amusing, because he'd intrigued her, because... it had been such a normal thing to do. She could be a normal woman, leading a normal life... with an impending wedding, and a home.

Sadness flushed over her.

The moment she confessed her identity, this semblance of normality, even though based on a lie, would be over.

Yet how could she continue this?

What a coward she was.

How, oh how, was she to get out of this fix?

Chapter Twenty-Four

Lord Livingstone, Tristan's father, did not throw supper parties often. But when he did, it was always in grand style. After he'd returned from Bath, he'd announced that it was time for him to meet his daughter-in-law. What better opportunity than at a lavish engagement party?

Ava was in a fix and wrung her hands. She could not let the engagement go that far. But when Tristan had told her about his father's plans, he'd been so nervous about it she'd taken pity on him.

"What happens if there is no lavish engagement party?" she'd asked him timidly.

"My father won't have it." He'd pulled his hand through his hair. "He can still cut me off if he sees fit."

Ava had digested that. "So, if we were to elope..."

Tristan had laughed hollowly. "Then we will stand here without a penny. What is worse, people depend on me for financial support. My donations to Dr Allan and the Children's Hospital will be frozen, for example. My father doesn't like scandal. He doesn't even like the whisper of a scandal. Our family name is hallowed, you see. We are to live the life of saints." He sounded bitter. "He's already berated me about the poetry tournament, even though I won the blasted thing. Instead of congratulations, he wrote a biting letter that I seem to be incapable of staying out of the scandal sheets. He insists the wedding date be brought forward."

Ava chewed on her lower lip, deep in thought. She could not desert Tristan now. It would be cruel. But what she could do was meet the father, play along with it for a while, and then somehow... break the truth to him gently.

That meant she was heading for certain disaster and heartbreak, but maybe things would pan out better than she feared?

The problem was that her moral support, Millicent, had fallen ill and would be unable to go to Livingstone's engagement party. She had caught a flu and lay feverish in bed.

"I must say, I am quite content not to go, Ava. I know it sounds churlish of me and you must forgive me. But I cannot abide these social occasions, as you well know. Especially if they are being hosted by Lord Livingstone." She shuddered. "The man terrifies me."

Ava placed her hand on her forehead. "It is a shame, for I would've dearly loved to have you there. But of course you must stay in bed. Would you like me to make you a fresh mustard poultice?"

Millicent shook her head. "Do go and enjoy yourself and tell me all about it later."

Ava placed a kiss on her forehead and tucked the blanket in about her.

COACH AFTER COACH DREW UP TO HIS MASSIVE townhouse in Grosvenor square.

Ava's fingers stroked the satin upholstery of the carriage seats to soothe herself. She wore her hair in the usual style, tucked away under her brown wig. Under her coat, she wore a simple blue dress with a Kashmir shawl draped over her shoulders.

Her brother Kit looked as glamorous as always, in a perfectly cut coat and pantaloons. His thick, dark-blond hair was swept back in a roll, and the tips of his collar were so high they nearly poked his chin. He looked at once dishevelled and elegant, fashionable, and extravagant.

"It's not too late to turn back," Kit murmured into her ears as he helped her out of the carriage. "Say but the word."

Ava swallowed as she looked ahead with trepidation. Her instincts told her to flee. She did not have to do this. Every step she took now would ride her deeper and deeper into this tangle of deception.

Kit looked at her with a raised eyebrow.

She opened her mouth when she glanced at the entrance and saw a tall gentleman emerge. He was dressed in elegant black, his style contrasting to Kit's flamboyant one. His hawkish nose, the high cheekbones, strong eyebrows, dark, thick hair, the sensitive lips. When his eyes fell on her, they lit up.

A feeling of warm honey oozed through her veins.

And that was when Ava knew she could never turn back.

Tristan made his way towards her down the stairs.

"I suppose that's that then," Kit mumbled, then relinquished her hand.

Ava reached out to Tristan, he took her hands and kissed them.

"Ready?"

She took a big breath and nodded.

Together they climbed the steps to greet Livingstone.

THE OLD MAN WAS IN A DIFFICULT MOOD, TRISTAN noted. It was almost as if he were nervous. Tristan wondered why.

His father had taken a hard look at Ava, said all the polite things, then waved her on. Tristan had been irked. After all the drama, his father hadn't seemed at all interested in his chosen bride.

"Is that it, then?" Livingstone had barked and looked at the door.

"It appears everyone has arrived, my lord," his butler had told him. "One may proceed to supper."

"Bah," Livingstone had uttered, which had mystified Tristan.

What ailed the old man?

In contrast, Miles showed an uncommon interest in Ava. He towered over her, and Ava took a step back. Miles stepped forward, gesturing as he talked. Ava stepped back. It was an odd dance they danced.

Tristan glowered at Miles. "We are to proceed to supper." He offered Ava his arm, which she took readily.

"Not wanting to be impolite to your friend, but sometimes he is a bit—intense," she told him.

Tristan frowned.

"You should have no compunction to send him away if he bothers you."

"He brought me flowers the other day and apologised rather prettily."

"He did?"

Ava nodded. "I am glad he did. He is your friend after all."

"I wonder what he is up to," Tristan muttered to himself.

"Goodness, what a beautiful table! What pity Isolde cannot be here tonight," Ava said as they sat. It was lavishly decorated with heavy golden candle holders, and an entire swan made of silver fondant graced the middle of the table, decorated with fruit and flowers.

"It is a great shame, but Isolde declined. She said it would make her feel exposed and awkward. But hush now, it appears my father is about to hold a speech."

Livingstone stood with a glass in his hand, his silver eyes glittering oddly.

"I thought I would never see the day in which my son announces that he finally intends to tie the knot of matrimony. It is with great pleasure and relief, therefore, that I am announcing his engagement to Miss Ava Sackville." The crowd applauded politely. He lifted a hand. "The Sackvilles are a most excellent family. You could not have chosen wiser." He nodded at Kit, who smirked. "After all the years of degeneration that my son, alas, has brought over our family line, I must confess I am relieved."

The guests chuckled awkwardly, not entirely certain whether he was joking.

Tristan gripped the fork in his hand even though the first course was not yet served.

"Miss Sackville. Ava." Livingstone nodded at her. "I may call you that, yes? For you are to be my daughter, soon. Let me ask you one question. Has my son been treating you well?"

Ava blinked. "Naturally, my lord. He has been nothing but courteous and kind."

"Hear, hear," Miles interjected.

Tristan furrowed his eyebrows.

"Has he given you some sort of token of his affection?" Livingstone probed.

"Er, yes, almost daily. He's sent me the loveliest violets—"

"I don't mean flowers. I mean something more substantial. A brooch, maybe?"

Tristan stiffened. "Not yet." He knew exactly where this was heading.

A sly smile played about Livingstone's thin lips. "No of course, you didn't. You couldn't if you wanted to. For the heirloom which has been handed down for generations to the Sydney brides is gone now, isn't it?"

A deathly silence fell over the table.

"Sir, I beg of you not to address this topic this evening," Tristan bit out.

But Livingstone disregarded him. "Disappeared. Stolen. It is a roaring shame, is it not?" He turned to Ava.

"I am so very sorry, my dear. Tristan is unable to give you our Sydney heirloom for he pawned it a long time ago." He took a sip of his champagne. "To pay off his gambling debts."

Tristan jumped up. "You have always believed the worst of me, and I daresay I'm no saint, but I'm no blackguard, and certainly no thief. I never stole the brooch."

Livingstone sneered. "Did you not? It wouldn't have been the first time you stole something. You once admitted to taking a purse filled with gold coins straight out of my safe. Never blinked twice, never apologised, simply took the money. So, when I decided not to give you a loan for your staggering gambling debts, you stole the brooch and pawned it."

"It is a lie. You seem to have forgotten that later I repaid you the money, every single farthing. And Mother herself gave me the brooch to help me out of my debt. If you hadn't been so tight with your pocket, none of this would have been necessary. Yes, I pawned it. I would have bought the brooch back, but the pawnbroker had already sold it." The two men glared at each other across the dining table, while the guests listened in petrified silence.

"I say, Livingstone, maybe this matter ought to be addressed in private between you and your son," Kit suggested. "As fascinating as this drama is, I fear the soup is growing cold, and I am monstrously hungry."

"I hold you in high esteem, Sackville, for you come from an honourable, noble family." Livingstone acknowledged Kit with a curt nod. "Frankly, it astonished me that my son has managed to haul in a Sackville." Turning to

Ava, he said, "You must know you are marrying into a family of rakes and philanderers." He raised a thin hand. "I do not exclude myself, either. Knowing this, are you still willing to marry him?" He threw Ava a mocking glance.

Ava stood up next to Tristan and took his hand. Her eyes sparked, and there were spots of red on her cheeks. She almost looked beautiful. "For shame, Lord Livingstone, to bring this up on our engagement supper, which is supposed to be an event of joy, of celebration. You have completely ruined it before it even started. And shame on you for publicly humiliating your own flesh and blood. I do not care for trinkets, jewellery, and family heirlooms. I've got the highest regard for your son. He is one of the most honourable men whom I have ever met. He is courteous and kind, not only toward his fellow human beings but also toward the weakest in our society, as well as towards animals. I do not believe for a second that he stole that brooch. If there is a man who has integrity, it is he."

Her eyes teared up as she turned to Tristan. "It is an honour to be marrying you. No, much more than that." She wiped a tear away with one hand. "I want you to know that—I love you."

He hadn't seen that coming.

For one moment, Ava looked startled she'd said those words. She flushed, and her hand flew to her mouth. But her eyes met his, and he saw it there, pooling out of her eyes. She'd meant every word.

Livingstone looked like he'd frozen to marble. "You love him, do you?"

"Hear, hear," Miles interjected.

"I do, sir." Ava drew herself up like a queen. "And I would appreciate it very much, on this engagement night, if you were to stop defiling my bridegroom's personality, because I find that very insulting."

One could have heard a pin drop in the silence.

Then something alarming happened. A creaky, crusty sound broke out of Livingstone's lips.

He laughed.

He laughed so hard that he slammed his hand on the table, rattling the chinaware.

Everyone jumped.

Then he wiped a tear away with his hand.

"Well, what are you waiting for? Sit down, both of you. As for the rest of you: eat! Like Sackville said earlier, the soup is growing cold. This is supposed to be an engagement supper, isn't it? So eat and be merry."

The footmen began serving the mock turtle soup.

Tristan sat down, dazed.

Kit shook his head. "Well, that has been one of the most appalling engagement speeches I have ever had the misfortune to witness in my entire life. Puts me in the frame of mind to not let you marry Ravenscroft after all. Not because I believe in any of his accusations, but because it would mean that Livingstone would become your father-in-law." He shuddered. "On the other hand, he makes up for this shortcoming by offering better entertainment than the theatre. Imagine every supper playing out like that. Makes the theatre quite redundant if you ask me." Kit picked up his spoon and ate his soup.

"Can't decide whether you are to be envied or pitied,

Tris," Miles proclaimed from the other side of the table. He had to raise his voice above the general forced chatter, for everyone was determined to be cheerful. "Envied because, by George, you've got a fiery defender there by your side. But that dragon of your father is quite beyond the pale."

"Eat your soup, Miles," Tristan said wearily.

Too late it occurred to him he might not have reacted appropriately to his bride's public declaration of love. She sat next to him with a lowered head and did not appear to be eating as much as a morsel.

Chapter Twenty-Five

STUPID, STUPID, STUPID, STUPID!

What on earth had she done?

Defending her betrothed with brimstone and fire was one thing, but a public declaration of love?

If she could only hide under the table, crawl along on the floor, safely hidden by the tablecloth, and sneak out of the dining room. For one crazy moment she considered doing that.

This entire evening was a disaster. Not only was Tristan's father the devil personified, but he clearly took enjoyment in humiliating not only his son but the entire party. The old man was toying with them. He was a cruel tyrant, and altogether hateful. He'd goaded her into this outburst she now deeply regretted.

Ooh, the look on Tristan's face!

Ava cringed.

He'd looked surprised, disbelieving, almost incredulous, but the worst had been that he'd hadn't known how to respond.

He'd met her eyes for a second, then quickly looked away.

He did not know what to say because he did not reciprocate her feelings.

They had kissed, but that did not mean he loved her.

Tears pricked behind her eyelids. She swallowed them down bravely.

AFTER SUPPER, THE LADIES WITHDREW TO HAVE TEA in the drawing room, while the men remained for some port and a cheroot.

Ava could not bear the pitying glances of the other ladies.

"I beg your pardon," she mumbled and stepped out of the room.

Her wig itched, she felt sticky under the paste and powder she'd applied to her face, and she felt tired, so very tired.

She paused in the hallway to regain her composure.

A footman stepped up to her and pointed at a half-open door. "Begging your pardon, Miss. But his lordship would like a word with you in the library."

His lordship?

Tristan.

Ava ran her tongue over her dry lips. Her heart was beating in a painful staccato.

"Thank you," she told him, and she stepped into the library.

A fire roared in the fireplace, and sitting in front of it, in an armchair, was not Tristan.

It was his father.

"Oh." Ava considered turning around on the spot and running away.

He must have read her thoughts. "Pray do not run away, Ava. Contrary to what you may think, I am not the monster I may at times appear to be. Come join me here."

After a moment's hesitation, she sat at the edge of the sofa.

For a while, there was only the spluttering and cracking of the wood in the fireplace, the popping and roaring of the flames. Ava fidgeted and wondered why he'd called her into the library.

The Marquess of Livingstone was insufferably proud, a man impossibly high in the instep. He had a stern Greek profile as if chiselled out of marble, a sharp eagle nose, and hair that was peppered with grey. He was tall, imposing and intimidating. Very much like Tristan, Ava thought, except his features could soften in unexpected moments, and his eyes could lighten up with laughter and pleasure as he appreciated the ridiculous.

"So, you love my son." He uttered that as a statement of fact, not as a question.

It was too late to retract her words. "I—I... I suppose I do," she whispered.

He lifted a bushy eyebrow. "That does not sound nearly as confident as the announcement you made at supper. Be that as it may. If you truly love my son, then he is a lucky devil, indeed." He studied her closely. "I did not believe he had it in him, to choose a woman like you."

"A woman like me. Pray, what does that mean?"

"A Sackville." He stared morosely into the fire. "Virtuous, honourable, and full of the best qualities a woman can have. An excellent bride to choose."

Ava blinked. "You seem to think inordinately highly of Sackvilles, and precious little of your son."

"I beg pardon for the scene I caused at supper. I am aware it was excessively bad mannered of me. Consider it —a test."

"A test. Whatever for?"

He twisted his thin lips into a sly smile. "To see whether he meant it, first of all. And to see your reaction. I would have expected you to drop him. Burst into tears. Run out of the room. Anything, but stand up bravely and defend him. You were quite ferocious in your defence of him. I daresay he doesn't deserve it."

"But—why?"

Livingstone sighed. "I am dying, Ava. I am suffering from a heart disorder, which was the reason for my stay in Bath. Tristan does not know."

Ava covered her mouth with her hand.

"I suppose I neglected him, when I should have spent time with him." He rubbed his neck. "I admit I should have tried harder. He has always been more his mother's son. Then, there is his sister."

"Isolde."

"You have met her?" He cast her an enquiring look.

Ava nodded.

"Isolde was a pretty, lively thing until she succumbed to a fever. Turned into a cripple and was incapable of walking afterwards. I had her sent to a private institution, thinking it would be the best for everyone involved. My wife refused to leave her alone there. Moved in with

Isolde. Cared for her. She contracted an illness and died soon after. Tristan blames me for her death. He went quite wild afterwards." He made a throwaway movement with his hand. "Clubs, gaming hells, prize fighting and all sorts of ridiculous exploits. Nights out drunk, all the Covent Garden women—I beg your pardon, but you should know the truth about your bridegroom—and in general, a kind of life that shows no responsibility for anyone or anything. All those childish, ridiculous pranks! It was getting out of hand. I am deeply concerned about what happens to Isolde when I am no more."

"But there you are wrong, sir," Ava interrupted him gently. "He cares for his sister. And he is a philanthropist who actively supports Dr Allan's children's hospital." She shook her head in wonder. "I do not see the same person you see. It is a mystery to me, for it appears you do not know your son at all, and we seem to be speaking of two different people entirely."

Livingstone sighed wearily. "I have known him his entire life, Miss Sackville, whereas you have known him for how long, several weeks?"

"I believe that should not matter. I believe it is possible to know a person in a short period, and to never know another during an entire lifetime. I believe Tristan is good at wearing a mask, at playing a role, quite possibly the one you always expected him to play. Either way, I know one thing for sure: deep down, he is a good person, and that is all that should matter."

Livingstone studied her. "You really do love my son."

Ava opened her mouth to reply that of course she did.

"Ah, here you are." Tristan stood at the doorway of

the library, surveying the room with cool eyes. "I have been wondering where you went." He gave a nod in the direction of his father.

Ava flushed. Goodness! How much had he heard?

"If you will excuse us, I'll take Ava back. The guests have been wondering where she has been off to, and this is supposed to be our engagement supper after all, isn't it?"

"Tristan." The father pulled himself up and leaned on his stick. His eyes glittered. "Well done, son. I approve of your choice."

"Then I am most heartily relieved that you approve," he retorted, his voice dripping with sarcasm.

"We will talk later, son."

"As you wish." Tristan offered Ava his arm. "Shall we?"

She took it.

Instead of taking her back to the salon, he took her to a balcony. "I think we both need a spot of fresh air, don't you agree?"

It was fresh outside; the air was crispy cold but there were stars above. That was a rare sight indeed.

"I must apologise for my father," Tristan began in a clipped voice.

"Don't. Please. Don't." Ava raised her hands and shook her head. "Yes, he made a scene, it was uncalled for, even bad form if you will. Your father is not particularly nice. But Tristan, he is an old, sick man."

"He is a vicious old tyrant," Tristan grated through his teeth.

She placed a hand on his arm. "He is dying."

Tristan stilled. "What do you mean?"

"He told me he had to go to Bath because he had heart troubles. He didn't say exactly what. But his physicians have told him he hasn't got much time left."

Tristan was quiet. "I did not know."

"I suppose he wanted you to be settled before he—before he—you know. Make sure your affairs are in order. And there is Isolde to consider. And who knows what else with his estate. In a certain way it is understandable, even though he went about it in a drastic way."

"I am not certain I can ever forgive my father for thinking of me as a common thief." He raked his hand through his hair. "Do you believe him? That I stole the brooch?"

"Of course I don't believe him."

"I promised my mother I would reacquire it as soon as I could. When I finally came into some money, I returned to the pawn shop, but it was gone." His shoulders slumped.

"It is just a piece of jewellery, Tristan. In the grand scale of things, it doesn't matter. I had the impression that on some level, even your father doesn't care that much about it at all. He said the entire scene at supper was a test."

Tristan stared. "A test."

"To see how we both reacted, I suppose."

"Confound it, that would be very like him." Tristan growled.

"Yet Isolde seems to get along with your father?"

Tristan grimaced. "She loves the old blighter." He sighed. "But he thinks I can't care for her. Thinks I am neglecting her. Thinks—" he gritted his teeth "—thinks she would be better off if she were put away."

Ava shook her head. Tristan and his father, they really did not see eye to eye. It was not to be helped. Both were stubborn, proud men.

He looked down on her, studying her face. Ava squirmed under his gaze.

"I've never had anything like this happen," Tristan suddenly said.

"What?" she asked breathlessly.

"Having someone stand up for me in public like you did. Defending me. Believing in me." He laughed huskily. "In one thing my father is right: I am a lucky devil."

His thumb stroked over her lower lip.

She wanted him to kiss her, again; she wanted him to hold her, tighter this time, and never let her go.

Instead, she stepped back and sucked in a breath before exhaling it again shakily. "Tristan. There is something you should know—" She struggled for the words.

"Devil a bit, there you are." Miles' jovial voice interrupted them. "The entire company is wondering where you are, and we are about to finish the entire champagne without you two lovebirds."

Tristan dropped his hands. "Very well, Miles. Let us return to the others."

"Let the Second Act begin." Miles smirked and winked at Ava surreptitiously.

She smiled back uneasily, not sure how to interpret that comment.

Chapter Twenty-Six

Tristan had wanted to take Ava to the opera, but he'd found her oddly reluctant.

"Oh my goodness, no!" she'd exclaimed with such horror as if he'd suggested they go watch a raucous cock fight at the East End Rookeries.

"But it's Mlle Winter's final performance and I am certain you'll enjoy it. You shouldn't miss it. In fact, I am berating myself that I haven't taken you and Millicent to the opera earlier." It had been a gross oversight on his part. Tristan had seen the same opera countless times already and knew it by heart. Yet *her* voice never failed to thrill his soul like it had done the very first time he had heard it. He felt ready to share that with Ava. No, he *wanted* to share that experience with Ava. See her reaction. But she was oddly disinterested in joining him. He found that perplexing.

"I am afraid of crowds." Ava had wrung her shawl in her hands and avoided his eyes.

"But the other day you were fine at Astley's Royal

Amphitheatre, and there was quite a crush." Tristan had taken her and Millicent to see some splendid performances involving tightrope walkers, clowns, jugglers, and equestrian performers. Kit had accompanied them, too.

"That was because we were sitting in the first row right by the ring, and that is not at all comparable to being confined in a tight, constricted space like the opera box." Ava had shuddered.

Tristan had frowned. "I fail to see the difference. But very well, I shall not force something on you that you might not enjoy, even though I strongly feel you are missing out on something good, Ava."

"I'll hear her when she sings for Isolde," Ava had argued. "That will be enough for me."

Tristan hadn't pressed her further. He would go to the opera alone, for Miles had other plans that night.

Like the seven previous times, he'd brought a bouquet of violets for Mlle Winter. This time, however, he would deliver the flowers in person and ask when she intended to perform for his sister. For after he'd been hailed the glorious tournament winner, he'd received no communication about how he was to get his wish granted, and he felt more than irritated about it. The diva owed him a personal answer. He'd have to find a way past that guarded door. Surely, the Viking would recognise him and allow him to pass?

In between the Acts, there was the usual crush in the refreshment room. Tristan espied a flash of a familiar waistcoat, a pink and yellow striped creation. Kit? Tristan frowned. What was he doing here? Earlier at the club, Kit had announced that he would spend the evening at home with his sister. Kit wasn't the person to break plans or to change his mind at the last minute.

Tristan wrestled his way through the crowd, but Kit had left the room and hurried down the corridor leading towards the back of the theatre. Tristan followed him. There were only a few lights lit in the corridor that led to the back of the theatre, and no one was there. Kit had disappeared.

Tristan turned with a frown. Where had he gone?

His eyes fell on the wall, where a tapestry depicting the muses hung crookedly. Tristan lifted it gingerly. Behind it was a door that was half shut. Without thinking twice, Tristan pushed it open and followed the narrow, winding staircase down.

This was an entirely different world, the world behind the stage. He found himself in an underground labyrinth, a network of dim corridors stuffed with props, painted scenery, rigging and piles of rope. It smelled of wood, fresh paint, whale oil and floor wax. The contrast to the glittering, glamorous front was stark. Here, the floors and walls were grey and bare, and there were no lush carpets, gilded mirrors, sparkling chandeliers, or brocade curtains. The glitter and glamour of the auditorium was deceptive. Behind it all, on its flip side, was the gritty, bone-breaking reality that created this illusion.

People hurried to and fro, stagehands, carpenters, upholsters, the crew that operated the stage machinery, costume painters, and dressers. Some performers stood around, rehearsing, a group of giggling ballet dancers nudged themselves when they saw Tristan.

One of them approached him. "La, my lord, are you lost?"

"Yes. No. I am fine, thank you." Tristan backed away and stumbled over a ladder that was propped against the wall.

He heard laughter, a tinkling, familiar sound.

He whirled. Ava? What the deuce was she doing here?

He turned around the corner, glancing around and crashed into someone hurrying toward him.

A familiar scent of violets filled his nose.

Gobsmacked, he realised he'd run into Violetta Winter herself, who flinched back with a look of horror on her face. She was dressed in a scarlet and black Spanish costume and looked divine.

He reached out his hands to steady her. "I most humbly beg your pardon—" he stammered, then broke off. "Sackville!"

"The devil. Ravenscroft! Why are you here?" Kit frowned at him ferociously as he stepped forward.

"I followed you. And she? And what?" He turned to Violetta again, who'd snapped open a black fan and hid behind it as she fanned herself with a rapid movement.

"I must go," she breathed, shook off his hands and rushed away.

"I don't understand." Tristan rubbed his forehead, looking after her retreating figure.

Kit grabbed him by the arm and pulled him back toward the winding staircase. "You'd better leave before they discover you, then all hell will break loose." Kit almost physically dragged him back to his box and

232

pushed him into his seat. With the words, "We will talk later," he left.

Hot, confused, a thousand thoughts rushing through his mind, Tristan barely registered when the curtains rose for the Second Act. When she finally came on stage and sang a heart-breakingly lovely aria, and she pressed the flowers to her nose in a movement that was Ava, all Ava, his world came crashing about him as the pieces of the puzzle suddenly came together.

TRISTAN STAGGERED HOME ON FOOT. HE WAS roaring drunk and something in his chest throbbed painfully, but he couldn't quite identify what that might be.

He could have taken a carriage home, for it rained. But he preferred to walk, though the truth was that he was reeling and swaying his way through the London streets. He ought to have arrived at Grosvenor Square by now, his fuzzed mind told him. Instead, that blasted muddy road never seemed to end, so he just walked on and on, until he bumped into a gate. He leaned against the lantern by the gate for a brief rest. He was certain if he continued walking, by some miracle, he'd end up at his house, then he could crawl into bed and sleep and forget this entire night, this fiasco, this unbearable pain in the area of his heart and—*her*.

"The thing is this," he told the lamp post, "when you're engaged to a woman who you did not want to marry, initially, but your sire forces you to become a tenant for life, so you choose London's ugliest hag to vex him, only to discover that actually, he doesn't give a tuppence about who you choose and now you're stuck with a spinster when you could've chosen some other high-flyer, so you do the honourable thing and get to know her and suddenly realise she isn't a bad sort and she grows on you and you even begin to like her a wee bit—" he paused and swayed "—very well, so you like her immensely, despite her warts and moles and buck teeth and all, for she turns out to be this rather sweet, warm, kind, funny little thing who, despite her odd quirks and foibles—not to mention all those cats! Horrid creatures—so despite all her oddities you wouldn't mind marrying her *at all*—for her kisses—" his voice turned hoarse "—by Jove, her kisses haunt you every minute during the day, and let's not mention the nights—and then you go to this cursed opera, and it turns out she is her?" He pulled on his hair. "How does this make sense? She has always been her. Or her she. Curse the day I first set eyes on either of them. Now both are her, for she doesn't exist. She's a lie. All, all—a lie. Even her moles are a lie." When he thought of her moles that were no moles, he suddenly felt like sobbing. "Am I mad?"

"Nah. Just rotten drunk," the lamp pole replied. It had a rough voice with a Scottish accent.

Tristan squinted against the weak yellowish light. "I must be," he mumbled.

"So, what happens now?" the lamp pole asked.

"What happens now?" Tristan repeated. "Give me a fool's cap so I can be crowned London's biggest fool. Twit. Numbskull. Goosecap." He sat on the floor with a groan and buried his head in his hands. Even Miles had figured it out long before he did.

After the opera, he'd gone straight to the club and, to his relief, found Miles lounging by the fireplace. After he'd got himself thoroughly drunk, Tristan had worked up the courage to broach the topic. "Am a lucky fellow indeed, Milesh. Did'ya know that my shweetheart, my love, my darling bride'sh that shinger, that what'sh her blashted name—Missh Winter?" he'd slurred.

"Of course, she is," Miles, blast the man, had said as if it were the most natural thing in the world. "Are you real-ising this now?"

"Does evry'one know 'xcept me?" Tristan had asked bitterly.

"If it is any consolation, no one else seems to know. There was something about the movement of her hands when she lifts the flowers to her nose that is identical to Violetta Winter's. The caricature reminded me of it. And then, when I visited Miss Sackville, she did exactly the same. I tell you, man. I don't know why you did not see it sooner."

Yes, why hadn't he? The signs had been all there.

Tristan groaned.

"Some pickled sheep's eyeballs will cure that hang-over in the morning," the lamp post suggested.

Tristan shuddered.

"Or else some good old Scottish Highland Fling works miracles."

"Don't need women. Whether Scottish, divas, or spinsters. They're all, all a lie." Tristan made a throw-away motion with his arms.

"Nah. A Highland Fling is buttermilk with cornflour, salt, and pepper. Drink it first thing in the morning. Works miracles. Then go to your woman and talk it out. If you love her, you'll find a way."

Tristan looked up and found that the lamp pole had transformed himself to a burly man who stood in front of him, arms crossed, a pipe at the corner of his mouth and a cap on his head.

"Love," he mumbled. "She'd said she loved me." That was a lie, too. The cruellest of them all.

"Aye, in love and war, things never ain't that simple. Best go home and sleep over it. Want me to call you a hack?"

"Who are you?" Tristan demanded. "And where am I?"

"At Hyde Park Turnpike, guv'nor." He tapped the pipe against the wall to empty it. "And I'm the gatekeeper."

Sensational, the critics raved in the newspaper the next day. This final performance was beyond the top. Mlle Violetta Winter had sung with a transparency, a pain, a desire that was unequalled on stage.

The *Morning Chronicle* wrote, "Mlle Winter sang with genuine emotion, like a woman who defied all hope and dared to love, only to realise she had lost it all."

Chapter Twenty-Seven

Ava set the Morning Chronicle aside. It was a copy from the morning after her performance several days ago, and she'd read and re-read it a hundred times, yet the words never changed. Announcing her love for Tristan at the supper party had been one thing. But having a newspaper trumpet that her singing had been so transparent that the entire world now knew that her heart had been broken was on another dimension altogether.

She felt vaguely ill.

She'd not heard from Tristan for a full three days. No note, no flowers, no rides in the park. Every time she heard a carriage clatter in front of her house, she'd jump up and run to the window of the drawing room. But it was never him.

She wasn't sure what she would tell him once he showed up. Was it better to pretend nothing had happened? Or would she finally be able to work up the courage and tell him the truth?

When she'd run full smack into Tristan at the opera

the other night, she'd been so appalled, she'd nearly given herself away. If Kit hadn't been there and intervened, stepping in front of her and giving her the chance to escape, her entire disguise would have unravelled there and then.

Surely, he hadn't recognised her... had he?

Ava stepped up to the window and bumped her forehead against the glass.

Hot tears welled up.

She had tried to fool herself and buy some time with him. She'd wanted to play along with the engagement because she had lost herself in the pretence, in the world of "what if".

She knew the time had come when she had to end it all.

TRISTAN'S CURRICLE FINALLY DROVE UP IN FRONT OF her house on the fourth day. She jumped up and with shaking hands arranged her hair, pulled her fichu straight, and pleated out her skirt. Her heart slammed painfully against her ribcage as she descended the stairs, gripping the rail. She paused when she heard his deep voice as he conversed with Millicent in the drawing room. Part of her wanted to rush down and throw herself into his arms, confessing everything. And the other part, the cowardly one, wanted to gather her skirts and scramble up the stairs and hide in the attic, in the half-witted notion that all her problems would go away if she hid there long enough.

She heard him utter her name.

The cowardly part won.

She pirouetted on the last step and scrambled back, her mind frantically working out the directions to the attic, for she did not know how to reach it, or whether they even had one.

"Ah, there you are, Ava. Tristan has just arrived." Millicent stepped out into the hallway. Ava froze on the stairs as Tristan stepped out, tall and large, and annoyingly handsome.

"Good afternoon, Ava," he said coolly. "I have come to take you on a ride." It sounded like a command, not a request. His amber gaze was on her dark, intent and unwavering, and did she imagine it, a tad condescending?

"Attic," she blurted out. "That is, of course, I meant, good morning, I mean, good afternoon, for it is afternoon, of course. A good afternoon for a ride out." Deep breath. She could do this. If she could sing on a stage for three thousand people, she could turn and descend those stairs regally and go out for a ride with him without making a fool of herself. Being a diva on stage was a thousand times easier, for she stumbled down the remaining stairs, her foot entangled in the hem of her skirt. He reached out and caught her deftly in his arms.

Her first thought was that he smelled divine. That clean, masculine scent of starched linen and cologne. Her second thought was that he was angry. No, not angry. There was a flash of cold fury in his eyes. He let her go abruptly as if he'd burned himself.

Ava gulped.

He knew. He knew!

Now what?

"Attic? Whatever for?" Millicent tilted her head like a puzzled bird.

"I, uh, was merely wondering whether we had one." Ava fiddled around with her reticule to avoid looking at him. "Might be good for, er, storing things, amongst others."

Millicent blinked. "Excellent question. I am not certain. I suppose the housekeeper would know. I'll ask her later. Well, then, enjoy yourselves for as long as the weather lasts." She opened the door and peeked at the sky. "It might snow again soon."

When Tristan handed her up into the curricle a moment later, he barely glanced at her.

He sat next to her, staring straight ahead. His profile, the stern jut of his chin, the classical nose and proud forehead, how dear he had become to her! Her heart clenched painfully.

She cleared her throat once or twice to begin a conversation, only to throw a glance at his thunderous brow, and fall silent again. She fiddled with the pompoms on her reticule.

She could bear it no longer.

"I'm so very sorry," she whispered miserably. "For everything." She peeked up at him, but his profile had frozen to marble. "Could you please say something?"

"Tell me," Tristan said, finally turning to her with burning eyes, "how much does an opera singer like you earn?"

She felt the blood drain from her face.

"It must be pathetically little if you have to go out of your way to fish for my inheritance using such trickery as you are using, Mademoiselle Winter."

Ava gripped the edge of the seat. She deserved it. She deserved every bit of his reproach, anger and disappointment. But the contempt in his voice shook her deeply. Her lips attempted to form words before she finally uttered, "That is not true. It is not like you think."

He uttered a short, hard laugh. "Is it not? Not that this ought to surprise me since it is no secret that all women are after my inheritance so why not you, too? The difference being that others are being straightforward about it. Whereas you need to resort to lies, deceit and subterfuge. Ayrton must be paying you a pittance if you must resort to such measures to line your coffers."

Nausea punched her in the stomach. "No. No. You've got it all wrong. I never planned any of this."

"You never planned to dress up as the plain and dowdy Ava Sackville?" He lifted his dark eyebrow, which she normally liked, but now she thought it made him look diabolical.

"I did it because of Kit," she said with a thick voice, "knowing that the *ton* would not consider my profession to be respectable enough and that it might mar his reputation. My intention was to disappear at the end of the season. But then you came and proposed, and events developed from there, and—" He lifted the second diabolical eyebrow which completely threw her. "Oh! very well, at first, I admit I did find it amusing. So, I accepted your proposal." Even to Ava's ears, this sounded bad.

"You found it amusing." A vein ticked in his temple. "It was all a game to you, of course. What else? You must have had a good laugh at the fool who fell so neatly for your ploy. Only to invite him to that tournament of yours, for further amusement. And let's let him win, shall we? The ultimate triumph, as we laugh over how that dolt doesn't even recognise his own fiancée on the public stage. Good Lord, how you must have laughed."

She lifted her hands to her cheeks. "I did not. It's not like that." She shook her head miserably.

"Your disguise is masterful. Naturally, a professional actress and opera singer like you would know how to use wigs, costumes, and paint to conceal herself. The only thing you could not disguise is your laughter. And there is a particular scent of violets and honeysuckle that hangs about you." He swallowed painfully. "It is what gave you away."

Ava twisted her hands in an agitated manner but did not reply.

The horses continued trotting down the lane, and the sun peeked through the clouds cheerfully as if they were not having this awful conversation.

"I never meant any of it maliciously," she said in a low voice. "I had nothing but admiration for you."

"Forgive me if I find that difficult to believe. Rest assured that whatever admiration I had for Violetta Winter has now crumbled to ashes. I have never, in my entire life, encountered a woman as treacherous as you, and taking as much enjoyment out of making fun of her admirers as you do. I congratulate you, Ava, on how skilfully you have played your part. Or shall I say Violetta? Is that even your real name?"

Her chin quivered. "I *am* Ava Sackville. I never

deceived you in that respect. Everything about Ava is true. It is not an invented personality."

"I don't believe you," he said coldly. "You are too consummate an actress. I do not know who you really are, ma'am. You seem to be no different from any of the other cyprians who exhibit themselves on stage to all and sundry with the exception that you've got a superior voice, but that is all."

His words cut her as if he'd plunged a sword into her heart.

"You forget yourself, sir!" she hissed. "I deserve your anger, but I'll not allow you to insult my name or my profession. It is thanks to men like you that my profession has received its bad name. Men like you who treat artists and singers like harlots merely because they choose to share their God-given gifts with the public. "

Something flared in his eyes. "Aye, you are entirely right, ma'am, they share their 'gifts' all too generously with the public. And in my experience, at any price, too." His glance raked up and down her figure, causing her body to smoulder with heat.

"Let me down. I do not deserve such insults. I'll walk back home." Her voice shook with rage and humiliation.

"Don't be ridiculous. We will finish this ride, then I'll set you off at home, and then we will continue with this engagement like nothing has happened."

She stared at him with wide eyes. "You cannot be serious."

His jaw clenched briefly. "I am very serious. How much do you want?"

Ava stilled.

He named a sum.

She felt as if something inside her died. "I am not for sale," she said tonelessly.

His face was stony. "You have no choice. We must maintain this charade of an engagement at all costs. You shall be reimbursed. It should not be too difficult. You merely continue doing what you were so masterfully doing up to now, deceiving everyone."

She flinched. "I intended to tell you."

"When exactly were you going to tell me? After our marriage?" he bit out.

She shook her head. "It never seemed to be the appropriate moment. I never intended this to go on for as long as it did."

Tristan looked up and narrowed his eyes. "Too bad, because now it is too late."

"What do you mean?"

"Precisely that," Tristan muttered as another carriage pulled up next to them. In it sat a tall, erect gentleman with silvery hair and bushy eyebrows. Livingstone lifted his cane in greeting. "Ah. My prodigal son."

"Father," Tristan bit out. "Excellent timing, as always."

Livingstone nodded at Ava. "Well met, Miss Sackville. After our successful supper the other night, it seems we are to repeat it all in more elevated company. We are going to Brighton this coming Saturday. His Royal Highness is inviting us for a gala supper at his Pavilion. You are to receive the royal blessing on your union. What do you say? Have you received the invitation?"

"I was just about to tell Miss Sackville about it." Tristan did not move a muscle in his face. "We will of course attend."

"Splendid." His father threw Ava a shrewd look. "Together with your brother and that elusive cousin of yours, yes?"

Ava stared at him, horrified.

Livingstone took that as a yes, gave a curt nod and moved on.

Ava turned to Tristan. "Brighton? His Royal Highness? You cannot mean it."

Tristan set his jaw. "Do you understand now? This is a muddle of tremendous proportions. If my father finds out who you are, he will think I have tried to run a rig on him yet again. He will cut me off on the spot."

"For how long is this to continue? He will expect us to get married eventually."

"The scandal will be greater if we throw his highness' invitation into the wind. The Prince insists on meeting my bride and does not take no for an answer. We continue this charade until we come up with some plausible reason the engagement has to be mutually, politely dissolved. Without a scandal. Without you revealing your identity. Miss Sackville changed her mind; she would prefer not to marry Ravenscroft after all and to remain a spinster for the rest of her life. Hopefully Father will swallow it. You can then quietly disappear to wherever it is you came from, and we can forget we ever met."

His words stung. She covered her hurt with a disdainful smile. "We will go along with your plans, Lord

Ravenscroft. And you may keep your money. For I've got a far better idea."

"You do?" he frowned.

"Oh yes. As you have so correctly judged my character, I am of course only interested in your fortune. Following this reasoning, why accept a paltry amount for a sham engagement when you can have the real thing, a tremendous fortune, and a title to boot? I am not willing to relinquish that so easily. For it is you who has no choice," she said softly as she turned the dagger.

"What are you saying?" He looked thunderstruck.

"I am saying, Lord Ravenscroft, that yes, our engagement will continue." She leaned back with a little smile playing about her lips. "But this time, it will be for real. No pretence. No calling off. Don't you see?" Her little laugh was brittle. "You will simply have to make an honest woman of me and marry me or else face the consequences. And we can't have that, can we?" She peeked up at him from under her eyelashes. She noted with a hint of malicious satisfaction that her words had thrown him into confusion, and he was entirely speechless.

Good.

Chapter Twenty-Eight

THE PAVILION IN BRIGHTON WAS AN ORIENTAL extravagance of the likes Ava had never seen before, and she had seen a lot in her time. Before Napoleon had made travelling through the Continent impossible, she'd been to the gardens in Versailles, the hall of mirrors in Schönbrunn, and the gilded ballrooms in Catherine's Palace. But this, she thought as she gazed at the glory about her, this was quite different.

She stood in a long gallery with salmon pink wall-paper decorated with blue birds in bamboo shrubs, massive lemon-yellow vases stood on lacquered oriental chests in niches between marble fireplaces, and the walls were fringed with edges of arched roof tops from which dangled little bells and lanterns. In the centre of the gallery hung a massive chandelier with scarlet pendants dangling from it.

It was an orgy of colour and chinoiserie and bad taste. Ava liked it.

But she was far too nervous to dwell on the extravagance of this place.

Tristan walked next to her, flint-faced and reserved. Beyond a quick sweep over her figure and the customary lifting of his diabolical eyebrow when he'd beheld her usual spinsterish outfit, which had left her jittery and cross and made her want to throw a vase at him, he had not said anything the entire trip. Come to think of it, he hadn't said much at all after her lofty announcement that he had no choice but to marry her. It appeared he had been brooding over her words ever since.

Kit, of course, had noticed the thick air between the two and had thrown much effort into making up for their surly silence by talking in a forced, cheerful monologue the entire trip. Ava had chewed her lower lip raw and answered in monosyllables, if at all.

Tristan, after a while, had rolled his eyes and interrupted Kit with the clipped words, "The charade is over, Sackville."

Kit's eyes flew to his sister, who stared doggedly out of the window. He lifted his hands. "Why are we going to Brighton, then?"

"The engagement is to continue." Tristan pulled his top hat over his eyes, leaned back, and crossed his arms, pretending to sleep.

"Ava? You're going to marry that churl, anyway?" Kit said with a stage-whisper.

She gave him a curt nod. "Yes."

Tristan's corner of his mouth pulled down into a sneer.

Kit looked from one to the other, then shrugged.

"Very well. If you say so. Where was I? Ah, yes. Let me describe the waistcoat Cumberland was wearing when Ambersford hit him..."

Ava sighed and wished Millicent were here. She would fuss over her, wrap her in a shawl and make her a poultice and feel sorry for her, and at the moment she very much wanted someone to feel sorry for her. But Millicent had emphatically refused to come along, claiming she had a monstrous headache.

The Prince of Wales greeted them in an opulent saloon which was overwhelming in its crimson, silver, and golden colours. He was a corpulent figure in a blue coat and white silken breeches, with a silver star pinned on his breast. He was talking to Livingstone, who had arrived earlier in a separate carriage, and both men looked up when they entered the room.

"Ah! Ravenscroft," His Highness said, "we have been talking about you and your charming bride."

Ava curtsied.

His Highness pulled his thick lips into a smile, waggled both his eyebrows, took her hand, and smacked his lips on it. It felt warm and wet, and Ava would have liked to pull her hand away and wipe it on her dress, except that would have been rather impolite, not to say an affront against his delicate royal sentiments. Tristan was already furious with her. She had to be careful and not direct any additional fury against her person, especially if it was royal.

Ava sighed.

The Prince stepped closely to her, and—winked.

It was definitely a wink.

Tristan had seen it too and scowled.

"It will be an evening of the likes none of you have ever beheld," the Prince proclaimed in his booming voice. "But first, ladies and gentlemen: supper. It will be a mere trifle."

The trifle of a supper consisted of a thirty-six-course meal, starting with a variety of soups, followed by fish, fowl, chicken, ducklings, pheasant, lamb, rabbit, boar, and turkey. The entire supper was rounded off by desserts and savoury entremets. Not to mention the eight centre-pieces of patisserie, creative creations that decorated the table and that were delicately crafted of spun sugar and fondant.

Between the rabbit pie on a bed of laurel and the Ducklings Luxembourg, Miles, who sat across from Ava, had surreptitiously broken off a corner of a miniature tower of the Royal Pavilion, crafted out of pastry and marzipan, and popped it into his mouth. "Not bad," he proclaimed.

Ava could barely swallow the exquisite food. Her nerves felt stretched, and her thoughts were preoccupied with Tristan, who sat next to her, eating his food in testy silence. Miles had originally been assigned to be her table partner, but just when he was about to offer her his arm to lead her into the dining room, Tristan had cut in. "We will change places, and I will sit next to Ava tonight." His curt voice had allowed no contradiction.

"Suit yourself." Miles had shrugged and strolled away.

Ava felt tired and hot in her disguise. She was sitting right in front of a massive fireplace in which a fire was roaring full force. Little beads of sweat formed on her forehead; her wig itched unbearably, and she felt the thick paste and powder on her face grow sticky and moist. When she felt something slide down her cheek, she knew it was one of the moles she'd stuck on her cheeks. Repressing a curse, she lifted a napkin to her cheek and surreptitiously picked it off.

An overwhelming sensation of dread overcame her. Her disguise was melting right in the middle of the third course, and there were many more courses to come.

While she was picking at her dish of pheasant in truffle and wine sauce, she felt something lodged between her dentures and her gums. It grated painfully against the flesh above her teeth, so she attempted to loosen it with her tongue.

Plop it made.

Her dentures swam in the wine sauce, bobbing between grey bits of pheasant and a sprig of parsley.

Petrified, she stared at her plate.

Now what was she to do?

She watched helplessly as a footman stepped up to her to clear the plate away.

"One moment." Without much ado, Tristan fished her teeth out of the sauce and let it disappear in his napkin on his lap before anyone could blink. Then he nodded curtly at the footman to remove the plate.

"Thank you," she whispered.

He looked at her with hooded eyes. "I think you look considerably better without them," he said dryly. "But that means you'd better refrain from speaking the rest of the evening."

"Yes," she croaked.

He bent his head closer. She could feel his warm breath on her temple. Her breath quickened. "You've also lost a mole, and that wart, which I now see is a beauty patch you stick on, how very clever, seems to be sliding down your other cheek." He lifted a finger and picked it off. His finger was white with her paint. He stared at it and shook his head, as if still not believing he'd been so gullible to fall for her disguise.

After supper, they gathered in the music room with its flamboyant crimson-golden walls with Chinese patterns and dragons, and a gilded domed ceiling. An orchestra awaited them.

"My ladies, my lords," the Prince announced, "what comes now is something truly special, something truly unique, something truly—what is the word I'm looking for? Extraordinary. Yes, there it is. It is something I promise none of you has ever experienced. For a little bird has told me that a goddess walks amongst our midst." The Prince grinned.

"What the deuce is he jabbering on about?" Kit asked Miles, who shrugged.

"He's already foxed, so expect anything."

The doors opened, and several footmen rolled in a small table on wheels with champagne glasses.

"This will be one of the most extraordinary experiences you will have ever encountered," the Prince continued. "It is a performance by a lady, a star, a nightingale, an angel's voice. I give you, ladies and gentlemen—Violetta Winter."

Ava gasped and clasped Tristan's arm tightly.

"Damnation," Tristan growled.

A general muttering rose among the crowd.

"Eh?"

"Where is she?"

"What does he mean?"

"You mean the singer?"

"Beg your pardon, Your Highness, but where is she?"

Prinny clasped his hands behind his back, pleased. "Where is she, indeed? She is among us. Has been all this time."

The Prince walked through the crowd, then stopped in front of Ava with glittering eyes. "Madam?" He held out his hand.

The muttering grew.

Ava backed away.

"Begging your pardon, Your Highness." Tristan stepped in front of Ava. "My fiancée isn't feeling well."

"Nonsense. I think she is the perfect person to sing for us tonight." He rocked back and forward on his heels. "I have looked forward to this event for months."

The crowd began to laugh.

"But Your Royal Highness," Lady Erskine interjected, "isn't it better to have someone like Mrs Townsend sing? It might be more amenable to us all. For let us be honest, Miss Sackville cannot really sing." Her announcement was met with the approval of those who'd heard Ava sing so horridly that evening so long ago.

"With all due respect, Your Highness, I don't approve." Tristan balled his hands into fists.

"Neither do I," Kit added hastily and stood next to

Tristan. "If Ava isn't feeling the thing, she should be left alone."

"Ho ho, will you call me out now, Ravenscroft? That would be most amusing." The Prince's enjoyment had reached its height. Far from being annoyed or angry at Tristan's resisting him, he seemed to enjoy the drama. "But I would place a wager that we are about to discover that you, Miss Sackville, are a divinely talented singer." He lifted her hand and kissed it. "Are you not?"

Ava pulled her hand away. "I would rather not sing if you don't mind, Your Highness."

"But I insist." The Prince grinned broadly.

"This is nonsense." Livingstone's rusty voice spoke up. "If she doesn't want to sing, then she doesn't want to sing, and I say one shouldn't force her to." For once he agreed with his son. "A gentleman never forces a lady to do what she doesn't want to do. I daresay I am old school, but a man of my age is allowed to say this, Your Highness." This was a sharp hit against the Prince, but he was either too drunk or oblivious to get the message.

Ava found she began to like Tristan's father tremendously.

"Oh, but this isn't a case of having to force a lady to do something. Not if it has been contractually agreed upon for weeks, and the lady still has to fulfil her agreement." The Prince's voice had cooled down considerably. "I am waiting, mademoiselle. All impatient and eager to hear your voice."

"No." Tristan folded his arms. "I forbid it."

An audible gasp rose from the crowd. Ravenscroft dared to contradict the Prince! It was unheard of.

"Like my father says, no one ought to be forced to perform if they don't want to," he added. "Especially if the lady in question is my betrothed."

"Especially if it sounds as hideous as she did that first time," a voice snickered.

"I agree, spare us the torture," said another.

All eyes were on Ava.

She gripped Tristan's hand tightly. She closed her eyes. She fought an inner battle. Then she sighed. "I shall have to do as the Prince asks."

Several people groaned.

Tristan looked grim.

The prince triumphed. "Why didn't you just say so to begin with. I want you to sing from Mozart's *The Seraglio*, 'The Aria of Constanza' where she declares to the Pasha, she will never be unfaithful to her lover."

"That is a hideously difficult aria, Your Highness," Kit interjected, lifting a finger. "May I suggest something a little less demanding on our ears—"

"Silence!" the Prince roared. "She will sing this to please me, and she will crack those glasses in the process like she did for *him* in Paris." He pointed with a fat finger at the table with the glasses. "Twenty glasses! It is a command."

Ah, therein lay the rub. The Prince Regent was notoriously jealous of Bonaparte even after he had been soundly beaten in battle.

Ava cursed the day she had to perform at the Tuileries. It hadn't been of her own volition, either. Bonaparte had been so delighted by her performance he hadn't wanted to let her go at all, and she'd had to leave in secret,

Sofi Laporte

with Kit, sneaking out of Paris at night. Prinny must have heard the story.

"You do not need to do this," Tristan told her in a low voice. He held her by the arm. "Say the word and I'll take you away."

She closed her eyes painfully. "It is too late," she whispered and shook his hand off her arm as she stepped to the front. "I am sorry."

"Well, this is going to be interesting," the Duke of Westington muttered. "The last time that woman sang, my ears needed a fortnight to recover. Is this another one of your jokes, Ravenscroft?"

But Tristan had his eyes fixed on Ava, who stood pale, with hands clasped, in front of them. Hot and cold flushed through her and she battled the sorrow that welled up at the depth of her soul.

The familiar strains of music started, and the violins played.

She closed her eyes and folded her hands in front of her.

Then the music swept her away.

She threw back her head and sang.

Twenty champagne glasses, three lorgnettes, and the chandelier cracked, they said later. It was phenomenal. It was never heard of before. It was, in one word: divine.

The guests, who, until the moment she'd opened her mouth to sing, had scoffed and sneered, had been prepared to dissolve in jeers and laughter.

256

Then those delightful tunes came out of her mouth, and the jeering died, and the magic worked on them.

They were all entranced.

This was no mere performer. This was a siren.

And then everyone realised the importance behind it all. The respectable Miss Ava Sackville, spinster by day, was Violetta Winter, a celebrated opera singer by night. She stood on the public stage of London, for everyone to see.

Didn't they say she had many lovers?

Didn't she hold that phenomenally scandalous tournament?

Wasn't she engaged to be married to the Earl of Ravenscroft?

An opera singer marrying an earl?

What was the world coming to?

Mrs Townsend's gloved hand crawled to her mouth. Her eyes glittered gleefully. "Oh, what a delicious, delicious scandal!"

Chapter Twenty-Nine

Livingstone, Tristan's father, had not stayed to hear her finish. He must have left mere moments after she'd begun to sing.

Tristan had sat through the entire affair, gritting his teeth. Throughout supper she'd appeared vulnerable, almost sad, and he'd felt like a cad. He'd been torn between wanting to flee and kissing her senseless.

But now when she sang, she was no longer his beloved Ava, but the bewitching siren. Her familiar, seductive voice shook his core.

Why? Why had she done it? Why had she given in? They would all have supported her: Kit, her family, himself, even his father had been on their side. They would have extricated her from this situation, and no one would have suspected a thing.

"My ears must be malfunctioning," Westington had mumbled as Ava's voice had climbed one arpeggio after another with ease. "Since when can that woman sing?"

Her bosom had heaved, her eyes had shone, and she'd looked altogether beautiful.

At that moment, Tristan had known he'd lost her for good.

Adding to the sense of betrayal that had gripped him ever since he'd uncovered her charade, he'd felt a sharp, sudden pain somewhere in his chest. But since this was all nonsense, he'd hardened himself against any feeling and met her silently pleading gaze with a stony, implacable expression.

When she was done, Kit jumped up and boxed himself through the crowd, attempting to extricate Ava from the mass of people that pressed about her.

The Prince Regent, drunk and ecstatic by a triumph that he claimed as entirely his, announced she was to repeat the entire procedure once more, this time with fifty water glasses.

"Miss Sackville is tired and needs to rest." Tristan cut into his speech without any compunction at all. Prince or no, to the devil with him. "Ma'am?" He offered her his arm.

He packed her and her brother into his carriage. "I'll sit outside with the coachman," he announced. He needed fresh air. He needed to think. He needed to get away from her.

THE NEXT MORNING, LIVINGSTONE SUMMONED Tristan and Ava to his study.

Ava appeared pale and red-eyed, for she hadn't slept a wink. She also hadn't bothered to don her disguise. She wore a simple, green, woollen gown, and her copper hair was tied in a loose knot, with several wisps curling at her swan-like neck. Without any sort of disguise or costume, she was a delicate, elfin thing, her skin translucent and silken without the paint, her eyes tremulous and dewy.

"Tristan," she'd said in a thick voice when they'd met in the foyer.

But he'd barely glanced at her as he'd strode past her to his father's library without a word.

Tears veiled her eyes, and a painful knot inside her pulled tight.

Despite the roaring fire in the fireplace, she shivered. Livingstone stood in front of the window, his back to them.

"Sit," he ordered without turning around.

Tristan remained standing. "There is an explanation," he began.

"Silence." Livingstone turned and studied Ava's appearance indifferently. "I do not want to hear your explanation. I have never, in my entire life, felt so mocked. You have made a laughingstock out of me, out of my honour, and my good intentions. Our family name."

Ava could not bear it any longer. "It is all my fault. Tristan did not know of my identity until recently. He—"

Livingstone lifted a hand. "Please. No more. I cannot bear to listen to any of this." He looked at her coldly. "You are in possession of an exceptional, God-given talent you certainly know how to use. My felicitations." He bowed his head. "But you are not a fit bride for my son."

Ava clenched her hands to fists until her knuckles

whitened. "I believe it is up to your son to decide who befits him, and who does not. Especially since he has been duped as much as you."

"You are a very talented actress, are you not, mademoiselle?" Livingstone gave her a wintry smile. "Whatever hold you exert over my son: release him. I beg of you. For I shall never countenance such a union, and well he knows it."

"May I remind both of you that I am right here with you in this room and capable of making my own decisions? I am not a child. I do not appreciate you speaking for me in this manner—either of you." He turned to his father. "I have promised Miss Sackville my hand in marriage, and I shall honour that promise. It was given a promise in good faith and when I gave it, I did not know of her identity." Tristan stared back stony-faced.

Livingstone steepled his fingers and stared at them moodily. In the room's silence, only the crackling of the fire was heard.

Then he drew himself up as if coming to a momentous decision.

"I don't believe you." His voice fell heavily like an axe on the executioner's block. He pointed a finger at her. "I do believe she is a fortune hunter, a beautiful but deceptive one at that, a dangerous siren, an immensely talented singer but disreputable to the core. And you—are a willing fop in her hands. You have made me the butt of your last joke. I understand, Tristan. I understand the message you have tried to send. You want your independence. Very well. As you say, you are no child and a grown man, after all. I have therefore decided to respect your decision. You will no longer have anything to do with me, nor I with you. I'll no longer feel obliged to support you financially. Be free of me and any obligation you feel weighs you down. I wash my hands off you."

"Very well, sir, if that is your wish, then so it shall be," Tristan replied coldly.

Ava jumped up. "No! No, no, no, this is a misunderstanding—"

"Quiet!" Livingstone roared, and jumped up as well, toppling over the leather chair. He slapped his hands on the desk and leaned forward. His grey eyes shot barbs of ice at her. "You said you loved my son. I daresay that was a lie, too, a most cruel one since I believed you. If you have ever, ever felt as much as a spark of affection for him that wasn't rooted in greed, you will let him go and leave him be."

"It was not a lie." Tears were running down her face, and she swiped at them with her hand.

Both men looked at her.

Tristan looked weary, tired. "Let us finish this game, I beg of you."

No matter what she said, they would not believe her. Every word that left her mouth was to be twisted and changed and interpreted in the light of who she was on stage: an opera singer not fit to be an earl's countess.

She pulled herself up proudly. "In that case, gentlemen, there is nothing left to be said." She made an exit worthy of the diva she was, slamming the door behind her with such force that the vases in the hallway shook.

Chapter Thirty

"Pack my bags," Ava told her maid after she returned to her house on Bruton Street. "We are leaving."

The maid threw her a worried look. "Miss Millicent is waiting for you in the drawing room, Miss."

Ava closed her eyes and leaned against the banister of the stairs wearily. Millicent. She had missed the drama in Brighton, but no doubt Kit must have filled her in. The last thing she wanted to do was to talk to her, to relive the entire evening again. Besides, she was not in her disguise.

"Tell her I don't feel well—" Ava began, when Millicent stepped out of the room. She paused on the threshold and took in Ava's appearance. There was such a worried look of compassion on her face that Ava burst into tears.

"Oh dear, oh dear, oh dear, come here, darling." Millicent rushed over to her and took her in her arms and rocked her back and forth, crooning.

Sobs racked through Ava's body. She hadn't cried like that since she'd been a little girl.

"Come, let us go inside and sit down. Mrs Brown, if you could kindly bring us a pot of strong vervain tea, that would help tremendously. Look who I have brought to cheer you up: Leonidas. He insisted on accompanying me." She placed the little white kitten on Ava's lap.

Ava chuckled through her tears, picked up the little bundle of fur and buried her face in it.

"I had to come to see how you are doing, for I knew you must be going through hell right now."

"Did Kit tell you?" Ava blew her nose.

"I read it in this morning's paper before Kit told me his version of the event. The other half I'd already figured out myself."

Ava lowered her handkerchief. "Did you now?"

"Ava. I spent almost every day with you since your arrival. My eyesight is not as weak as one might think, and I am not yet a crone who sleeps the entire day. Of course, I knew about your disguise." She tugged at Ava's shawl. "Quite early on, too. Your awful wig was crooked more than one time and I was quite tempted to pull it straight! I must say, your natural hair is so much prettier!"

"But why... did you not say something?"

"I figured you had your reasons and that you would share them with me in time. I did not know you were that singer, however." A look of awe crossed over Millicent's face. "I have never heard you sing; you know. They say your voice is spectacular. I now wish I'd gone to Brighton with you yesterday. But there is no point in crying over spilled milk."

Ava took Millicent's hands in hers. "I never meant to deceive you out of malicious intent, you know. I thought it was best, to keep our identities apart, on account of Violetta Winter's reputation. It would help Kit get a foothold in society, and I would get some respite from prying eyes under an anonymous disguise. It worked well, at first, and now it's such a muddle." Tears welled up again, and she groped for her handkerchief. "Ravenscroft is furious; though he initially insisted we uphold the charade, everything unravelled yesterday. Someone must have whispered a word to the Prince about my identity; I daresay it was Miles Davenport. And Livingstone —" Ava sighed.

"What about Livingstone?" Millicent enquired.

"Enraged and feels he has been made a public laughingstock by his son and says he will cut him off." Ava wrung her hands. "Oh, Millicent! I shall never forgive myself if he does."

"Livingstone." Millicent drew her eyebrows together. "That man can be more stubborn than a cat waiting for a mouse to come out of its hole." She patted Ava's hands. "I suggest you drink up your tea and go to bed even though it is in the middle of the afternoon. You will see, after a good, long sleep, things won't appear quite as horrible as you think they are."

Ava, exhausted, thought this was an excellent idea.

MILLICENT GOT READY TO GO OUT, THEN STOOD IN front of the house undecided. No one who saw the spinster in her grey, drab pelisse and bonnet would see the epic battle that raged inside her. She shook her head, sighed, then drew her narrow shoulders up resolutely.

"To Lord Livingstone's residence," she told the coachman as she climbed into the carriage.

"A Miss Millicent Sackville is here to see you," the butler announced.

Livingstone looked up from his papers and stared at his butler as if he'd just said the Queen herself was waiting in his drawing room. "What? Who?"

The butler repeated what he'd said.

The papers fell from his hands. "Are you certain it is not the other Miss Sackville? Ava?"

"No, my lord. It is Miss Millicent. She would like to talk to your lordship."

Livingstone shot out of his leather chair. "Good heavens. Show her in."

He pulled his hand through his wiry grey hair with a jittery hand and tugged on the lapels of his banyan. Why wasn't he wearing an evening coat? It couldn't be helped. There was no time to change into something more elegant.

Then she stood in his study, a tall, willowy figure, out of place, out of time. Time had passed her by. Her forehead was still smooth, her lips still had that sweet curve. How long had it been? Thirty years?

"Millicent," he croaked.

"Alastair," she whispered, staring at him as if she, too, saw a ghost of the past. She took one, two hesitant steps into his study.

She held out her hand. "I came to give you this." Something small and glinting lay in her little hand. It was a delicate golden brooch with a blue flower. "I found it in a shop in the Burlington Arcade the other day. I recognised it immediately."

Steel grey eyes met soft brown ones.

"Marianne's brooch."

Millicent nodded. She dropped it into his palm. The brooch Tristan had pawned, and over which he'd quarrelled so bitterly with his son, had made its way back to him.

Then a quarrelsome spark entered her eyes. She lifted her chin. "And now this is done, we are going to talk about my cousin Ava and Ravenscroft."

Tristan had spent the entire night at the Club, or so he thought, for he inexplicably found himself on the sofa in Miles' drawing room the next day with a roaring headache. At least the man had had the decency not to load him off on a bank in St James' Park.

The afternoon sun streamed through the windows. He blinked and groaned. His hand clutched his head.

The smell of coffee revived him a little, and a hand held a cup of the brew under his nose.

"Drink," he heard Miles' voice say. He was bathed, shaved, and dressed to perfection in boots and riding clothes, blast the man. Tristan looked down at himself and saw his wrinkled clothes and loosened cravat. He pulled it off and took the coffee cup.

"What happened?" he said after he drank up the entire cup.

"A night of gambling at Watier's. You were drunk as a wheelbarrow."

Tristan groaned. "Don't say it. In my stupidity, I gambled away Ravenscroft Hall."

"You've got more luck than you deserve, my friend. When you are in your cups, you throw all caution in the wind and play deep. You won yourself a small fortune."

"I did?" Tristan rubbed his forehead.

Miles shrugged. "Fleeced Rotherham and several others down to their shirts." He pointed at the coffee table that was littered with IOUs, several golden pocket watches, and an emerald ring.

Tristan picked up the ring and inspected it. "That's his family insignia. Don't tell me he gambled that away?"

"Probably worth a fortune, too." Miles sat down and crossed his legs.

"I'll return it to him, of course." Tristan inspected the slips of paper that recorded how much each of the men owed him.

"I daresay you did not know half of the time what you were doing. Hauled you home afterwards." He lifted a hand.

Tristan got up. "Thank you. I had best be going."

"Sit. There is something I want to talk to you about." Miles pushed him down on the sofa again, then pointed at his chin. "Here."

"Here, what?"

"You may punch me here, once. But only once, mind you."

Tristan frowned. "You are clearly out of your mind.

But I find it hard to resist such an invitation. Very well."
He buffed him lightly on the chin.

"Excellent. But keep in mind you already punched me, so you've got no right to punch me again after what I tell you."

"Oh no. What folly is this? What have you done again?"

Miles lifted a hand. "This was for having croaked to Prinny about your betrothed. I am afraid it was me, and I take responsibility for that evening's disaster. You see—" he took a big breath "—I discovered her identity a while ago, and when Prinny invited me to Carlton house for one of his parties, I may have inadvertently let her identity slip."

Tristan jumped up. "You what?"

Miles raised his hands. "Remember what we said about punching! Prinny was so hell-bent on having her sing for him, you see, and no one could get a hold of her. So, when I visited her that day, after she'd sprained her ankle, it came to me out of the blue, and everything fit together."

Tristan raked his hand over his face. "I discovered it a while later."

"Took you a while, didn't it? Not that I blame you," he added hastily when Tristan glared at him, "for her disguise was excellent and she is a consummate actress."

"She is, isn't she," Tristan said bitterly.

"That is why Prinny planned that evening at the Pavilion." Miles shrugged. "You know the rest. Had no idea your old man would take it as badly as he did."

"I daresay the story is splashed all over the papers as well."

Miles winced. It was quite bad, as the newspapers exploited the story with glee. Miss Sackville's reputation was entirely gone, and Kit had best disappear for a while to weather through the whole disaster.

Tristan got up. "What is done is done. I need to go to Ravenscroft Hall to explain everything to Isolde. She will be heartbroken to learn that Ava was false to the core."

Miles nodded. "You love her."

"I do not!" Tristan jumped up and walked around agitatedly. "That is, dash it! I don't know her! The opera singer, I mean. Of course, I know Ava! She is nice and sweet and good and an excellent sport, by Jove, and everything a man could want! I have grown used to cat hair sticking to her clothes, and find neither her figure, moles, nor her buck teeth objectionable in the least. Even if her hair is coarse as straw and sticks out in all directions. She smells of violets and has a wonderful sense of humour, and somehow that seems to be more important." He rubbed his neck.

Miles crossed his legs, propped his elbow against his knee, leaned his head against it and smiled. "Like I said, you love her."

"Nonsense," Tristan snarled and took another turn about the room. "Don't you understand? She doesn't exist! None of it! Not even her cursed moles and buck teeth. And you know what is the saddest, Miles? How much I wish they would exist, her warts and moles, I mean. I would trade in the dashing opera diva for the homely Miss Ava any day. Except, of course, Ava doesn't exist, she never existed, and it was all a lie. Every word she uttered was a cursed lie. And now I'm stuck with that diva. What the deuce am I to do with her? I don't want that—that—that—fancy piece of an opera singer!" he spat.

Miles placed a finger on his lips and motioned with his head to the door.

"What?" Tristan whirled about.

The butler stood in the doorway, uncertain whether to announce the newest guest.

Next to him stood Violetta Winter, her gloved hand covering her mouth, with a stricken look on her face. She turned without a word and left.

Tristan blinked. "I just had a vision. She wasn't really here, was she? She didn't just hear me say all those horrible things, did she?"

"Aside from the fact that I think you are a mutton-headed numbskull whose brains need to be inspected, for there isn't a single man who wouldn't love to be in your shoes right now, being betrothed to the loveliest woman on this earth, I think you are greatly deluding yourself. And yes, she most definitely heard the latter part of your speech. Bad luck, old chap. You really bungled it this time." He clapped Tristan on the shoulder.

AVA HADN'T BOTHERED TO LIGHT A LAMP. SHE SAT IN the dark room, a woollen scarf about her shoulders, staring out the window with sightless eyes.

So, that was it.

Their English adventure was over.

After she'd overheard Ravenscroft say that he did not

273

want "that fancy piece of an opera singer" in a voice so full of loathing, she'd rushed home from his house and locked herself up in her room. She'd been sitting in a chair here ever since.

He didn't love her.

That was clear.

The worst thing was not his rejection, she decided, for she'd expected that. The worst had been the contempt in his voice.

I love him, she thought, *with all my heart. But I deserve better than that.*

She had not cried, for there were no more tears to shed, but her heart had wept blood.

And so, she'd sent a note to Kit, who'd come, looked at her wordlessly, and knelt next to her, wrapping his arms about her. "Say the word, sister dear, and we'll go."

"Let's go, Kit," she'd said muffled. "Let's go back to Vienna."

He nodded and left to arrange the trip.

They would leave tomorrow morning.

Chapter Thirty-One

THEY WERE PLAYING A NEW OPERA AT THE OPERA house: Rossini's *La Cenerentola*, and no one liked it at all. They'd booed the new leading lady and pelted her with apple and orange peels. The poor woman had broken off after five minutes and left the stage, sobbing.

"We want our Violetta," the crowd howled.

Phileas Whistlefritz, Mlle Winter's former manager, had been summoned by the former Prince of Wales, who was now George IV, for the old king had died two months ago.

"Get her back," King George ordered. "She's a jewel of the English stage and we want her back. Besides, she still needs to smash my fifty champagne glasses."

Was there ever another English king so enthusiastic about having his crystals broken?

Whistlefritz wiped his sweaty forehead and wrung his hands. "But your majesty, Violetta Winter has refused to renew her contract and left the country months ago. No one knows where she is because she never stays anywhere for longer than three days. And even if we knew her whereabouts, we'd have to kidnap her for she said she refused to return. Ever." She'd thrown a final porcelain rider at his head to underscore her words. Whistlefritz shuddered at the memory, for it had grazed the tip of his carefully coiffed curls.

"Excellent notion, Whistlefritz. Do whatever it takes to get her back, even if you must kidnap her! For the opera has become truly unbearable without her."

TRISTAN HAD BROKEN HIS HEAD OVER HOW ON EARTH to tell Isolde. She'd been pestering him, asking for Ava, asking why she had not returned after the first visit. Tristan sat down next to her bed and told her the entire story. She did not take it well.

Setting her mouth in a mulish line, she said, "She still has to sing for me. She owes at least that to me. And to you as well. After all, you won that contest. She owes you the prize."

Tristan looked at her helplessly. "She's already left."

"Then get her back."

Tristan raked his hand through his hair. "It isn't that easy." He sighed. "Sometimes it is better not to pursue. Sometimes it is better to let people go."

"I used to think so too. Lying here, day in, day out, unable to walk. Feeling sorry for myself, feeling hurt that people forgot me, that no one ever came to visit. I've had to let many, many people go. People I thought were my friends. People I thought were family. My dreams. My entire life." She stared at the light blue embroidered canopy of her bed. Then she pushed back the quilt that covered her.

"What are you doing?"

She pulled herself up and attempted to lift her legs out of bed. They dangled thin and white over the edge.

"Isolde."

"If you are not going, then I shall," she said through gritted teeth. "Because you are foolish to let someone go who loves you."

"Yes, that is what she says, but what she really wants is my fortune."

"Tristan." Isolde fell back into her pillows with a sigh. "Yes, she lied. But she could not lie about her emotions. She loves you. I saw it myself. It's how she looked at you. She couldn't bear *not* to look at you. She was smitten. How could you not have seen that? How could you have been so blind?"

The Adam's apple in his throat bobbed as he swallowed. "I... do you really think so?" Miles believed so, too. As had his father, until he'd confirmed his worst fear that it had been a lie. She'd also announced it publicly she'd loved him but somehow his mind had refused to believe it.

Isolde slapped her forehead. "You are my big brother, and I love you. But you are such a hopeless dolt-head that I can't help but scream with frustration sometimes."

He clenched his fingers into a fist and unclenched them again. "I am not sure I can trust—"

"Tristan." She looked at him sternly. "Do you love her?"

"She is an opera singer."

"What has that to do with anything?"

"It has everything to do with everything!" He jumped up, took a turn about the room, pulled both hands through his hair and sat next to her. "I am sorry. I didn't mean to shout. Dash it! Was ever a man so plagued with women." He got up, took a turn again, stared out of the window, pulled his hair again. He repeated this in alternate order.

Isolde watched him with growing hope. "You love Ava."

He stopped, blinked, bemused. "Ava." His face softened and a wistful feeling rushed through him.

Ava, with her gentle smile, her humour, her stubbornness, her strength. How she bit on her lower lip when she pondered on something. How her eyes lit up first before her lips curled into a smile. How she smelled of violets and how she loved those little purple flowers—and all those cats, especially homeless ones! He wanted to tell her that he'd picked up a homeless kitten in the gutter the other day and forced his groom to adopt it; that Achilles had grown into a self-confident cat who stalked about his rooms as if he were the tiger of a maharajah. And the litter of kittens that they'd saved together so long ago are tumbling around in the stable yard at the very moment, to the joy and frustration of the grooms. He wanted to tell her that the opera was no longer the same without her, that it had become a scruffy, contentious place where no one could produce the quality of singing she had. Most of all, he wanted to tell her that there was a hollowness in his heart at the thought of having lost her forever. A terrible fear rushed through him. He'd hurt her terribly. All those things he'd said! Tristan groaned.

"Judging from your star-struck expression, I conclude you are absolutely besotted," Isolde concluded, satisfied. She lifted her legs back into bed and covered them with a quilt. "When are you leaving?"

"Leaving for where?" He blinked.

Isolde groaned. "To Vienna. To fetch back Ava."

Tristan stared at his sister. She was right. He had to get her back. Right now. Immediately. On the spot. Why hadn't he already done so yesterday? When did the next ferry cross from Dover to Calais?

He rushed to the door. Then he turned around, returned to Isolde, and planted a kiss on her head. "Thank you. You are wonderful."

TRISTAN STORMED DOWN AND NEARLY RAN OVER A lady and a gentleman who had just begun to climb the stairs. He had no time to greet them properly because he had a ferry to catch.

"Tristan!"

The lady wore a deep dark-blue coat and held a muff. She had flushed cheeks and was pretty when she smiled. He had to look twice before he recognised her.

"Miss Millicent Sackville!" Tristan caught himself. "I beg your pardon. I didn't recognise you."

She clung to the gentleman's arm, who was none other than his father's.

"Father." Tristan bowed stiffly. They had not spoken

since his father's furious outburst. "I gather you have come to visit Isolde."

"That, too. But we have come to find you as well." His father cleared his throat. "We've got some news. Miss Sackville and I, well, we have decided—in short, it may come as a surprise to you—considering that we have known each other for quite some time..." His normally so-eloquent father bumbled.

"We're married," Millicent burst out. Her eyes sparkled. "Isn't it famous?"

Tristan's jaw dropped. "You're what?"

For the first time in his entire life, Tristan had the satisfaction of seeing his father blush. "Millicent is right. I asked her to be my wife, and she graciously acquiesced. After—" he calculated "—nearly thirty years, she has finally said yes. I never thought I'd live to see the day." He swallowed, visibly moved. "I am the happiest man on Earth."

Tristan stood thunderstruck. "Millicent is your very first lost love?" He'd known that his father had suffered a disappointment in love when he was younger and then continued to marry his mother Marianne out of duty. It hadn't been a bad marriage at all, but it hadn't been a love match, either.

"She took some persuasion." Livingstone's face softened as he looked down on Millicent. Tristan had never seen his father so soft, so human before.

"He can be very persuasive." Millicent smiled and blushed. Then she took Tristan's hands in her own. "I am your stepmother now."

"Well..." Tristan groped for words, "then I give you my heartfelt congratulations."

Livingstone beamed at him, evidently relieved. "I would have a word with you unless you are in a hurry to leave."

"I'll visit Isolde in the meantime and tell her of the news," Millicent told them and continued climbing the stairs.

His father led him into the library.

"When did you marry?" Tristan asked.

"Yesterday. Millicent came to me to give me a nasty scolding on account of how I treated you. The worst of it is... she was right." He pulled himself up to his full height. "Son. I have thought about this, and I have come to the conclusion that I have been too hard on you. Not only now, but—always." He swallowed.

Tristan stood thunderstruck. "What prompted this sudden change of mind?"

Livingstone fumbled around in his pocket and handed it to Tristan.

His mother's brooch.

"Millicent found it in a shop and returned it to me. She helped me realise it would be very much like Marianne to lend you her brooch to help you. I... I owe you an apology. Instead of expecting the worst of you, I should have helped you."

Tristan stared at the delicate piece of jewellery in his palm with burning eyes.

"This is the reason why our relationship is not as good as it could be," his father continued. "The responsibility is entirely mine, and I want to ask your forgiveness for the terrible words I uttered the last time we met. They were said in anger."

His mother would have wanted them to reconcile. So, with a lump in his throat, he was capable of not doing more than giving a curt nod. His father took a sharp breath of relief.

"There is another thing you should know." He hesitated before continuing. "Because you like to throw at my head that I had Isolde institutionalised and deserted Marianne when she decided to join her there so she would not be alone."

"Father, I—" Tristan began but Livingstone interrupted.

"Let me finish, then you may have your say. The truth is that Marianne gave me no choice. The hospital was said to have the best doctors at the time, and we were helpless. We did not know how to deal with Isolde's illness. I was truly convinced I was doing this for the best of everyone involved." He swallowed. "Marianne agreed and insisted on being with Isolde. It was a harsh, long, cold winter, and she fell ill. She might have fallen ill anyway if she had not gone with Isolde. We will never know. But you are right that her death lies on my shoulders. I should have never sent Isolde there to begin with but ordered the doctors to set up at Ravenscroft Hall instead." He passed a hand over his brow.

Tristan watched his father silently, understanding for the first time that behind his emotionless façade, he'd flagellated himself heavily for the death of his wife. It dawned on him how little he knew the man who was his father. And how similar they were on the other hand when it came to stubbornness and pride.

As if reading his thoughts, Livingstone continued. "I am a foolish man, someone told me recently, driven by my pride. That someone is Millicent." A smile broke out over his face, making him twenty years younger. "Millicent reminded me that the Sackville name is an honourable one, and I did her family a great disservice by not recognising Ava as a fit bride for my son. Millicent was furious. Have you ever seen her furious?"

Tristan shook his head, dumbfounded.

"It is not something one would ever want to experience again. I confess I was shaking in my boots." He shuddered.

"Millicent! Giving you a fright! Now that is difficult to believe."

"You have no idea." He remembered the scene and shook his head. "After she gave me the verbal thrashing of a lifetime, she scolded me for being a terrible father. The worst is that she is right. Forget what I ever told you about finding the perfect Sydney bride. It is balderdash. Find the one who loves you and who you love. The time we are given in this life is too short for anything else. I may only have several months left, who knows. I pray they are years. I intend to live them happily. And I would like nothing else than for you to be happy, too." He sighed. "Even if it is with that opera singer. You should give her the brooch; Marianne would have wanted you to. Provided you choose to marry Ava after all? For if you do, you will have my blessing."

Tristan stared at his father with amazement. He was

married not twenty-four hours to Millicent and, all of a sudden, the iron rod that was his father turned into butter? Not just mere butter, but clotted cream of the finest sort. How did that happen? "Repeat that. It was Millicent who prompted you to change your mind about Ava?"

His father dug with the poker in the fireplace, and a wistful smile played about his mouth.

"She reminded me that a younger Alastair would not have minded the union at all. We were secretly engaged when she was seventeen. We were deeply in love, but it was not to be. A series of circumstances made it impossible for us to continue our engagement. Both our families were against it. The pressure was too high. Millicent's mother fell ill. She called it off, and I accepted her decision, resigning myself to my fate of having to marry someone my parents chose."

"Mother." Tristan swallowed.

"I was truly fond of your mother. She was a fine, lovely woman."

"The perfect Sydney bride," Tristan said dryly. "But fondness is not quite the same as love. You loved Millicent."

His father nodded. "I never could forget her."

Tristan pulled himself up. "While I appreciate being reinstated in your good graces, I would like to inform you that I'll attempt to live an independent life from now on."

His father looked at him with a raised eyebrow. "How do you intend to do that?"

"You know of my interest in minerals. I have been thinking that I would like to help the British museum establish a mineral collection. Not only that, but to establish a mineral dealership with the support of some investors. It would require some travelling, but I believe it could be a success."

Livingstone narrowed his eyes. "In other words, you intend to work. An aristocrat who works like the average John, Dick, and Harry."

Tristan stiffened. Of course, his father would object to any sort of proposal he put forth. His father seemed to have changed much lately, but it was too much to ask for him to loosen all of his proud aristocratic sentiments.

"I am aware that gentlemen of our class do not work," Tristan said. "If the *ton* considers it disreputable, then so be it. As far as I am concerned, there is not much of a reputation for me left to lose anyhow. But, sir, this seems to be the only venue available when one would like to lead a certain lifestyle and be financially independent. I am therefore determined to follow this path." He thought for a moment and then added, "In addition to marrying Ava, of course. Provided she'll still have me."

Livingstone assessed him grimly for a while. Then a smile broke out over his face, and he clapped him on the shoulder with such unexpected force that Tristan nearly stumbled into the fireplace.

"My son has finally grown up."

Chapter Thirty-Two

Ava was tired.

She had been touring the past few months and given impromptu concerts in Berlin, Leipzig, and Prague. She had received an offer from the Opera in Paris, which she had toyed with accepting. Kit, however, was less than enthusiastic about the prospect of moving to Paris.

"I must say, now that we're back in Vienna, I've begun to miss the smell of good old English soil. And that feeling of the perpetual drizzly rain and the gritty fog seeping down your damp collar. You get that feeling only in London. Or that rancid smell of the Thames," Kit waxed nostalgic. "Makes me almost homesick for London when I think of it. Then there are all these wondrous activities like smashing each other's noses to pulp at Jackson's and getting fleeced in the clubs and at prize fights. Strutting with the other beaux along Bond Street in boots that pinch something awful but that one must wear for some reason that no one really knows but everyone does so anyhow. And all the pretty turtle doves in Covent Garden." He sighed deeply. "I wonder whether Hetty thinks of me sometimes. Ah, the good old times."

But Ava wasn't listening. She shoved aside a pile of letters, all of which came from the King's Theatre in London, begging her to return. The sum they'd offered her, should she accept the contract, was immense. There was a letter from Phileas Whistlefritz, who implored her to accept the contract. "Do it for my sake, Ava," he wrote, "for the King has threatened to throw me into the tower if I fail to get you back." She snorted. It would do him good to languish a little in the tower. She opened another letter with more eagerness, while Kit continued talking.

"I never thought I'd see the day, but I am even beginning to miss that English stiff upper lip and their penchant for nonsensical rules and etiquette, and the custom of perpetually guzzling tea. Say, are you listening, Ava? You're behaving like you swallowed a frog or worse."

For Ava suddenly jumped, clapped her hands, jumped again, clapped her hands in front of her mouth, clapped them to her cheeks, clapped while jumping, then finally stood rooted on the spot as she clutched the letter in one hand, while wiping tears away from her cheeks with the other.

"Kit, you won't believe this news! Millicent is Lady Livingstone now! Am I reading this correctly? It does say Livingstone, doesn't it? Dear sweet heaven! 'We married rather quickly with the butler and the housekeeper as witnesses,' she wrote. Can you believe it?"

"Wait. Cousin Millicent married the father of the

man who you'd intended to marry?" Kit snapped his fingers. "What's his name again?"

"Lord Livingstone. T-Tristan's father." It was the first time she'd uttered his name since they'd left England.

"But, as far as I recall, he was of the cantankerous kind, the sort who makes milk curdle by merely smiling at it, and I recall he spoiled a perfectly happy party with his bellow and bark. Not fun to have around at all. Do you think Millicent will be happy with him?"

"Oh, I hope so! She certainly sounds happy. She says they used to be engaged, once, and that he was her first love." She lowered her letters as a line appeared between her eyebrows. "I wonder what she will do with all the cats because she said, once, that one of the reasons why she did not marry him was that he detested cats."

Kit grinned. "Maybe she will convert him. Turn him into a cat-lover. That is the best story ever. Millicent is now Ravenscroft's stepmother!"

"It does seem rather odd." Ava would rather not think or talk about Tristan. Every time they did, her heart ached. She stood up abruptly. "I must go to the opera for the rehearsal."

Walking through the streets of Vienna, she marvelled at how displaced she felt. Yet nothing had changed. Her lodging in the Kohlmarkt was exactly as she'd left it, with Martha cooking the same meals day in and day out. The same chestnut vendor stood by the corner at the end of the street, and in the Burgtheater they played the same plays, the same operas, attended by the same audience.

Yet she'd changed; she was no longer the same.

She had lost some of the joy of singing and performing, knowing a certain person was no longer in the audience, no longer listening to her. She received countless letters, many of admiration, many invitations, but never a letter from him.

Only the bouquet of violets that she received regularly made her heart hammer. The violets had begun to arrive in Leipzig. Someone threw them on stage after every performance; a small, simple, delightful bouquet. In England, they'd always come with a short note, signed with a scrawled R. But these flowers bore no notes. Surely, they were tokens of admiration from other admirers? Violets were common flowers, after all. She scolded herself for attaching too much importance to them.

After the rehearsal that afternoon, Ava remained on stage. The lamp boy put out the lights in the pit, casting the auditorium into gradual darkness.

"Leave the lamps on the stage for a little while longer," Ava told him. She needed to be alone, she needed some silence, she needed to ponder on what had happened during the rehearsal, why she had felt out of touch with the music, why she'd had to break off and ask the conductor three times to start the aria over again. She'd lost her thread, her concentration. Nothing like that had ever happened before.

In the end, the conductor had broken off, shaking his head. "You need to rest, Violetta," he'd said.

She'd agreed.

"I mean a long rest." He'd packed up his music sheets, throwing her a meaningful look. "From singing."

She'd remained behind, aghast.

A long rest.

She rubbed her eyes wearily. What would she do during a long rest? Her mind never rested. It would go round and round and rehash every single memory, every single word, it would try to recapture the details of his face before it would be blurred in the forgetfulness of time. Tears welled up, she pinched the bridge of her nose with two fingers and swallowed.

"You can put out the lights now," she told the lamp boy as she descended the stairs. It was best to return home, and to do as the director said: lie down and rest.

The lamp boy hovered in the pit.

"You know, I can't help but wonder all this time whether in the end you let me win because it was me, or because you really liked my poem better than everyone else's. I've had some sleepless nights over that, pondering on that question."

Ava whirled around. "Tristan?" she whispered. She bent to pick up the lamp by the stairs and held it high.

A tall, shadowy figure leaned nonchalantly against the boxes in the pit with crossed arms.

She clenched her fingers about her lamp and bit on her lower lip, for it trembled.

"I like to think that it was because you truly liked my poem. Granted, 'sausage rolls' was not the most poetic expression, but it was the only term that popped into my mind then, so it had to do."

"Tristan." Her voice choked with tears.

His gaze was burning through her.

"It was a brilliant poem." She sounded breathless. "I enjoyed it, and it made me laugh." She could not move one more step, not for the life of her.

"That does set my mind at ease, then." His eyes never left her face.

Ava took a big breath. "Is that why you had to come all the way here, to get an answer to this most important question?"

He looked as tall and handsome as always. His hair was ruffled, but there were dark rings under his eyes as though he hadn't slept much.

"That is why I had to come all the way here to ask the question," he repeated softly. "Granted, there are more important questions that have kept me awake." He uncrossed his arms and took a step towards her.

Ava nearly dropped the lamp and melted on the spot.

After swallowing once, twice, she dared to ask: "Oh? And what would that be?"

He took another step forward. "The question I have," he said slowly, "the question that has kept me awake night after night—" another hesitant step "—after all things were said and done—" another step "—and every-thing was over like a long, beautiful dream..." He'd reached the bottom of the stage and stopped in front of the stairs, looking up at her.

"Yes?" Her breath came quickly.

He grasped the edge of the stage to support himself, and his knuckles whitened. "I wondered whether I was wrong about it all and you might have meant it. I wondered whether Ava really was the person you were when you were not Violetta."

She licked her cracked lips. "Violetta Winter is a stage name. The persona I adopt when I am in the theatre. I lied through omission, yes. I omitted telling you where I had to go every few nights and what my profession was, and that I sing under another name. And I am so, so sorry for that. But I have never lied to you about being Ava."

He took the steps up the stage, and stood in front of her now, and she looked up, smiling through her tears. "You are still as ridiculously tall as always."

He wiped a tear away with his thumb.

"I have seen this face in my dreams night after night —" his voice was rough "—Ava's face, without the paint. And then Violetta's face, and then both merged. And then I woke one morning and realised what a fool I'd been. It doesn't matter what you choose to call yourself, it doesn't matter what you look like or what you wear. I have fallen in love with Ava. And I've been thinking, even if Ava never existed, you invented her and were able to embody her. And that means that a part of you *must* be her. And I thought, maybe that is all that matters." He cupped her face in his hands and he devoured her face with hungry eyes.

"Tristan. I am Ava. I always have been. It is Violetta who doesn't exist."

"It took me some time to realise this. Can you ever forgive me, dear heart?"

She lifted her hands and drew down his face. She kissed his nose, his eyes, and finally, his lips. With a groan, he gathered her into his arms and crushed her in a triumphant embrace. He devoured her, demanding, caressing, nibbling her lips, her ears, her neck, leaving her quivering, tingling, burning.

She dug her hands into his thick, soft hair and sighed

against his lips, while his mouth continued to possess hers with urgent kisses. A moan escaped from his throat. Then he buried his face in her neck, inhaling her scent deeply.

"Ava. My Ava."

Epilogue

It was summer, and everything was in full bloom. Millicent, now Marchioness of Livingstone, was hosting her first garden party at Ravenscroft Hall. It would be followed by a full-fledged opera performance in the amphitheatre across from the lawn where the tables were set up.

Millicent ran back and forth, checking for the hundredth time whether the chairs were arranged properly and whether the tea cakes were sitting at the right angle on the silver platters.

"But Millicent, it's just us!" Ava had laughed.

Millicent wrung her hands. "It isn't 'just' you. I want you to enjoy yourselves and no one should be hungry or thirsty or want for anything. Besides, everything needs to be perfect, and the little ones aren't helping." She picked off a little white and black kitten that had managed to climb one of the tables to reach the milk jar. Leonidas had already stolen a sausage roll, which he was devouring under the tree as they were speaking.

All of Millicent's cats had moved with her to the Livingstone residence. It turned out that Alastair tolerated them as long as they made his Millicent happy. Alastair had nearly sat on one earlier, but they'd all stormed towards Tristan as soon as he appeared.

"He seems to be their prime favourite," Ava said, puzzled, as they watched Tristan wrestle with three kittens simultaneously.

"And Kit, too," Millicent said. "It is a fact my cats seem to prefer the men of the family, forgetting entirely who raised them." She sighed. They watched Kit as he stood in front of Isolde, who lay on a divan. She looked up at him through her eyelashes and laughed.

"And not only the cats seem to like Kit, apparently," Millicent added after a thought.

Kit was dressed in a short, padded hose and a doublet over a linen shirt with a ruff. He looked like he stepped out of an Elizabethan portrait. He pretended to act out a scene from the opera by playing on an invisible mandolin and going down on his knees in front of Isolde. She clasped a hand to her mouth and giggled. Two spots of red appeared on her cheeks and her eyes sparkled. She looked lovely.

"You think?" Ava tilted her head aside. It wouldn't be the worst match. They were both spirited and lively and seemed to share the same ridiculous humour. "If it helps Kit settle down, I'm all for it."

"All for what?" A pair of arms crept up from behind her in a warm embrace. Ava turned her head to her husband with a brilliant smile. They had married quietly in Vienna, with only Kit and two witnesses in attendance. Upon Livingstone's insistence, they'd repeated the wedding in England. "One cannot be more thoroughly married than that," Tristan had announced afterwards, satisfied.

"All for *that*." Ava nodded at Kit and Isolde, and Tristan followed her glance with a frown.

"I hope they come to an agreement before we have to leave again," she murmured against his ear.

They would spend the summer in Ravenscroft Hall, and then Tristan would accompany her on a concert tour to Stockholm—Helsinki—St Petersburg. After that, she would take the conductor's advice and rest.

Her hand crawled over her stomach.

It might be a long rest, she thought, as joy rushed through her.

Everyone sat down and stared at her expectantly.

The orchestra began to tune the violins. The choir stood by the side. The conductor lifted the baton.

Everyone was ready.

Isolde clapped her hands, her eyes glistening with joy. "An opera only for me, all for me!"

"Indeed, we've had to hire half of the opera house to bring the props and the costumes and the additional singers, and not to mention the scenery!" Kit groaned. He was participating and singing the part of Leporello, Don Giovanni's servant.

Ava had kept her word.

Her eyes met Tristan's, who smiled at her encouragingly.

"Sing," he said, leaning back proudly.

And Ava sang.

* * *

WHEN A HOPELESS SPINSTER ENLISTS HER BUTLER'S help to turn her life around, it invariably leads to great trouble... but can it also lead to a chance at love? Don't miss Lady Avery's story in the next instalment of the Merry Spinsters, Charming Rogues series: *Lady Avery and the False Butler*.

Also by Sofi Laporte

The Wishing Well Series:

Lucy and the Duke of Secrets

Arabella and the Reluctant Duke

Birdie and the Beastly Duke

Penelope and the Wicked Duke

A Christmas Regency Novella:

My Lady, Will You Dance?

A Mistletoe Promise

Wishing Well Seminary Series:

Miss Hilversham and the Pesky Duke

Miss Robinson and the Unsuitable Baron

Merry Spinsters, Charming Rogues:

Lady Ludmilla's Accidental Letter

Miss Ava's Scandalous Secret

Lady Avery and the False Butler

Miss Louisa's Final Waltz

Georgians in Paris

The Vicomte's Masquerade: An 18th Century Romance
Novella

About the Author

Sofi was born in Vienna, grew up in Seoul, studied Comparative Literature in Maryland, U.S.A., and lived in Quito with her Ecuadorian husband. When not writing, she likes to scramble about the countryside exploring medieval castle ruins. She currently lives with her husband, 3 trilingual children, a sassy cat and a cheeky dog in Europe.

Get in touch and visit Sofi at her Website, on Facebook or Instagram!

amazon.com/Sofi-Laporte/e/B07N1K8H6C

facebook.com/sofilaporteauthor

instagram.com/sofilaporteauthor

bookbub.com/profile/sofi-laporte

Made in United States
Orlando, FL
08 January 2024

42238748R00166